MATTHEW ARNOLD

Literary Lives
General Editor: Richard Dutton, Professor of English
Lancaster University

This series offers stimulating accounts of the literary careers of
the most admired and influential English-language authors.
Volumes follow the outline of the writers' working lives, not
in the spirit of traditional biography, but aiming to trace
the professional, publishing and social contexts which
shaped their writing.

A list of the published titles in the series follows overleaf.

Matthew Arnold

A Literary Life

Clinton Machann
Professor of English
Texas A&M University

St. Martin's Press
New York

St. Martin's Press, Scholarly and Reference Division,
175 Fifth Avenue, New York, N.Y. 10010

First published in the United States of America in 1998

This book is printed on paper suitable for recycling and
made from fully managed and sustained forest sources.

Printed in Hong Kong

ISBN 0–312–21031–0

Library of Congress Cataloging-in-Publication Data
Machann, Clinton.
Matthew Arnold : a literary life / Clinton Machann.
p.   cm.
Includes bibliographical references and index.
ISBN 0–312–21031–0
1. Arnold, Matthew, 1822–1888—Biography.   2. Poets, English–19th
century—Biography.   3. Critics—Great Britain—Biography.
I. Title.
PR4023.M28 1997
821'.8—dc21
[B]   97–18187
                                                              CIP

In memoriam Robert H. Super (1914–96)

Contents

Abbreviations of Frequently Cited Sources

The following abbreviations have been used throughout this volume to indicate editions of Arnold's works and frequently cited secondary sources. All quotations from poems are taken from *P*.

CPW   Arnold, Matthew, *The Complete Prose Works of Matthew Arnold*, ed. R. H. Super. 11 vols (Ann Arbor: University of Michigan Press, 1960–77).

LMA   *Letters of Matthew Arnold, 1848–1888*, ed. George W. E. Russell, 2 vols[1] (New York and London: Macmillan, 1895).

MAAL Honan, Park, *Matthew Arnold: A Life* (Cambridge, Mass.: Harvard University Press, 1983).[2]

MAB   Buckler, William E. (ed.), *Matthew Arnold's Books: Toward a Publishing Diary* (Geneva: Droz, 1958).

MAHC Coulling, Sidney, *Matthew Arnold and His Critics: A Study of Arnold's Controversies* (Athens: Ohio University Press, 1974).

MAP   *Matthew Arnold: The Poetry*. The Critical Heritage, ed. Carl Dawson (London: Routledge & Kegan Paul), 1973.

MAPW *Matthew Arnold: Prose Writings*. The Critical Heritage, ed. Carl Dawson and John Pfordresher (London: Routledge & Kegan Paul), 1979.

P   Arnold, Matthew, *The Poems of Matthew Arnold*, ed. Kenneth Allott, 2nd edn, revised by Marian Allott (London: Longmans, 1979).

SL   Arnold, Matthew. *Selected Letters of Matthew Arnold*, ed. Clinton Machann and Forrest D. Burt (London: Macmillan, 1993).

Notes

1. Because the texts of letters in *LMA* are not always reliable, I have used the recently published and accessible *SL* whenever possible. The manuscript of *Matthew Arnold: A Literary Life* was completed prior to the publication of volume 1 of Cecil Y. Lang's edition of Arnold's letters by the University Press of Virginia.
2. The manuscript of *Matthew Arnold: A Literary Life* was completed prior to the publication of Nicholas Murray's *A Life of Matthew Arnold* (London: Hodder & Stoughton, 1996).

Preface

The posthumous reputation of Matthew Arnold has developed in ways that increasingly set him apart from other Victorian figures in the canon of English literature. It is curious that a nineteenth-century English poet should figure in late twentieth-century debates about political and social issues, but such has been the case. Of course it is not his poetry but rather his critical prose that is at issue. 'The Function of Criticism at the Present Time' and *Culture and Anarchy* remain much-quoted texts, even in controversial prose written and read outside the academy. American intellectuals in particular continue to argue about Arnold's concept of 'culture' and even of 'the State'.[1]

This book, however, is not about modern versions or applications of Arnold. Instead it is an attempt to show how Arnold's poetry and prose grew out of his personal life and his engagement with the world. It is easier to deal in this way with his prose than with his poetry. Of course one can trace poetic influences and occasions, but the prose, however abstract its applications may be today, is firmly rooted in contemporary concerns and controversies, not least importantly those associated with his profession of school inspecting. At the same time, however, there are unifying concerns and purposes in Arnold's career as a writer, and his transition from poet to critic makes sense in terms of the circumstances of his life.

Although only one substantial modern biography of Arnold had been published prior to 1996, certain interesting features of Arnold's life and literary career have been widely discussed: the problematic influence of his headmaster father, his intense and uneasy friendship with the poet Arthur Hugh Clough, the identity of 'Marguerite' (in the 'Switzerland' poems), his retraction of the important poem *Empedocles on Etna* in 1853 and his subsequent 'failure' to write introspective poetry. I attempt to show how these familiar features figure in the evolution of Arnold's writings and also try to cast new light on the forces that shaped the career of this extraordinary man of letters. Although a brief study like this one cannot possibly be as exhaustive in life detail

xi

as a full biography or as scholarly or theoretical as a critical monograph, it can at least be aimed at providing the reader with a better understanding of the writer's literary development in the context of his personal, social and professional life.

I first became interested in the works of Matthew Arnold in the early 1970s while studying under the direction of David J. DeLaura at the University of Texas at Austin (although I wrote my dissertation on Ruskin, not Arnold). While writing this book at Texas A&M University more than two decades later, I was chairing the doctoral advisory committee of Walter Kokernot, who was completing his dissertation on Arnold's early poetry. In the intervening years I have met, and in some cases worked with, several Arnold scholars, including some of those cited in this study. This has been one of the genuine pleasures of my professional career, and I want to express my thanks to everyone who has helped me to understand and appreciate the subject of this book, with special emphasis on the editor of Arnold's prose, to whom it is dedicated. I came to Victorian studies as the product of a Czech-American, working-class family from rural Texas: Arnold seemed exotic and aloof but interesting. After all these years, I still cannot exactly describe myself as an 'Arnoldian', and indeed, although that term crops up in academic discourse from time to time, Arnold, unlike some other literary icons, does not inspire fan clubs. But whenever I return to Arnold's works, the experience is always bracing and worthwhile.

Charles Snodgrass and Hyon-Jin Kim, both graduate students at Texas A&M University, assisted me in the research for this project.

CLINTON MACHANN

Note

1. A new edition of *Culture and Anarchy* was published in 1994 by Yale University Press. Edited by Samuel Lipman, the volume includes interpretive essays which as a group acknowledge the continuing (though controversial) relevance of Arnold. Reviews and related articles quickly appeared in publications such as *Commentary* and *The New Republic*, which focus on political and controversial issues, as well as in scholarly journals such as *Comparative Literature* and *New Literary History*. A recent critique of Arnold's 'apology for a deeply authoritarian ... notion of the State' is found in Edward W. Said, 'Nationalism, Human Rights, and Interpretation', *Raritan*, 12 (1993), 26–51.

1
Juvenilia

Although the growth of a writer's mind can never be fully mapped and explained, it is easy to see that Arnold's early family life and schooling helped to establish literary and critical directions taken in his mature work. Arnold was born on Christmas Eve, 1822, at Laleham-on-Thames, the second child and eldest son of Thomas and Mary (*née* Penrose) Arnold. This chapter will briefly trace his development to the time he went up to Oxford in 1841.

As a child Arnold was described by his parents as active and restless, but at the age of two he was hobbled by iron leg braces designed to straighten a 'bent' leg, and he wore them for nearly two years. No doubt the 'incumbering irons' encouraged a deep sense of competitiveness in Arnold as he contended with his more mobile younger brother Tom and other siblings for the attention and approval of his mother. Later Arnold's clumsiness in sports and other physical activities, as well as his often dejected disposition, helped to justify his family nickname of 'Crabby' (*MAAL* 13). Early in Arnold's life, intellectual pursuits were more accessible than vigorous outdoor games, but he was not permanently crippled, and, although he remained relatively slight and unathletic as a young man, he was by no means a weakling. It may be that the heroic exertion often associated with walking in Arnold's mature poetry is related to this childhood ordeal. As an adult Arnold was nostalgic about Laleham and the surrounding country-side where he had spent the first five years of his life, and the images of peace and security he uses to describe the place in his letters are almost Edenic. One of the sources of the water – and, in particular, river – imagery that runs through his poetry is in his idyllic early memories of the Thames. (His real love of rivers is also connected with his lifelong hobby of fishing.) Like many of his contemporaries, Arnold developed a passion for landscape scenery, especially wild flowers, descriptions of which abound in his adult correspondence. Throughout his life, Arnold enjoyed

1

occasional visits to the place of his birth, especially with his sons, and he was eventually buried there (near the three sons who preceded him in death).

Both of his parents were powerful forces in determining young Arnold's intellectual and emotional life. Mrs Arnold was frail of body but energetic and vivacious, ambitious for her husband and for her children. Her Celtic ancestry (she was born in Cornwall), her broadmindedness and intellectual curiosity, her emotional energy balanced by a strain of melancholy, her taste for foreign travel combined with a deep love of home, her sympathy for political reform, her literary bent (she kept a journal and wrote religious and occasional verse): all these qualities influenced her children, especially Matthew, as is abundantly demonstrated not only in his later creative and intellectual works but most directly in his adult correspondence with his mother.

Just prior to his marriage in 1820, Thomas Arnold, in partnership with John Buckland, his sister's husband, had established at Laleham a small university preparatory school. He was an intensely dedicated schoolmaster, destined for great achievements in his short life, and not especially tolerant of the idleness or restlessness he perceived in his children. But he was also openly affectionate and playful with them, giving them silly nicknames and encouraging a special kind of wit and humour within the family. Arnold would grow up to be a similar kind of father and family man, though with less of his father's capacity for sternness.

Thus from earliest infancy Arnold was exposed to an academic atmosphere of schoolhouses and classrooms but also immersed in the intense life of a close-knit Victorian family. As might be expected in a highly literate family, Arnold's first lessons were taught at home by his parents. Early exposure to Biblical allusions came through family readings of the Bible and the devotional poetry of John Keble in *The Christian Year*. (Keble was a family friend and one of Arnold's godfathers but, later, as an Oxford Tractarian, he was harshly criticized by Thomas Arnold.) At the age of six, Arnold had his first formal Latin lesson from his father.

During this same year – 1828 – Thomas Arnold's dream of heading a renowned preparatory school was fulfilled when he was appointed to replace Dr Wooll as headmaster of Rugby School on the south bank of the Avon in Warwickshire. He had plans for reinvigorating the school, where enrolment had declined in recent years. Dr Arnold (he took a DD degree shortly after his appointment) was to be largely successful, raising the academic standards – and the prestige – of Rugby and making himself the most famous headmaster in England. At the age of six, little Matthew was already learning a great deal from this remarkable man, but it is never easy for an ambitious son to grow up in the shadow of an eminently successful father. Some of the strategies adopted by Arnold to cope with the psychological pressures of his position as eldest son would help to determine his personality as an adult man and writer.

After the move, the Arnolds resumed their home instruction of Matthew and the other children. While his governesses, first Miss Robertson and then Miss Rutland, helped him to learn and recite his catechism, Arnold and his older sister Jane were also privy to the Rugby boys' syllabi of history, geography, arithmetic, Italian, French and German. Some of Arnold's early texts were Sellon's *Abridgement of Holy Scripture* (a prize for catechism recital), Bewick's *British Birds and Quadrupeds*, a Bible *Bilderbuch*, and Bunyan's *Pilgrim's Progress* (*MAAL* 17–18).

However, by the early part of 1831 Dr Arnold was not satisfied with his son's progress in Latin and Greek and, with Mrs Arnold's approval, sent him back to the Reverend John Buckland's school in Laleham, where he might improve his study habits. Arnold was miserable away from home in the confinement of Laleham school. Furthermore, he continued to resist diligent study and frequently violated the school's rigid regulations. Dr Arnold was not pleased with the unsatisfactory reports he received on his son's behaviour, and on that account Mrs Arnold sometimes withheld from her son the letters from home that he craved. Nevertheless, during Arnold's two years at the Laleham School, he was introduced to texts by Virgil and Ovid that he would hold dear for the rest of his life. In particular, Arnold's appreciation for Virgil's fourth *Eclogue* seemed to represent a breakthrough in his struggle with the classics.

At the end of 1832, Dr Arnold recalled his son to Rugby in order 'to familiarize him with home feelings' (*MAAL* 20). Herbert Hill, a cousin of the poet Robert Southey, was brought in to tutor Matthew and his brother Tom. Hill, who knew little of mathematics, concentrated almost exclusively on the literary classics. Arnold may have been intimidated by the Rugby students surrounding him – his father tended to think of them all as part of the family – and he apologized to Hill for 'dullness in learning orally', but over the course of the next three years he became adept at 'construing' Homer, Herodotus, Xenophon, Aeschylus and Persae (*MAAL* 21).

He also began to write poems. In 1835 Arnold wrote (in Latin) a birthday poem for his little sister Frances ('Fan') and then lyrics in which he emulated Byron's *Childe Harold*. A more substantial effort in 1836 was 'The First Sight of Italy', heavily influenced by both Scott and Byron:

> Italy, Italy,
> The mountains echo thy name!
>   In the depths of the sea,
> Where the whale and the dolphin are rolling in glee,
> Is stored thy never ending fame.   (ll. 27–31)

If this is evidence of the future poet's innate proclivities, it also reflects a literary environment. At this time, Dr Arnold was composing his own Romantic lyrics in imitation of Coleridge, and Mrs Arnold followed suit. The family's poetic activities were inspired by vacations at Fox How, their new holiday home, which they first occupied in July 1834. Fox How is situated between the Rotha River and Loughrigg Fell in the Lake District. William Wordsworth, whom Arnold met at the age of eight, was a neighbour and became a family friend. Young Arnold responded both to the natural beauty and the literary associations of the area. Although he apparently never developed a strong attachment to the Warwickshire district around Rugby or the school itself, Arnold had loved his early Laleham home, and the new holiday house – later the permanent residence of his mother – would be a delight to him for the rest of his life.

In 1836, Arnold, along with his brother Tom, attended Winchester College, his father's alma mater, for a year of study before entering Rugby. A preparatory visit by the family to Winchester and nearby Eaglehurst (the home of Dr Arnold's sister, Lydia) moved Arnold to compose 'Lines Written on the Seashore at Eaglehurst', precursor to 'The Strayed Reveller' and other mature lyrics dominated by landscape imagery. Upon his matriculation at Winchester, Arnold penned 'Lines Written on First Leaving Home for a Public School' and sent the poem home to his parents.

Arnold apparently excelled in the early days at Winchester, and he wrote to ask his father's advice about applying to be a Heathcote Scholar, a tuition-free status unlike that of commoner. But Dr Arnold advised against the application since it involved a test on the Church's Thirty-nine Articles, the study of which seemed to him a waste of time since virtually all of the articles had been disputed; thus, Arnold declined that offer of preferment. After leaving Winchester for the Christmas holiday of 1836–7 and his fifteenth birthday, Arnold returned to Rugby, where he became acquainted with an unusually bright and sensitive boy named Arthur Hugh Clough, more than three years his senior, who had also come for a visit. Clough was one of Dr Arnold's star pupils and had recently won a Balliol College scholarship at Oxford. Their friendship later developed into one of the most interesting literary relationships in Victorian England.

Back at Winchester Arnold applied himself to literary studies. After plodding through classroom readings of Virgil's *Aeneid*, Horace's *Satires*, and Sophocles' *Electra*, Arnold distinguished himself by reciting a passage from Byron's *Marino Faliero* at Easter. In the meantime, however, he had committed the unpardonable sin of informing Mr Moberly, the headmaster, that the class assignments were too light, and in consequence he had been harassed by his classmates. Before leaving Winchester, he also managed to burn his hand quite seriously in an accident involving the discharge of a firearm.

Arnold was now to enter his father's school, but first he holidayed in France with his family for ten days in August 1837. The sights of Paris made a great impression on the fourteen-year-old, who had already learned to appreciate the enlightened and liberalizing traditions of France (though his father had a higher regard for the German people). As a young man Arnold was to become something of a Francophile, mimicking French mannerisms and customs and pursuing a refined sense of aesthetics unavailable in England.

In late August 1837 both Matthew and Tom entered the fifth form at Rugby, not taught by their father but under his close observation. Arnold's composition tutor was James Prince Lee, and his mathematics tutor Bonamy Price. Although Arnold grumbled over his mathematics, he took to his composition themes with skill and talent. The next summer he was promoted to the sixth form while still fifteen; now he was under the direct instruction of his father. During this time at Rugby, Arnold apparently met his father's rigorous expectations and won several writing and oratory prizes; however, he also showed an independent streak and probably was jealous of some of the older Rugbeian students favoured by his parents.

At Fox How during the Christmas holiday of 1838, each of the Arnold children contributed to a literary collection which would be distributed to friends and read aloud on New Year's Eve by Dr Arnold. The *Fox How Magazine* was issued twice a year by the Arnold family for the next four years and contained much of Arnold's most interesting juvenilia. In general the pieces in the *Fox How* were light and humorous – Dr Arnold included a satire of his eldest son, entitled 'Crab' – but among Arnold's contributions were poems on religious subjects which, Park Honan suggests, reflected the darker moods of his father. In a Christmas 1838 poem that begins 'Land of the East! Around thy shores are flung/By fancy's hand the glittering stores of song', Arnold described the departure of the Spirit of God from Jerusalem as the Romans prepared to capture and destroy that city in AD 70: 'But hark – yon sound of rushing mighty wind./Say, tells it naught to thy despairing mind?/God leaves his People desolate, forlorn.'

Back at Rugby, Arnold continued to excel in his literary pursuits. He developed a reputation for being self-possessed but lazy. In the spring of 1840 his poem 'Alaric at Rome' won for him a sixth-form prize in verse and his father's praise. 'Alaric' represents Arnold's attempt to treat seriously the tragic history of the conquering Visigoth king related in Gibbon's *Decline and Fall*. Late in life, Arnold retained a high regard for his first published poem, which already reflects the complex cultural background of his mature works. Although it is still noticeably Byronic in style, 'Alaric' can be linked to Arnold's later fascination with the *Zeitgeist* that challenges traditions and institutions.

Arnold's ambitions to attend Oxford were encouraged by his parents, although his father, an alumnus of Corpus Christi College, was not sanguine about his son's chances of success when he decided to compete for one of the two Open Balliol scholarships to Oxford, like the one his friend Clough had won four years earlier. Dr Arnold hired a tutor, William Lake, to help prepare his son for the November competition, but Arnold did not apply himself, and his family became even more pessimistic about his prospects. Arnold surprised them by taking the second scholarship after a gruelling competition among semi-finalists. This prize out-shone all his other accomplishments thus far and gave him the confidence he needed to pursue his literary studies at a higher level.

It also must have made him feel more worthy of his loving but demanding father. Much has been written about Dr Arnold's influence on his son, who would one day eulogize him in that most 'Victorian' of poems, 'Rugby Chapel'. Although Arnold did not adopt the unquestioning Christian faith or Broad Church activism of his father, he inherited both ideas and intellectual habits from him. Dr Arnold was a staunch classicist in his approach to educational curricula. He fused secular and religious elements in his social thought and was a strong advocate for reform, occasionally disturbing his neighbours in the town of Rugby with controversial ideas. Influenced by Samuel Taylor Coleridge, he insisted on the inseparability of Church and State. As a historian, he followed the German Niebuhr and the Italian Vico, developing his own organic concept of the nation whereby its life is analogous to that of a person: the nation's history must be told in terms of its developing mental and moral personality or spirit. In spite of these influences, he did not attach himself to a specific school of thought. He was convinced that he lived in a civilization that was similar to the classical civilizations of Greece and Rome; for him there was an 'ancient' and 'modern' period in the history of every people. In his *History of Rome* he was more concerned with moral issues than with military tactics. One can find echoes of all these positions and tendencies in Arnold's works.

In spite of his deeply felt family affections, Dr Arnold must have been in some ways a difficult father for a sensitive and ambitious son. His local prominence at Rugby, enhanced by a growing public reputation as an educator and thinker, exposed his eldest son to current ideas and enabled him to meet famous people, but it also encouraged high expectations for the son's success. The accomplishments of former students such as Arthur Penrhyn Stanley and Clough, to whom the headmaster was a kind of surrogate father, added to the pressure. The headmaster's religious-based views towards corporal punishment and expulsion were particularly stern and occasionally led to excesses, while his lack of tact and unwillingness to compromise often made even his friends uncomfortable. Of course, these same qualities enabled Dr Arnold to effectively reform a school which had developed a reputation for drunkenness and disorder prior to his arrival. Dr Arnold always placed 'religion and duty' above intellect in his priorities as an educator. As a youth, Arnold countered his father's sternness with an affected nonchalance and dandified dress and habits. Later in life – even after Arnold had in his own way become a moralist – his insistence on intellectual delicacy and tact in his writings as a counter force to rigidity and zeal undoubtedly owes something to the father–son relationship during this formative period.

According to various scholars, Arnold's personal relationship with his father informs future pivotal works such as *Empedocles on Etna*, the Preface of 1853, and 'Sohrab and Rustum'.[1] The poet W. H. Auden blamed Arnold's limitations as a poet squarely on his dominating father: Arnold determined that nothing should contradict his father's 'holy final word' and he 'thrust his gift in prison till it died'.[2] But this claim is extravagant and unfair. It may be true that the influence of his father to some degree stunted Arnold's potential as a poet, but it is more accurate to say that Arnold's success as a writer and intellectual was to a large measure due to his ability to negotiate the various and sometimes conflicting traditions and influences he inherited from his family and from the society in which he grew up. One of the most striking examples of his ability to accommodate and creatively make use of seemingly incompatible influences is covered in the next chapter. At Oxford, while holding on to central ideas and concepts inherited from his father, he was to come under the powerful influence of his father's old adversary, John Henry Newman.

It is tempting to speculate that the Celtic–Germanic dichotomy in the English character that Arnold wrote about in the 1860s (and which anticipates that of the Hebraic–Hellenic) had its origins in two potentially conflicting but complementary traditions within his own family. There is nothing surprising in the fact that Arnold's nurturing mother encouraged his poetry-writing, proudly copying passages of his verse into her letters to family relations, and the apparent contrast between the sensitive, emotional mother and stern, moralistic father reflects familiar Victorian gender stereotypes. However, in forging his identity as an artist, Arnold could build on certain associations with his 'Celtic' mother – dreamy melancholy, inwardness, emotional expressiveness – as a way of distancing himself, or protecting himself from, his overpowering 'Germanic' father who seemed to dominate the lives of so many young Rugbeians. In addition to his strident Anglo-Saxonism and often-expressed disdain for the Irish and other Celtic peoples, Thomas Arnold was a Germanophile who openly admired nineteenth-century German society and scholarship (especially the historiography of Niebuhr, although as a Christian believer he could not go too far in his acceptance of Higher Criticism). The friend for whom he expressed the highest esteem was Baron Bunsen, the German intellectual who served as ambassador to England.

The tendency to embrace French society and literature in Arnold's young adult life can be seen as related to this same strategy of reaction against his father's habits and world view. Later Arnold would emphasize what he took to be the large Celtic component in French culture, and he tended to think of both Celtic and French elements as essentially feminine. But lest we overemphasize these 'Oedipal' elements in young Arnold's development, we should remember that the French and Celtic and feminine associations with poetry's 'natural magic' are more than balanced by dominant masculine and classical ones early in his poetic career, and the dialogue between Hebrew and Hellene in his most famous 'cultural' criticism is one anticipated by his father's version of ethnology. At any rate, Arnold never showed much interest in exposing the origins of his mature ideas and intellectual habits in his early life. Reticence about one's private life is typical of Victorian writers and intellectuals, and yet many of them wrote autobiographies in which they attempted to trace the development of their dominant ideas as well as their publications. Arnold not only resisted the impulse to analyse his own development in this way but he also made it clear that he did not wish anyone to write his biography (*LMA* 1:vii). His private diaries and journals, although they are fairly extensive, consist primarily of literary quotations, reading lists, schedules of activities, financial calculations, and so on, with very little introspective commentary. In 1880 he wrote to his sister Frances that 'I never write a journal, but I tell my stories in letters, which is the better and pleasanter way' (*SL* 258). But even after reading the private letters in which Arnold most fully reveals himself, scholars are left to speculate about young Arnold's conscious strategies for dealing with his complex childhood heritage.

One reason for this may be that Arnold never passed through a stage of open rebellion or rejection of his home or parents. Regardless of his far-ranging interests and the sophisticated, cosmopolitan public image that he cultivated in the course of his career, Arnold retained a powerful emotional attachment to his family. Apart from the considerable influence of father and mother, Arnold as an adult continued to feel a close bond to his siblings. In particular, as will be seen, his older sister Jane (1821–89) remained one of his closest friends, and he always associated her with his earliest memories of childhood at Laleham. His youngest sister Frances (1833–1923) became especially important to Arnold when she remained at Fox How after the death of their mother in 1873, and he addressed his frequent 'letters home' to her. Other sisters were Mary (1825–88) and Susanna (1830–1911). As for the brothers, Arnold was closest to Tom (1823–1900), who followed him to Oxford and later led a rather exotic life, living for a time in New Zealand, converting to Catholicism and later lapsing, only to return to the Catholic Church and work under J. H. Newman at Birmingham Oratory School before becoming a professor of English at University College, Dublin. Other brothers were Edward Penrose (1826–78), who, like Arnold, became an inspector of schools; William Delafield (1828–59), who emigrated to India and became Director of Public Education in the Punjab; and Walter (1835–93), who went to sea as a boy sailor at the age of twelve and later married and settled down in Kent.

Throughout Arnold's adult life, it seems that strong bonds with his family and a few close friends provided him with the emotional security he needed to anchor his intensively subjective life of the mind for, despite his commitment to society and to humanity, Arnold as artist and critic is a solitary wanderer and thinker. As a nineteen-year-old Oxford undergraduate in the autumn of 1841, Arnold was poised at the brink of the first mature phase of his poetic career, a phase marked by anonymity and 'quiet work'. If he did not seem to be a particularly brilliant student and scholar, we know that he had already developed a strong inner life and a passion for reading that remained with him to the end of his days. As he approached the age of 60, Arnold would write to his sister Frances:

> The importance of reading, not slight stuff to get through the time, but the best that has been written, forces itself upon me more and more every year I live; it is living in good company, the best company, and people are generally quite keen enough, or too keen, about doing that, yet they will not do it in the simplest and most innocent manner, by reading. (*SL* 260)

2

The Strayed Reveller (1849), *Empedocles on Etna* (1852), *Poems* (1853)

Arnold's years at Balliol College (1841–4) were decisive for his subsequent literary career and the formation of his mature thought. This is not to say that he was very successful as a student. Arnold went into residence at Oxford after distinguishing himself at Rugby and winning an open scholarship, but his formal studies seemed to stagnate at Balliol. He earned a reputation there not as a scholar but as a dandified dresser, a flippant wit, and an avid fisherman and whist player. He ended by obtaining a disappointing second-class BA in 'Greats'.

Nevertheless, this was a time of great changes and turning points in Arnold's life. First, there is the matter of his father. Thomas Arnold was appointed Regius Professor of Modern History at Oxford in August of 1841, and he made an impression with his lectures on 'modern history' before his sudden death from heart disease in June of the following year. The enhanced reputation and occasional presence of his father at Oxford must have made Arnold's already sensitive intellectual and emotional position even more vulnerable as he was being introduced to the thought of the controversial John Henry Newman, who would become one of the most powerful and persistent influences in Arnold's life. The early, unexpected death of Dr Arnold probably had a liberating effect, leaving him less constrained in the development of his ideas as well as his poetic ambitions. Ironically, he was even freer to adopt some aspects of his father's legacy, such as his views on the 'classic' and 'modern', without fear of being overwhelmed or overshadowed by Dr Arnold. But it was also a profound psychological blow to a loving son and a challenge – cultivated by the widowed mother – somehow to carry on the

11

work and assume the mantle of the father in the name of the Arnold family. After the death of his father, Arnold's letters to his mother begin to take on an enormous importance in his life; the evolution of his career and of his *ambition* as a writer and thinker gradually becomes a major theme in this correspondence. Another apparent effect of Dr Arnold's early death is that it intensified the strain of fatalism and melancholy that mingled with lightheartedness and *joie de vivre* in the son's personality. Arnold expected that he would die of the *angina pectoris* that struck down his father (and his grandfather William Arnold as well) in the prime of life. One of the habits he adopted later in his career was jotting down in his diary the ages of various authors and other famous men when they died. However, Arnold's relative success in coming to terms with the early death of his extraordinary father can be contrasted with his brother Tom's abrupt crisis of faith, emigration to New Zealand, and conversion to Catholicism.

Clough was another young man who would have had to adjust to Dr Arnold's death, but many years would pass before Arnold fully appreciated the complexity of his friend's relationship with the departed leader. Arnold's friendship with Clough, who was elected a fellow of Oriel in the spring of 1842, solidified and began to develop into an important literary relationship. Although Arnold was a only a mediocre student of the classics at this time, he was reading and absorbing a great deal of literature by writers who would influence his work for the rest of his life: Carlyle, Emerson, George Sand and Goethe. Winning the Newdigate prize for his poem 'Cromwell' in 1843 provided the impetus he needed to pursue poetry as a vocation. Most of his important poems would be written within the next ten years. Finally, the tradition of Oxford University itself as a force in English culture would become central to Arnold's identity as a writer and thinker.

Balliol itself was a centre of resistance to the Tractarians, who were making their influence felt throughout the University at this time. Archibald C. Tait, senior tutor at Balliol, joined in a public protest against the infamous *Tract 90*, in which Newman attempted to show that the Thirty-nine Articles were capable of a Catholic interpretation. Tait and others of his party were of course keenly aware of Arnold's identity as the son of one of Newman's great enemies. The pressure that Arnold must have felt in this situation did not prevent him from joining the students who went to hear Newman preach at St Mary's. Arnold admired the sermons for their charm and intellectual power but, unlike his brother Tom, was never drawn into the Oxford Movement. Instead, in the midst of the very serious religious debates raging at Oxford, he adopted a detached attitude and avoided definite allegiance to either the social-activist Broad Church Anglicanism of his father or the High Church party of Newman and E. B. Pusey. It would later become clear that Arnold was in fact closer to his father than to Newman on the key issue of recognizing the English church as a fundamental national institution. The nonchalant personal style exhibited by Arnold during this time was surely related to his strategy of avoiding serious engagement in intellectual and religious issues and might be interpreted as a kind of defence mechanism. By the end of his Balliol years Arnold had probably ceased to believe in the key Christian doctrines of the Resurrection and the Atonement, which his father apparently had accepted without question (*MAAL* 73).

Arnold's complicated grounding in religious controversy at Oxford would be central to his life's work as a writer and thinker, but his growing friendship with Clough had an obvious and immediate impact on his budding career as a poet. Clough had come to Rugby in the summer of 1829, when he was only ten years old, and, having no real home in England, formed especially close ties to the school and its famous headmaster. His friendship with Arnold, however, did not begin until Arnold came up to Oxford as a Balliol scholar in the autumn of 1841. Clough had won the Balliol scholarship in the autumn of 1836, but as Arnold was following him to that college, Clough was disappointing both himself and his Rugby friends by failing in his second attempt to win the Balliol fellowship. Clough was, however, elected a fellow of Oriel in the spring of 1842 (as Dr Arnold had been and as Matthew Arnold would be in 1845).

The curriculum at Balliol, which included Divinity, Mathematics and Morals, in addition to Latin and Greek, was not especially challenging. However, Arnold, though he was always an avid reader, did not always apply himself to the assignments, and from the beginning developed the reputation of a brilliant but idle young man who did not live up to his potential. He was joined at Oxford by his brother Tom, who came up to University College in the autumn of 1842. The brothers were closely associated with Theodore Walrond (a former Rugbeian and Balliol man who remained one of Arnold's closest lifetime friends) and Clough. The four spent much time together and engaged in free-ranging discussions of ideas: Clough and Tom were much more susceptible to the radical and utopian politics of the 1840s than was Arnold, who remained sceptical, although he admired the Romantic idealism of George Sand. Other friends and associates included the classicists John Campbell Shairp and William Young Sellar, the historian and man of letters James Anthony Froude, the poet and anthologist Francis T. Palgrave, and former Rugbeian A. P. Stanley, who would publish the *Life and Correspondence* of Arnold's father in 1844 and later become an important Church official. Arnold and some of the others belonged to a debating club known as 'The Decade', as did the Balliol tutor (and later master) Benjamin Jowett, who had attended Dr Arnold's inaugural lecture at Oxford. Clough was one of the most influential university men in this circle and had the reputation of being both a promising poet and a profound thinker in religious and political matters. In contrast to Clough's earnestness, Arnold was known for his playful mockery and banter, which his acquaintances found both entertaining and irritating, a foreshadowing of the 'vivacities' that would later characterize his critical prose.

Arnold came to respect Clough more as a classicist than a poet, and in future years he was impatient with Shairp and others from the Oxford group who admired Clough's 'novelistic' treatment of contemporary life in his narrative poems. Nevertheless, the friendship between Arnold and Clough which developed during this time at Oxford continued to be a major factor in their lives and careers for at least a decade. During the course of this decade, Arnold wrote most of his important poetry, and there is no doubt about Clough's influence on his aesthetic and intellectual development. By 1853 Arnold was attempting to arrest the growing estrangement between the two men when he wrote to Clough, '[T]his I am sure of: the period of my development ... coincides with that of my friendship with you so exactly that I am for ever linked with you by intellectual bonds – the strongest of all' (*SL* 80).

Arnold had completed 'Cromwell', his Newdigate Prize poem, by February 1843 and it was published at Oxford later that year. He was prepared to recite the poem at Commemoration in the Sheldonian Theatre on 28 June, but an uproar among the students over the controversial award of a complimentary degree to the

American ambassador made this performance impossible. The assigned topic of Oliver Cromwell reflected current interest in Carlyle's treatment of the Puritan Lord Protector in *Heroes and Hero Worship* (1841) but also may have been intended as a criticism of the Puseyite cult of King Charles the Martyr. Arnold's poem, written in heroic couplets, depicts Cromwell standing on the banks of the Thames, looking at the 'tall dark ships' that were soon to set sail for America. As he approaches middle age, he is contemplating emigration to America, but after falling into a reverie in which he foresees his historic destiny, he of course decides to remain in England. His was

> A Life – whose ways no human thought could scan,
> A life – that was not as the life of man;
> A life – that wrote its purpose with a sword,
> Moulding itself in action, not in word!   (ll. 219–22)

The main significance of 'Cromwell' is that its success built up Arnold's confidence in his poetic powers. Although Arnold was not wholly satisfied with the poem and never reprinted it, it has interesting qualities. 'Cromwell' incorporates water imagery in a way that adumbrates his more mature work: Arnold begins with a Romantic image of the sea as the site of Freedom and later describes Cromwell's outer life first as a 'dark current', then as a 'silent plain' through which a 'swift river' (his inner life) flows. This is the awkward beginning of the river and sea imagery that figures so prominently in many of Arnold's best known poems.[1] It is worth noting that, although Arnold based the incident in his poem on a hint he found in Hume's *History of England*, Arnold's father had once toyed with the idea of emigration to America, and it is as a courageous leader of men that Arnold would later portray his father in the elegy 'Rugby Chapel'.

By the time Arnold faced 'Schools' (final examinations) in November 1844, he had already written several of the poems that he would publish in his 1849 volume, most notably the sonnet 'Shakespeare', with its arresting image of Shakespeare as a lofty mountain 'Planting his steadfast footsteps in the sea'. Not all critics have praised this poem – F. R. Leavis thought it was 'an orotund exercise in thuriferous phrases and generalities'[2] – but Arnold's attempt to deal with the enigmatic power of Shakespeare's art is a major early work:

> Others abide our question. Thou art free.
> We ask and ask – Thou smilest and art still,
> Out-topping knowledge.   (ll. 1–3)

In later life as a celebrated critic, Arnold would have rather less to say about Shakespeare than one might expect, but at this early stage of his career the poem shows he has been thinking deeply about the Shakespeare criticism of Hazlitt, Coleridge and Carlyle, and it also shows his personal fascination with the mysterious origins of artistic genius. Jovial in his social life, Arnold – in the tradition of the great poetic genius described in his poem – was very reserved about his own creative writing. His reticence helps to explain why the time of a poem's composition often cannot be precisely documented, but other poems written by the end of 1844 include 'To a Gipsy Child by the Sea-shore', 'Mycerinus', 'Stagirius', 'The Voice', 'A Question', 'To the Duke of Wellington', 'Written in Butler's Sermons', 'Written in Emerson's Essays', and probably 'The Hayswater Boat' and 'In Harmony with Nature.'

Arnold drew his subjects from a variety of sources, and he measured his own responses to life against those of the major influences on his mind. His poem about the Gypsy child was inspired by a mother and child he saw at Douglas on the Isle of Man while on holiday with his family. The child's sad face made him recall Wordsworth's notion of the soul's pre-existence as expressed in his 'Immortality Ode', but Arnold's poem is less hopeful. 'Mycerinus', based on a story from Herodotus about the son of the Egyptian king Cheops, also has Wordsworthian overtones but, again, implies an un-Wordsworthian pessimism. This poem about a young man who responds to Fate's arbitrary decree – that he die in six years' time – by abandoning his duties and dedicating himself to revelry probably is related to young Arnold's own role as nonchalant 'swell' at Oxford and to his expectation of an early death. 'In Harmony with Nature' is even more openly pessimistic about a possible beneficent relationship between humankind and nature: 'Nature and man can never be fast friends.'

The 'voice' of the poem by that name almost certainly belongs to Newman: his 'lute-like tones' 'Blew such a thrilling summons to my will,/Yet could not shake it'. Like many other undergraduates, Arnold was charmed by Newman's sermons at St Mary's yet not persuaded by his religious opinions. Nevertheless, Arnold would later name Newman, along with Goethe, Wordsworth, and the French critic Sainte-Beuve as the figures from whom he had learned 'habits, methods, ruling ideas, which are constantly with me' (*SL* 233). Arnold's poem on Emerson reflects his mixed reactions to reading the 1841 and 1844 volumes of that amazing American's *Essays,* and the one on Butler's *Sermons* – a textbook for 'Greats' – indicates that he had been pursuing at least some of his assigned readings at Oxford.

Unfortunately, Arnold was generally unprepared for the 'Schools' examination, and three weeks of desperate cramming did not save him from a second-class degree, which was awarded in November 1844. After this sobering experience, Arnold decided to compete for an Oriel Fellowship that would be decided the next spring. While preparing for the examination, he took the temporary position of assistant-master at Rugby, where he taught fifth-form classics under his father's successor, Dr A. C. Tait, who would later become Archbishop of Canterbury. When Arnold was elected Fellow of Oriel College in late March 1845, he modestly wrote to his Uncle Trevenen Penrose, his mother's brother, that his success 'may in some measure atone for the discredit of a second class in the Eyes of those who felt most the discredit of it, yet in real truth it leaves me, as to my reading, very much where I was before' (*SL* 27). (There was no prescribed reading list for the Oriel exam.) The long-term significance of Arnold's accomplishment would be primarily symbolic: at this critical juncture in his life he reaffirmed his status as a competent and accomplished young scholar and gentleman. Furthermore, at Oriel he was following in the footsteps of both his father, who had been granted his fellowship there 30 years before, and Clough, who had been at Oriel since 1842. (In addition, Oriel was J. H. Newman's old college.) Nevertheless, though he later would use an idealized image of Oxford in some of his most important lectures and essays, Arnold, like Clough and many others there at the time, realized full well that the general academic level left much to be desired, as a very critical report from the Royal Commission on the University of Oxford would point out in 1852. Arnold himself, comparing the English universities with those of Germany and France in an 1861 report, wrote 'So entirely have Oxford and Cambridge become mere *hauts lycées,* so entirely has the very idea of a real university been lost by them, that the professors there are not even organized in faculties; and their action is . . . perfectly feeble and incoherent' (*CPW* 4:323–4).

The atmosphere at Oriel under Provost Edward Hawkins was conservative and evangelical, not congenial to lively conversation, but Arnold was not unhappy there (*MAAL* 82–3). Arnold maintained a dandified style of behaviour, but he was reading deeply in works that would ground his future poetry. During these Oriel years he began the practice of keeping a diary in which he recorded reading lists, along with comments on literature, religion and the meaning of life. Not only was Arnold eclectic in his reading of George Sand (whose liberal idealism appealed to him and whose version of feminine sentimentality may have reminded him of his mother), Goethe (who had largely displaced his earlier interest in Byron), the French poet Beranger (who reinforced his affectation of French culture), and the Hindu classic *Bhagavad Gita* (where he found a discipline of resignation congenial with his developing stoicism): he typically balanced his studies of Kant, Lucretius, Descartes, and the Epicureans and Stoics with critical refutations of their positions (*MAAL* 93), following the dialogic impulse that would lead him to his later work as critic. The culmination of Arnold's relatively carefree bachelor life came in these years. In July 1846 he travelled to France, where he was able to arrange for a short visit to George Sand at her house in Nohant. Although in his later career as a critic Arnold had little to say about novels, he read them with pleasure throughout his life and was something of a disciple of Sand in the 1840s. In particular, he took her *Lelia* (1833) seriously, finding solace in this novel, which he came to associate with the Alpine imagery and brooding Romanticism of Senancour's epistolary novel *Obermann* (1804). After teaching again at Rugby to earn money in the autumn of 1846, he returned to Paris in late December and stayed until February 1847, indulging his infatuation with the French actress Elisa Rachel – whom he had seen perform in London – by attending all her performances. Arnold was attracted to her 'profound emotional force and inward concentration' (*MAAL* 110) and later wrote sonnets about her, one of which suggests that he identified with the 'contending powers' that clashed in her soul, not 'the radiant spirit of Greece alone' but also 'Germany, France, Christ, Moses, Athens, Rome' ('Rachel III', probably written in 1863).

By April 1847 he had begun to work as private secretary to

the Marquis of Lansdowne, elder statesman and Lord President of the Council in Lord Russell's Whig government. Arnold's mother was anxious that he find regular employment and may have written to Lansdowne on his behalf. Arnold's duties were fairly light, and he had time for his literary pursuits. At the same time, he was able to observe at first hand the workings of aristocratic Whig politics, an experience that would later inform his social and political writings. Though he was influenced by Conservative thinkers like Edmund Burke and though he often quarrelled with Liberal contemporaries and especially with the Nonconformists who made up a key constituency in the Liberal party, Arnold would always describe himself as a Liberal and could never bring himself to vote for the Tories.

Two of Arnold's brothers were striking out on bold new courses during this period. In November 1847, Tom, in search of social ideals and a new way of life, emigrated to New Zealand. The following February, Willy emigrated to India as an ensign in the Bengal Army of the East India Company. Apparently Arnold was less adventurous and ambitious, but he eventually found his way to a deeper engagement and commitment in life. Through the connection with Lansdowne, Arnold in 1851 would be appointed Inspector of Schools, a position that would enable him to marry and one that he would keep until he retired late in life. In the meantime, he underwent an enigmatic and disappointing (but creatively fruitful) romantic affair, and, at the age of 26, published his first volume of verse, *The Strayed Reveller, and Other Poems*. The author was identified by the pseudonym 'A'. In February 1849 the book was released in 500 copies by B. Fellowes (the publisher of Dr Arnold's sermons, Roman history and *Miscellaneous Works*), apparently at Fellowes' expense.

The title poem takes its setting from Book 10 of Homer's *Odyssey* and its dramatic form represents an early attempt by Arnold to capture a 'classical' style in English verse. The poem is also important as a young poet's attempt to reconcile two modes of poetry. The central character is a Youth who wanders into Circe's palace and drinks her magic wine. The wine enables him to imagine the clear and purely beautiful vision of the gods, a vision Arnold associated with the poetic ideals of Richter and with the spontaneous 'natural magic' he found in Maurice de Guérin's 'Le Centaure', which he had read in 1847. But what of the all-too-human, inward-feeling poet who sees with empathy and moral conviction? The 'wise bards' also 'Behold and sing' but with 'what labour!' and 'what pain!'. The price exacted by the gods for this poetry is 'To become what we sing'. But Arnold does not indicate whether the Youth is to become a 'wise bard'. He would continue to express the tension between Romantic introspection and a classical ideal of detached lucidity in various ways during the coming years.

In addition to the earlier poems from the Balliol days which have already been mentioned, the volume included the sonnet 'Quiet Work' (asking Nature to teach the poet the lessons of 'Tranquillity' and 'Repose' in his work); 'Fragment of an "Antigone"'; 'The Sick King in Bokhara'; the sonnets 'To a Friend', 'To George Cruikshank', 'To a Republican Friend' (and its companion 'Continued'), and 'Religious Isolation'; 'To my Friends who ridiculed a tender Leave-taking'; 'A Modern Sappho'; 'The New Sirens'; 'To Fausta' (later reprinted as 'A Question'); 'The Forsaken Merman'; 'The World and the Quietist'; 'In Utrumque Paratus'; and 'Resignation. To Fausta'.

The 'Friend' and 'Republican Friend' addressed in the poems by those names is Clough. Alluding to the political turmoils of 1848, the poet has his friend ask the (rather awkwardly phrased) question 'Who prop, thou ask'st, in these bad days, my mind?' The answer is Homer, the Stoic philosopher Epictetus, and Sophocles. In the 'Republican Friend' poems, the poet expresses sympathy for his friend's revolutionary optimism but is 'Rather to patience prompted, than that proud/Prospect of hope which France proclaims so loud'. 'The World and the Quietist' is directly related to Clough as well. This elusive poem is informed by the doctrine of 'holy work' which Arnold found in his exploration of *The Bhagavad Gita*, but a March 1848 letter to Clough shows that his friend was not favourably impressed by Arnold's 'Oriental wisdom' (*SL* 34). And 'Religious Isolation', which advises giving up the hopeless search for a personal enlightenment which will resolve all religious doubts, is written against the background of Clough's impending resignation of his Oriel fellowship in the summer of 1848 because he could no longer subscribe to the Thirty-nine Articles. (Clough finally took this rather impractical and self-defeating step the following October.)

Arnold's letters written to Clough between late 1847 and the time he published his 1849 volume suggest that he was forming his own political and aesthetic opinions against the works and ideas of the older poet. Arnold combines references to politics and aesthetics in a variety of ways that convey ambivalent attitudes. As Arnold develops an aesthetic that is detached from the 'Time Stream', he is simultaneously deeply interested in revolutionary developments in the France of 1848 and in social unrest at home. He tells his mother that he admires the French (with reservations) and sides with London crowds against the police (*SL* 35–6), but expresses scepticism about the very category of a 'people' to his 'Republican Friend' (*SL* 39–40). On a personal level, as he strives for practical wisdom in 'these damned times' (*SL* 59), Arnold seeks to retain the friendship of a man whom he seems impulsively to push away from him. His friendship with Clough was stormy and passionate; he makes cruel pronouncements on Clough's poetry (*SL* 28–9), and then attempts to apologize (*SL* 29–30). Arnold scolds Clough for trying 'to *solve* the Universe' in his poetry (*SL* 29), feels a 'growing sense of the deficiency of the *beautiful*' in Clough's poems (*SL* 32), ridicules Clough's Oxford friends who 'rave' about his 1848 poem *The Bothie of Toper-na-Fousich* (*SL* 49), and declares that Clough's poems 'are not *natural*' (*SL* 51). It seems that Arnold is projecting his own uncertainties and his own weaknesses on to Clough, or at least using Clough in an attempt to work through his own intellectual dilemmas. It is irritating that Clough tries to solve the universe, as it is fatiguing to witness 'Tennyson's dawdling with its painted shell'. And yet the remaining, apparently more positive, alternative associated with Shakespeare is also inadequate: 'to *reconstruct* the Universe is not a satisfactory attempt either' (*SL* 29). Arnold's formulations during this period are sometimes confusing, but at least one principle is clear: the Keatsian sort of lyric poetry should be rejected in favour of a classical *style* that is capable of producing 'grand moral effects' (*SL* 50, 53).

'The Forsaken Merman', which turned out to be one of the more popular and significant poems in the 1849 volume, is atypical of Arnold's poetic works and has been classified with some Romantic ballads as nineteenth-century 'poems of the supernatural'. Drawing on a Danish folk ballad, Arnold has a merman father speaking to his beautiful children of the sea, lamenting the absence of Margaret, their human mother, who has left their colourful and exciting underwater world to return to a dull, grey life with her own kind on land. Arnold's charming but troubling contrast of the natural pagan world of beauty and the controlled and pious human world (which ironically leads Margaret to abandon her family) has continued to fascinate readers, but it also figures at this early stage of his career the complex tensions between a life of the imagination and the adult duties and responsibilities that would haunt him for the rest of his life.

Like Wordsworth's 'Tintern Abbey', Arnold's 'Resignation' is a poem addressed to a favourite sister ('Fausta' is Arnold's older sister Jane) about revisiting a place and the reflections which follow the two occasions. But unlike Wordsworth, who finds that Nature leads 'From joy to joy', Arnold reflects that natural objects 'Seem to bear rather than rejoice' and ends his poem with an enigmatic but chilling reference to 'The something that infects the world'. Arnold never rejected all of Wordsworth – he continued to believe in the primacy of authentic experience and feeling, for example – but even more strongly than the 'Gipsy Child' poem, this melancholy lyric reinforces the impression that at least one of Arnold's projects in his early poetry was to revise Wordsworth's poetic vision of nature.[3]

The other poem in the volume addressed to Jane as 'Fausta' is concerned with lost joy and 'False and hollow' dreams. Arnold's surviving letters to Jane from the late 1840s on confirm his habit of revealing to her the melancholy side of his outwardly jovial personality. From the beginning of Arnold's literary career, Jane, whom he always addresses in correspondence by her family name 'K', was his closest confidante (*MAAL* 101–4). Like Clough, she is an intimate friend with whom he shares his inner feelings and thoughts, though with her Arnold drops his defensive posturing and adopts a tone of utter frankness and occasionally that of meditation or confession: 'I am subject to these periods of spiritual eastwind when I can lay hold only of the outside of events or words' (*SL* 60). She is the Arnold family member who is best able to understand his ambitions and fears. In the summer of 1849 he writes to her that 'my poems are fragments . . . I am fragments, while you are a whole' and asks that she not look for an internal consistency in his work that is absent (*SL* 57). Along with Clough and a few other university friends, such as Froude and Shairp, she was one of a very small group whom Arnold could expect to understand his poetry. Jane is perhaps the audience and the critic whom Arnold takes most seriously, particularly in his early poetic career. In 1853 he would write, 'I seem to want to see *you* and be with *you* more than anyone when my Poems are making their way ... you were my first hearer' (*SL* 93).

As shown by his letters to his sister Jane and to Clough, Arnold was passionate in his art, but like many young poets, he was tentative and full of self-doubts when it came to publication. He published under the pseudonym 'A' – which his father had once used when publishing social criticism in periodicals – but he sent copies of the book to selected friends. In critical retrospect, *The Strayed Reveller* as a first book of poetry was an outstanding artistic success, but it found few readers when it appeared in 1849. Although the book was not widely discussed in print, some of the reviewers anticipated future contemporary criticism of Arnold. In an unsigned piece in *Fraser's*, Charles Kingsley referred to A as 'a true poet' but asked, 'To what purpose all the self-culture ... What has he taught us?' (*MAP* 42). The critic for the *English Review* found A to be too doubting and full of melancholy (*MAP* 1–32). Writing for the *Germ*, William Michael Rossetti referred to A's self-consciousness, a legacy of Byronism: an acute observation, given Arnold's subsequent judgment of his own work along the same lines (*MAP* 56–66). Overall, the critical comment was mixed but not especially unfavourable. William Aytoun found A inferior to Elizabeth Barrett Browning but acknowledged that he had the potential to become a successful poet (*MAP* 47–55).

The Strayed Reveller was never reprinted, but of the 27 poems it contained, only 'The Hayswater Boat' was not used by Arnold in later editions (probably because of its 'Tennysonian' romanticism). The major themes of Arnold's mature poetry were already present in this first volume: the need for stoic detachment, the buried self, the primacy of universal law over personal desire, the inadequacy of human love, the transience of human life, the exhaustion produced by inner division. *The Strayed Reveller* already provides plenty of evidence of the interior tension between rational and intuitive thought, between the moralist and the lyricist in the poet, to support variations of the 'divided self' or 'two Arnolds' theme that has been prominent in Arnold criticism.[4]

Arnold sensed that his stoic manner and emphasis on ideas would not appeal to a wide audience and he was envious of the measure of popular success achieved by his friend Clough. He was convinced that his was not a favourable age for good poetry, and in a letter to Jane, he described himself as 'rather a reformer in poetical matters'.[5] At the same time, he was keenly aware of what it could mean to be recognized as an important poet. The

great poet-prophet Wordsworth had been a friend and neighbour to the Arnolds in their Lake District home. Like many of
his young peers at Oxford he had felt the power of the 'hero as
poet' ideal promulgated by Carlyle. While writing his earliest
poems he had still been under the spell of the fiery Byron, and
he continued to acknowledge the emotional force of Byron's poetry
even after he had all but abandoned the writing of poetry himself.
After his identity as a poet became public and his reputation
grew slowly but steadily in the coming years, he measured himself
– with mounting frustration – against Tennyson, the contemporary poet with the highest status.

At a deeper level Arnold had absorbed Romantic, Kantian ideas
about poetry that elevated the status of the poet while ensuring
that he always faced his limitations. As he would later put it,
'The grand power of poetry is its interpretative power; by which
I mean . . . the power of so dealing with things as to awaken in
us a wonderfully full, new, and intimate sense of them, and of
our relations with them' (*CPW* 3:12–13). The poet has the power
to open up his readers to increased consciousness and the possibility of a unifying self-knowledge grounded in human experience, but this 'criticism of life', as he would call it, involves a
constant struggle. Long after his own poetic powers had diminished, Arnold kept this belief in the power of poetry to transcend common speech and scientific discourse at the centre of
his literary criticism. However, as a practising poet Arnold was
hampered by the inherent contradictions between his assumptions about painful Romantic engagement with the dilemmas of
life and the standards of calmness, serenity and poise he associated with the greatest poets of the past.

In spite of perceiving his own limitations and the inadequacies
of his age, Arnold was already a very ambitious poet in 1849.
But how could he achieve fame and help to reform English poetry?
He would draw on the great classic tradition and develop a
modern English version of the grand style, and at the same time,
like Goethe, he would focus on the most important *ideas* of his
own day. While writing the poems that made up *The Strayed
Reveller* he was reading Lucretius's *De Rerum Natura* (*On the Nature
of Things*) and dreaming of one day writing a major poem on
the Roman poet and philosopher (*SL* 318). Lucretius was a care-
ful observer of nature, interested in how human beings ought to
live, free of superstitious fears; Arnold found his views congenial.

However, by the time Arnold published his first book in February 1849, he was already engaged in another major poetic project, a series of poems that apparently grew out of a profound personal experience. Arnold had spent a brief holiday in the Swiss Alps in the autumn of 1848 and again in the autumn of 1849. In a letter to Clough dated 29 September 1848, Arnold mentioned a planned rendezvous on the following day with a blue-eyed lady at the Bellevue Hotel in Thun. This is almost certainly a reference to the 'Marguerite' figure at the centre of the 'Switzerland' poems. The poems chronicle a series of meetings and partings that apparently concluded during the 1849 visit. The 'Marguerite' experience has long been seen as an important turning-point in Arnold's poetic career. Until the late 1970s, when Honan began to publish articles in which he argued that Marguerite was really a young neighbour of the Arnolds who lived with her mother at Rothay Bank, near Fox How, it was generally assumed that Arnold had indeed met a young French woman in Switzerland, although he may have substantially fictionalized their relationship in his poems. Whether or not the woman was real, the Marguerite episode was seen to mark an important turning-point in Arnold's career because the unhappy affair led him to renounce the world of passionate romance and turn to his writing with a new dedication.[6] Since the real drama in the poem is interiorized, the poet grappling with the idea of his unrealized passion, the actual identity of Marguerite did not seem crucial.

Although his version of the Marguerite story remains controversial and has been contested by some other Arnold scholars, Honan is convinced that Arnold was passionately attached for a time to Mary Claude, a young lady of French Huguenot origin who had moved with her mother and siblings to England after living in Berlin (*MAAL* 144–67). According to Honan, when she failed to meet him for their rendezvous in Switzerland as planned, Arnold was teased by friends and family members. The incident was never publicly discussed, and any romantic intimacy must have ended in 1849. After Arnold's marriage in 1851, it was more important than ever to suppress the story. Another possibility, however, is that Arnold was briefly infatuated with his mother's attractive neighbour in Westmorland but that the Marguerite of 'Switzerland' was an entirely different woman. Claude, a writer who had already published poems and stories for children by the autumn of 1848, never married and continued to live in England.

Whatever the facts of the matter may have been, the resulting love poems are important works in which Arnold takes a new direction. Honan rightly sees in Arnold's story of frustrated love a variety of 'reflective passion': *'la passion réfléchissante, la passion qui se juge elle-même'*, borrowing a phrase that Mme de Staël used to describe Goethe's *Werther*. This mode of feeling, that of an isolated hero who in the process of judging his own passions arrives at deeper self-knowledge, is also associated with Senancour's *Obermann* (a particular favourite of Arnold's at this time) and other works of European sentimental romanticism.

Arnold had written at least three, and perhaps more, of the 'Switzerland' lyrics before he published *The Strayed Reveller*, but he chose to include only 'To my Friends, who ridiculed a tender Leave-taking' (later renamed 'A Memory Picture'). This poem (which later was placed first in the series and later still taken out of it altogether) sets at once the tone of resignation to the limitations of romantic love: 'Quick, thy tablets, Memory', says the poet, who wants to preserve a precious memory of Marguerite, knowing that 'Time's current strong/Leaves us fixed to nothing long.' Other poems written before 1850, in approximate order of composition, were 'Meeting', 'Parting', 'A Dream', 'A Farewell', 'Isolation. To Marguerite', and 'To Marguerite, in Returning a Volume of the Letters of Ortis' (later renamed 'To Marguerite – Continued').

The last-named lyric would come to be regarded as a classic nineteenth-century expression of estrangement and isolation:

> Yes! in the sea of life enisled,
> With echoing straits between us thrown,
> Dotting the shoreless watery wild,
> We mortal millions live *alone*.   (ll. 1–4)

Arnold took the original title of the poem from Ugo Foscolo's *Letters of Ortis* (1802), the story of a melancholy Italian who commits suicide after a disappointing love affair. This and other poems in the series that express individual isolation and desperate longing for union with another through romantic love anticipate 'The Buried Life' and 'Dover Beach', both of which were composed within the next two years. In addition, the self-analysis that characterizes the series as a whole looks forward to *Empedocles on Etna*, the title poem from Arnold's second volume of poetry, published in 1852.

Arnold did not finish his grand poem on Lucretius, but the ambitious *Empedocles*, composed during the period 1849–52 along with several other major poems, represents his most substantial effort to develop a 'classical' poet-philosopher figure who would adequately address the spiritual ailments of humankind in the mid-nineteenth century. In fact Arnold converted stanzas originally intended for 'Lucretius' into his poem about the sceptical philosopher-poet of Sicily in the fifth century BC who, according to legend, despaired of attaining truth and flung himself into the crater of Mount Etna.

The period 1849–52 is also pivotal in Arnold's personal life. Although he was planning and writing some of his best poems at the time, 1850 was a frustrating year. Following the Marguerite episode, he began to court Frances Lucy Wightman, daughter of Sir William Wightman, Justice of the Queen's Bench, but Judge Wightman interrupted the courtship because he thought Arnold's income was insufficient to support his daughter and a family household. Arnold was receiving £120 per quarter from his Oriel appointment, but he would have to give up the stipend when he married, and he had only £72 per quarter from his post as Lansdowne's Private Secretary (*MAAL* 217). Like his friend Clough and other young intellectuals of his day who lacked independent means, Arnold faced a problematical economic future. In 'The River', later incorporated into the series of love poems entitled 'Faded Leaves' based on his relationship with Miss Wightman, Arnold describes a boat ride down the Thames during which he complains of his unresponsive companion: 'My pent-up tears oppress my brain,/My heart is swollen with love unsaid.' (Arnold suppressed the first six stanzas of the manuscript poem when it was published, presumably because he decided details about the setting and the clothing worn by the young woman were too revelatory.) It seems that Miss Wightman did in fact respond favourably after Arnold declared himself, but the young couple would nevertheless have to wait for the Judge's blessing. Meanwhile Arnold was very unhappy about the marriage of Jane Arnold to William Forster – a Quaker who would later become a Liberal statesman and education reformer – in August of that year, and refused to attend the wedding, temporarily estranging himself from his favourite sister and close confidante. In addition, Arnold may have been envious of his two far-flung brothers who also married in 1850: Willy in the Punjab and Tom in Tasmania.

In 1851 events took a more favourable turn for Arnold. In April he was appointed Inspector of Schools by Lord Lansdowne. This appointment, with a base salary of £450 a year plus travelling expenses, cleared his way to marrying Miss Wightman, and Judge Wightman agreed to provide an additional annual allotment of £100. The wedding took place on 10 June. In the early autumn, the couple took a late honeymoon journey to France, Italy and Switzerland, and on 11 October 1851, Arnold began his 35-year career of travelling widely, inspecting elementary schools and training colleges conducted by Nonconformists and Methodists.

At this time elementary schools were regulated according to the Council on Education's Minutes of 1839 and 1846. The first inspectors were appointed in 1839, after it was decided that no monetary grants would be made either to the schools or to the Training Colleges for teachers unless they accepted government inspection. The inspectors were not supposed to intervene in the management or discipline of schools, or interfere directly with religious instruction which was left to ecclesiastical authorities. Their primary duty was to observe and collect facts, which they reported to the Council. After 1846 inspectors had the additional duty of examining the pupil teachers – exceptional students, thirteen to eighteen years of age – who continued their own education while assisting the adult staff of the schools. Arnold was one of three lay inspectors assigned to schools not affiliated with either the Church of England or the Roman Catholic Church, and the district for which he was responsible at the beginning consisted of thirteen English counties, all counties of South Wales, and all except two counties of North Wales. Over the next three years, the Welsh counties were replaced by counties in south-east and south-central England.

In the early days Arnold's wife often accompanied him on his tours of inspection, but he sometimes travelled alone. He also occasionally travelled as Marshal to his father-in-law on circuit and earned additional income in that way. Whenever possible, Arnold spent a few days at Oxford, and he treasured long holidays at Fox How, although he often brought work with him. At the end of each school year, he was required to submit a general report on his inspections, and he had to spend a week each December administering and grading examinations of pupil-teachers at training colleges. In his new career Arnold maintained close ties with some of his Oxford friends, including Walrond and the barrister Wyndham Slade – both of whom were companions during European travels – as well as Clough, though Arnold and Clough had become less intimate since Arnold's courtship of Fanny Lucy had dramatically curtailed the amount of time the two poets spent together.

Although Arnold did not inherit his father's interest in schools as institutions, he enjoyed travel, and he was broadly sympathetic to the wide range of society with which his inspectorship brought him in contact. While he was only mildly interested in specific issues relating to the schools' curriculum, he was idealistic about the overall 'humanising' and 'civilising' effects of education. In particular, he was convinced that British elementary schools were going to play an essential role in 'civilising the next generation of the lower classes, who, as things are going, will have most of the political power of the country in their hands' (*SL* 67). One of his persistent complaints was about the fees (typically, 2*d*–8*d*, or 1–3p, per week) charged by some of the schools which excluded the poorest students. From the beginning Arnold strongly advocated free, compulsory elementary education, supported by the State, and, for him, education combined fundamentally social, political and moral purposes. Although he did not know it, Arnold was entering his last productive period as a poet, but he was also beginning the practical research that would help to generate the socio-political ideas of *Culture and Anarchy*.

Arnold assured his wife that 'I intend seriously to see what I can do . . . in the literary way that might increase our income' (*SL* 67), but the commitments and pressures of Arnold's new profession were not congenial to his poetic career. From this time onwards, the rigours of his inspection duties would be a continual motif in his correspondence, especially to his mother. He would no longer have the luxury of quiet, leisure time for literary pursuits that he had enjoyed as part of University life and in his sinecure with Lord Lansdowne. In future years, Arnold would become increasingly envious of poets like his great rival Tennyson who were not tied down by professional, non-literary careers. However, unlimited free time does not necessarily lead to artistic productivity, and the hustle and bustle of Arnold's new mode of life brought him into contact with a variety of people and places that would feed his interest in social issues and serve to hasten his transition from poet to critic. Before that happened, the exhilaration accompanying such important life changes helped to bring about the flowering of Arnold's poetic art. Arnold had a strong, rugged body and a driving ambition to continue his 'real' life's work in literature while succeeding in his new profession. In spite of nagging doubts about the direction he was taking as an artist and thinker, Arnold wrote one important poem after another.

While *Empedocles* was taking shape in his mind, Arnold was writing in reaction to a variety of experiences. In the autumn of 1849 he wrote 'Stanzas in Memory of the Author of "Obermann"', in tribute to Senancour, who had died three years earlier and whose novel had originally attracted Arnold's attention because it had 'charmed' authors such as George Sand and Sainte-Beuve, whom Arnold admired. This poem, which associates the fairly obscure French author with Wordsworth and Goethe as exemplars of sensibility and self-possession, calls to our attention the distinctive and somewhat unexpected nature of the nineteenth-century literary influences that told most strongly on Arnold. Senancour had a 'gravity and severity' that separated him from other sentimental writers, but the melancholy genius after all had an 'unstrung will' along with his broken heart. Finally he is an unsatisfactory model for Arnold in his search for just the right version of the intellectual as solitary quester in these 'damned times', as he described them to Clough.

When Wordsworth died in April 1850, the poet's son-in-law Edward Quillinan, a neighbour of the Arnolds at Fox How, asked Arnold to write an elegy, and 'Memorial Verses' was published in *Fraser's Magazine* the following June. Once again Arnold contextualizes the subject of his elegy within a group of three: this time, it is Byron, Goethe and Wordsworth. Byron 'taught us little – but our soul/Had felt him like the thunder's roll'. Goethe, 'Physician of the iron age', diagnosed the fatal illness of Europe and advised '*Art still has truth, take refuge there!*' Wordsworth, on the other hand, had 'healing power'. Now that he is gone, 'who, ah! who, will make us feel?' Arnold's method is to assess the importance of his great predecessors in terms of their overall significance to their historical era. This is simultaneously an intellectual exercise that will carry over into Arnold's criticism – the continual measuring of the writer's 'adequacy' to his age – and an attempt to place himself in relation to the writers that he most admires and respects, the ones whose influence he has most felt. Arnold's habitual comparisons and adjustments of assessment over time helps us understand the nature of his later claim in a well-known 1869 letter to his mother that his own poems 'represent, on the whole, the main movement of mind in the last quarter of a century' and that they will appear so in retrospect as people become increasingly conscious of that movement (*SL* 217).

Two major poems are closely associated with the beginnings of Arnold's married life. He wrote at least a portion of 'Dover Beach' on a honeymoon trip with his bride to the seaside town of Alverstoke following their wedding in June 1851. (Later in the month they visited Dover as well.) In September of that year, during their Continental wedding journey, the couple visited the monastery of the Grande Chartreuse in the French Alps, and Arnold's experiences there led him to draw together ideas he had been mulling over for several years and produce 'Stanzas from the Grande Chartreuse'. Arnold delayed the publication of 'Dover Beach' until 1867, but eventually it became one of his best known poems. In it he weaves together allusions to the present, classical Greece, and medieval Europe. Critics have found echoes of Sophocles, Thucydides, Milton, Wordsworth, Keats and J. A. Froude's novel *The Nemesis of Faith*, among others, but Arnold achieves unity by effectively juxtaposing sight and sound imagery. And in spite of a very bleak, 'modern' view of the human condition, the poem does after all affirm romantic love:

> Ah, love, let us be true
> To one another! for the world, which seems
> To lie before us like a land of dreams,
> So various, so beautiful, so new,
> Hath really neither joy, nor love, nor light,
> Nor certitude, nor peace, nor help for pain;
> And we are here as on a darkling plain
> Swept with confused alarms of struggle and flight,
> Where ignorant armies clash by night.   (ll. 29–37)

In his 'Grande Chartreuse' poem, Arnold allows himself to identify imaginatively and emotionally with the Carthusian monks while understanding rationally that it would be impossible to give himself up to a Newmanesque Catholic faith. In what came to be one of the defining phrases of the Victorian age, the poet is

'Wandering between two worlds, one dead,/The other power-less to be born'. The poem was first published in *Fraser's Magazine* in April 1855.

Even without the honeymoon poems, *Empedocles on Etna, and Other Poems*, published by Fellowes in October 1852, according to the consensus of critics today, represents Arnold at the height of his poetic powers. However, Arnold, who once again published under the pseudonym A, became dissatisfied with the volume soon after it appeared and began to plan a new one in which he would take a bold new direction. By November of the following year he had published a new volume which conspicuously omitted the title poem and a few others from the previous one, added what he considered to be a major new poem in his new mode, and explained his actions in a Preface that can be considered his first important critical essay.

Arnold's arrangement of poems in the 1852 volume reveals the divisions and tensions in his poetic programme at this volatile moment in his literary career. The ambitious long poem *Empedocles on Etna* comes first. It is followed by a block of sixteen lyrical poems, the first thirteen of which can be classified as love poems. Of the love poems, the first six are related to the crisis in Arnold's courtship of his wife Fanny Lucy and the following seven to the earlier 'Marguerite' episode. Four of the Fanny Lucy poems will find their way into the five-part series 'Faded Leaves' in Arnold's 1855 collection, while the others will become the more celebrated 'Switzerland' series (six poems in the 1853 edition, seven in 1854, eight in 1857). In retrospect it is easy to distinguish between the two groups of poems but the dividing line was not so clear in 1852. What seems missing from both groups, however, is the sense of an overwhelming or uncontrollable passion. The love poems, with their dominant mood of longing and regret, are followed, appropriately enough, by three lyrics in which the poet expresses doubts about the meaning and purpose of life. The sonnet later named 'Youth's Agitations', along with 'Self-Deception' and 'Lines written by a Death-Bed' (part of which was later published as 'Youth and Calm') perhaps reveal more about Arnold's personal and artistic doubts ('We but dream we have our wish'd-for powers./Ends we seek we never shall attain') than do his greater artistic successes.

Next comes Arnold's contribution to Arthurian romance, 'Tristram and Iseult', which he had begun in Switzerland in 1849, and, finally, a group of seventeen poems that includes the elegies on Wordsworth and Senancour and other interesting works such as 'Self-Dependence', 'A Summer Night', 'The Buried Life', 'Lines written in Kensington Gardens', 'The Youth of Nature', 'The Youth of Man' and 'Morality', in which Arnold as solitary observer continues his exploration of the boundary between man and nature. Overall, Arnold's *Empedocles* volume incorporates a remarkable range of significant new poetry.

It is widely assumed today that *Empedocles* is Arnold's most important and successful poem, an honest exploration of deeply-felt contradictions and inadequacies. Clearly Arnold saw the plight of his ancient philosopher as analogous to that of the Victorian intellectual. Among the traits of 'modern consciousness' are scepticism concerning ultimate truths, acute self-consciousness, a sense of isolation and loneliness, suspicions of 'pure' intellectualism, the desire for 'wholeness', and nostalgia for a lost world. It is no wonder that many readers have identified Empedocles with the author himself. As Arnold explained in the 1853 Preface, Empedocles had 'survived his fellows, living on into a time when the habits of Greek thought and feeling had begun fast to change, character to dwindle, the influence of the Sophists to prevail' (*CPW* 1:1). However, Arnold's original plan had been to present his protagonist as a man 'who sees things as they are – the world as it is – God as he is: in their stern simplicity'.[7] Arnold wanted to express a classical ideal of harmony and fulfilment, and he intended that Empedocles possess some of the qualities that he later associated with the disinterested critic, who strives to see the object 'as it really is'. But Arnold was unable to imagine this positive sage figure as he developed him in the poem itself. The confusion and folly of the world are too much for Empedocles, who is now 'dead to every natural joy'. When (inspired by the songs of his youthful friend Callicles) he does momentarily recover a feeling of joy in union with nature, he captures the moment in a sort of Browningesque move and takes his suicidal plunge into Etna's crater. A century later, it was easy to see this poem, which does not flinch from its desperation, as the culmination of the poetry of experience, and to condemn Arnold, who was dissatisfied with his creation, for repressing his exploration of the egotistical imagination. This view was particularly tempting when a connection was made between the idealized and lofty but inaccessible Greek culture that Arnold hopelessly pursued and the strict moral aspirations, manliness and high ideals of Arnold's father. It was said that Arnold was attempting to escape from his (feminine) emotional side, from the unresolved problems of his personality and his art. Ironically, the impulse to resist Arnold's criticism of his own work has been a major factor in securing his reputation as an important Victorian poet.

Arnold's version of the 'Tristram and Iseult' story antedates those of Wagner (1865), Tennyson (1872) and Swinburne (1882). However, it is not so much the narrative itself but the persona of its narrator that has interested critics. The poem represents Arnold's most successful effort to move away from a lyrical voice and create a narrator who maintains aesthetic distance from the emotions generated by the dramatic action of the poem. The poem is also interesting for the implications of the storytelling by Iseult of Brittany at the end – what cannot be endured in life can be endured when it is transformed into art – and for Arnold's uncharacteristic insights into the female psyche. In his implied contrast between Iseult of Brittany and the two romantic lovers, Arnold probably meant to juxtapose a model of the moral and responsible artist with the discredited Romantic model he associated with Keats. At a more personal level Arnold's fascination with the story of 'the two Iseults who did sway/Each her hour of Tristram's day' may have had its roots in the Marguerite/Fanny Lucy contrast in his own life. Miss Wightman was an eminently respectable and responsible young lady with High Church sympathies.

Echoing the 'Switzerland' sequence, 'The Buried Life' is also about estrangement: 'Alas! is even love too weak/To unlock the heart, and let it speak?' wonders the speaker, 'and yet/The same heart beats in every human breast'. The speaker searches for his genuine, unified *self*, this time figured as a 'buried stream'. He assumes that people in general are alienated not only from others but from themselves, but he cautiously asserts that in rare cases, 'When a beloved hand is laid in ours' we are able to experience and express our deepest sense of selfhood. Ironically, it is only by looking outward (into our lover's eyes) that we are enabled to achieve the inward vision. Like 'Dover Beach', 'The Buried Life' makes a powerful claim for romantic, sexual love. 'Lines Written in Kensington Gardens' is at once one of the last important pastoral poems in English and a lyric about the city. The gardens provide the illusion of a pastoral setting in the heart of London but offer no Wordsworthian sense of participation in the life of nature. 'A Summer Night', closely related to 'The Buried Life', is also about the urban experience: 'In the deserted, moon-blanched street,/How lonely rings the echo of my feet!' Arnold goes on to lament the emptiness of modern urban life and asks, 'Madman or slave, must man be one?' The slaves devote their lives to 'unmeaning taskwork', while the intellectual who attempts to escape from the prison of meaningless work is like a mad helmsman 'Still bent to make some port he knows not where, /Still standing for some false, impossible shore.'

Arnold's own dissatisfaction with the 1852 volume – and its title poem in particular – was heightened by some of the negative criticism it received. As with the 1849 book, reviews were mixed, but George David Boyle's opinion that the book 'constantly disappoints us' was not unusual. Boyle (whose review was published in the *North British Review* of May 1853 after Arnold had already withdrawn the volume) also echoes Arnold's own view that the age 'seems unfavourable' for poetry. Arnold knew that Clough – who after resigning his fellowship at Oriel had moved to the United States in search of academic employment – was reviewing *Empedocles* for the *North American Review* in December 1852 when he wrote to him, 'As for my poems they have weight, I think, but little or no charm ... I feel now where my poems (this set) are all wrong, which I did not a year ago.' And yet Arnold claims he was only being honest: 'But woe was upon me if I analysed not my situation: & [Goethe's] Werter [Chateaubriad's] René and such like none of them analyse the modern situation in its true *blankness* and *barrenness*, and *unpoetrylessness*' [*sic*] (*SL* 78). Nevertheless, Clough's review essay (which included commentary about Arnold's 1849 volume as well as the 1852) dealt a blow to Arnold when it appeared in July 1853. Clough made public his longstanding disagreements with Arnold over the proper subject matter of poetry: like the increasingly popular novel and unlike the poems of Arnold, modern poetry should deal with 'the actual, palpable things with which our every-day life is concerned'.[8] Worse, Clough compared Arnold's poetry unfavourably with that of Alexander Smith (a poet associated with the 'Spasmodic' school) whom Arnold did not respect. Clough did make useful comments about 'Tristram and Iseult' which Arnold politely thanked him for and used in revising the poem for future editions, but the review further weakened the already fragile friendship between the two men.

Arnold had already withdrawn the *Empedocles* volume, however, and the review that mattered most was Arnold's own. He focused on the 1852 title poem itself in the preface to his rapidly prepared 1853 volume, which was meant to supplant rather than merely follow that of 1852. By the end of the summer of 1853, Arnold had completed both 'Sohrab and Rustum' and 'The Scholar-Gipsy', important new poems. In August he wrote to Clough from Fox How, announcing that after being 'nearly stupified by 8 months inspecting' he was planning the new preface (*SL* 87), which he had finished by early October. 'How difficult it is to write prose', he wrote, 'because of the *articulations of the discourse*: one leaps these over in Poetry – places one thought cheek by jowl with another without introducing them – but in prose this will not do' (*SL* 90). Arnold had completed the preface by early October and *Poems by Matthew Arnold. A New Edition* appeared in November. Gone was 'Empedocles', along with the 'Obermann' stanzas, 'A Summer Night', 'The Buried Life', 'Kensington Gardens' and other 1852 poems, and Arnold made various revisions, reprinting fragments of the 1852 'Youth of Nature' as 'Richmond Hill' and 'The Power of Youth'. He did lift one of Callicles' songs out of *Empedocles* and reprint it as 'Cadmus and Harmonia'. He also reprinted most of the 1849 poems, including 'The Strayed Reveller', 'Mycerinus', 'The Forsaken Merman' and most of the sonnets. He omitted the Fanny Lucy poems but for the first time assembled the Marguerite poems under the heading 'Switzerland'. Overall, only nine of the poems were new, while 25 had been previously published.

Among the new poems in 1853 were 'Sohrab and Rustum', 'The Church of Brou', 'The Scholar-Gipsy', 'The Neckan' (a companion-piece to 'The Forsaken Merman') and 'Philomela', all of them based on legend or myth. Arnold intended 'Sohrab and Rustum' to be the centrepiece of his new book. The tragic story of the poem, in which a heroic warrior learns that the adversary he has mortally wounded in individual combat is his own father, is taken from the Persian *Shah Nameh of Firdousi* and other sources. Arnold was proud of the epic characteristics of his blank-verse narrative, which he called – in the Homeric tradition – an 'episode'. He created elaborate similes that are reminiscent of Milton's: in the opening section, Sohrab rises from bed and 'Through the black Tartar tents he passed, which stood/Clustering like bee-hives on the low flat strand/Of Oxus'. Arnold believed that he had achieved his newly formulated poetic goals in this poem, with its noble subject, its heroic characters and action, and its precision; he told his mother that it was 'by far the best thing I have yet done' (*LMA* I:34). Even so, there is some ambiguity in the way the meaning of the poem is generated by heroic actions; presumably the heroism is not found in the son's slaying of his father but rather in both father and son's acceptance of their tragic fate. Arnold was quick to contradict Clough's opinion that the poem was 'Tennysonian' and invited his friend to compare 'Sohrab and Rustum' with 'Morte d'Arthur' to 'see the difference in the *tissue* of the style of the two poems, and in its *movement*' (*SL* 90).

Arnold was less satisfied with 'The Scholar-Gipsy' because it did not 'animate' and 'ennoble' readers but instead offered only a 'pleasing melancholy', as he wrote to Clough (*SL* 92). Never-theless, the poem had a special significance for him, because it was associated with Clough and the Oxford years; both he and Clough were familiar with the source of the scholar-gypsy legend, Joseph Glanvill's seventeenth-century book *The Vanity of Dogmatizing*, and the two young poets had walked together in the Cumnor countryside near Oxford where the story is set. (When Arnold later wrote 'Thyrsis', his elegy on Clough, he made it a companion-piece to 'The Scholar-Gipsy'). Although he was not finally satisfied with the poem – anticipating some critics who would see his scholar-gypsy as irresponsible – Arnold clearly was attempting to create a more adequate version of the solitary questers who wander through his early poetry. For Arnold the myth of the scholar-gypsy stood for unity, stability and creativ-ity in a world of change and frustration, and this poem antici-pates his notion of the 'best' self, as distinct from the 'ordinary' self, which he developed in his critical prose. At the same time, in spite of Arnold's earlier critical remarks about Keatsian lyri-cism, which he had contrasted with the classical grand style, 'The Scholar-Gipsy' shows evidence of Keats's influence.

In the Preface, Arnold explains the exclusion of *Empedocles* by showing how the poem does not measure up to his ideal of what poetry should be. One major point is an emphatic denial: he did *not* reject the poem because its story is too historically remote for modern audiences. On this issue, Arnold heartily disagrees with a critic recently writing in the *Spectator* (later identified by Arnold as the editor, R. S. Rintoul) who thought that 'the poet who would really fix the public attention must leave the exhausted past, and draw his subjects from matters of present import' (*CPW* 1:3). *Empedocles* was not to be condemned on that score, but, according to Arnold, a poem must not only interest the reader by the accuracy of its representation but also 'inspirit and rejoice' him, 'convey a charm, and infuse delight' (*CPW* 1:2), and this *Empedocles* does not do. While it may successfully represent a time when 'the calm, the cheerfulness, the disinterested objectivity have disappeared' (*CPW* 1:1), it does not provide 'poetical enjoyment' because the suffering it portrays finds no vent in action. A successful poem must portray action: human actions are 'the eternal objects of poetry' (*CPW* 1:3), and expression must be subordinate to the delineation of the actions themselves in order to achieve unity and a profound moral impression. The hopeless, morbid situation of Empedocles and his reaction to it is painful, not genuinely tragic, representing the discouraging 'dialogue of the mind with itself' characteristic of nineteenth-century England (*CPW* 1:1).

Although the Preface itself is a bold and compelling attempt to justify, specifically, the exclusion of *Empedocles* and, more generally, a new theoretical position for its author, it bears a curiously problematic relation to the volume as a whole. Arnold did not make it clear in the Preface that he, with Aristotle on his mind, was referring only to narrative and dramatic – not lyric – poetry when he laid out his precepts. Most of the poems in the 1853 volume were of course reflective, philosophical lyrics, framed by the introductory 'Quiet Work' sonnet and concluding with 'The Future'. In fact the latter poem is much more compatible with 'Quiet Work' than with 'Empedocles', which had occupied the initial position in the 1852 volume, though neither short poem fits comfortably with 'Sohrab and Rustum'. But in spite of its internal confusions and tensions, the 1853 volume is the first published under Arnold's name and the first published by Longman (replacing Fellowes, Dr Arnold's old publisher). A new assertiveness replaces the tentativeness of the earlier productions, as Arnold makes a bold new move in his literary career. Later Yeats – no friend of Arnold's poetry – cited the precedent of Arnold's *Empedocles* when he decided to exclude the War Poets from his edition of an Oxford anthology of poetry.[9] In engaging contemporary critics on the issue of 'modern classicism' in the 1853 Preface, Arnold anticipated the pattern of critical dialogue that would generate most of his important prose works, though he did not begin this process in earnest until a few years later.

The 1853 *Poems* was too controversial to be considered a great critical success, but it was recognized as an important book and was widely reviewed. Clough noticed that critics could be roughly divided into two groups: 'one praising Sohrab highly and speaking gently of the preface; the other disparaging the preface and the general tone, and praising Tristram'.[10] As Clough implied, even some of the critics who applauded Arnold's search for a classical style were uneasy about the Preface or, in some cases, the whole idea of introducing a book of poems with a theoretical preface. Writing in 1864 of Arnold's Preface and his rejection of *Empedocles*, Walter Bagehot commented that 'Arnold is privileged to speak of his own poems, but no other critic could speak so and not be laughed at.'[11] Bagehot expressed a popular opinion when he argued that, aside from the problematical nature of Arnold's poetic theories, they were not really applicable to Arnold's poems in any case. Even Arnold's friend John Duke Coleridge wrote in the *Christian Remembrancer* that Arnold was 'fallacious and inadequate' as a theorist.[12] Those who wrote negatively of 'Sohrab and Rustum' tended to attack Arnold's concept of the 'modern' as false and comment on Arnold's apparent denial of present realities. Some critics, like William Roscoe, did praise the preface itself, emphasizing Arnold's classical approach and recognition that poetic art has intrinsic rules that should be recognized.

It was undeniable that Arnold had become a highly visible writer. By calling into question the relation of a poet to his times and by forcefully rejecting the personal, lyrical mode that had dominated English poetry since the ascendancy of the Romantics, he invited debate and made himself a target for controversy. He had come a long way since his timid presentation of poems by A less than five years earlier, and his demonstrated flair for probing sensitive aesthetic and cultural issues would lead him to a major shift in the direction of his literary career.

3

Poems, Second Series (1854), Merope (1857), On Translating Homer (1861), The Popular Education of France (1861)

Arnold's sensitivity concerning 'Sohrab and Rustum' during the composition process and his eagerness to seize upon praise of the poem after its publication revealed his anxiety about the new direction he was taking in his poetry. The years 1853–7 can be seen as an interregnum in his literary career. In 1853 Arnold was primarily a poet; four years later he would begin the prose phase of his career in earnest. This was not a calculated change, however. Arnold had every intention of vigorously pursuing his new poetic program as announced in the 1853 Preface. Once more he wrestled with his Lucretius materials to no avail, but by early October 1854 he had completed a poem which he thought 'will consolidate the peculiar sort of reputation that I got by Sohrab and Rustum' (*SL* 95). Again he had turned to legend and myth for his subject, basing 'Balder Dead' on the story of the Scandinavian sun god Balder from the *Edda* of Snorri Sturluson, through the French version given by Paul Henri Mallet in *Northern Antiquaries*. Arnold wanted to follow up on his success in 'Sohrab and Rustum', once again attaching the subtitle 'An Episode', calling attention to the epic qualities of the poem (although he later decided that the term was less appropriate in this case and removed the subtitle in 1869). Although it was a Northern European myth that had fired his imagination, Arnold as before longed to emulate classical models. He was not very concerned about fidelity to his sources and, instead of studying the Islandic narrative in any depth, prepared for his treatment of Balder's death, burial, and descent to Hell by reading heavily in Homer. He was highly pleased with the poem but critics – beginning with friends and family members – were less so (although old family friend A. P. Stanley agreed with Arnold that it was better than 'Sohrab and Rustum').

When Arnold published a second edition of his 1853 poems in 1854, he added a short new preface to that of 1853, acknowledging that his previously stated opinions about the proper subjects for poems did not apply to lyric poetry. He reminded his readers that *sanity* was the great virtue of the ancient classical writers but did not attempt a substantial response to the critics of his new poetic creed. *Poems. Second Series* was brought out by Longman in December 1854 (with a title-page dated 1855), but 'Balder Dead' was the only important new poem. Arnold included four of Callicles' songs from *Empedocles* as a series of lyrics entitled 'The Harp Player on Etna'. In the spring of 1855 he finally published his 'Grande Chartreuse' poem in *Fraser's Magazine*. He also wrote and published in the same magazine 'Haworth Churchyard', a sort of double elegy on Charlotte Brontë, recently deceased, and Harriet Martineau, who seemed to be mortally ill at the time but surprised Arnold and many others by living on until 1876. However, Arnold spent most of his creative energy in 1855 and 1856 trying yet again to shape his Lucretius project. By the autumn of 1856 he still had not produced a manuscript, but he was determined to write a verse drama, and he turned to a new subject. About one year later, he had completed *Merope*, and he published it with Longman in December 1857. The protagonist is a mother who awaits the return of her son Aepytus to avenge the murder of his father, Cresphontes, by his step-father, Polyphontes. Three versions of the Greek myth had been given in eighteenth-century plays by Maffei, Voltaire, and Alfieri.

Just as he had immersed himself in the reading of Homer while writing 'Balder', Arnold studied Sophocles in preparation for *Merope*, and after he was elected Professor of Poetry at Oxford in May of 1857 he used his new forum to explain and defend the approach to literature to which he was now committed in his creative work. In the election, members of Oxford Convocation cast a sizeable majority of votes for Arnold over his opponent, the Reverend John Ernest Bode, author of *Ballads from*

Herodotus. Despite his deeply-felt ties to Oxford and to the classical curriculum, Arnold was the less traditional, more progressive candidate. He was in fact the first holder of the post who was not an ordained minister. In his inaugural lecture, 'On the Modern Element in Literature', delivered in November 1857, he further developed his idea that classical literature is 'modern' when it manifests tolerance, a critical spirit, and intellectual maturity. Like his father's lectures on 'modern history' sixteen years before, it was delivered in the Sheldonian Theatre at Oxford. In the spirit of his 1853 Preface and with *Merope* on his mind, Arnold declared that drama, although narrower in scope than the epic, 'exhibits, above all, *the actions of man as strictly determined by his thoughts and feelings*; it exhibits, therefore, what may be always accessible, always intelligible, always interesting' (*CPW* 1:34). Ironically, Arnold's critical attempts to justify his own failing poetic programme led him away from poetry to concentrate on criticism itself. In spite of Arnold's passion for his subject, his manner of presentation was not effective, and the first series of lectures was not very successful. Nevertheless, he had made an important innovation: he was the first holder of this post to lecture in English rather than Latin.

In the meantime, his *Merope* was proving to be a critical failure. Unfortunately for Arnold, though there was considerable sympathy for his attempt to find a new direction for English poetry, many of his readers were predisposed to question any new works in the tradition of 1853. There was something prophetic in the review of a *New Quarterly* critic who wrote of 'Sohrab and Rustum' that Arnold's 'original strain resembles the bald, bad translation of a Greek chorus'.[1] Much the same thing was said about *Merope*. Reviewing *Merope* for the *New Quarterly*, William Roscoe wrote that Arnold's 'powers have everywhere shown that he is deficient in the higher power of conception' (*MAP* 17). Early in 1858, Arnold scoured the reviews, anxious that the 'unfamiliar stranger' he had introduced to the public would find favour, and he even had hopes that it would be performed on stage. He complained to his sister Frances that he was misunderstood by critics who falsely believed that he wanted to 'substitute tragedies *à la Grecque* for every other kind of poetical composition in England' (*SL* 107). Arnold maintained a stubborn loyalty to his play, and even late in life he hoped that some wealthy amateur would stage it after his death. Nevertheless, now he had to acknowledge *Merope*'s negative reception, and he protected his pride by making flippant remarks to friends; he wrote Fanny Du Quaire (sister of his old college friend, John Blackett) that she was not bound to like the play because it was 'calculated rather to inaugurate my Professorship with dignity than to move deeply the present race of *humans*' (*LMA* 1:69). He complained to his mother of the '*grossièreté*' of English reviewing but said he was 'determined in print to be always scrupulously polite' (*SL* 105). Arnold was always sensitive to criticism and eager for praise, but he also had the capacity to change and redirect his energies. In mid-January he wrote to his mother saying that he would 'now turn to something wholly different' (*SL* 106) and assured his sister Jane that he did not intend to 'keep preaching in the wilderness' (*SL* 107). Still, he persisted in his plan to complete his verse tragedy on Lucretius one day.

In his Oxford lectures Arnold continued the 'Modern Element' line, following his introductory effort with five additional lectures in this series (the texts of which have not survived), the last of which was delivered in May 1860. Arnold continued to struggle with the lectures; after elaborate preparation he spoke to small audiences. His wife urged him to appeal more to the emotions of his listeners (*MAAL* 295). At the same time, however, the conditions of Arnold's family life were improving. For the first seven years of his inspectorship Arnold and his wife had lived in temporary residences, as he carried out his duties. In 1855, a typical year, he examined a total of 173 'elementary schools', 117 'institutions', 368 pupil-teachers, 97 certified teachers, and 20 000 pupils (*MAAL* 262). Arnold was not a gifted bureaucrat, and sometimes he was careless about details, but he worked hard and took his responsibilities seriously. His letters to his mother and sisters frequently complain of overwork and exhaustion. There were other worries as well. Arnold – who had chronic financial problems throughout his adult life – had borrowed money at the time of his marriage, and he worried about his debts. He also worried about the health of his wife and children, who moved with him from one lodging to another. His son Thomas, born in July 1852, was a sickly child and remained a semi-invalid until his death in 1868. Another son, Trevenen William, was born in October 1853, and Fanny Lucy's domestic burdens increased. Arnold often felt restless and frustrated with his mode of life. In the spring of 1856 he seriously considered accepting a government post on the island of Mauritius in the Indian Ocean.

However, in February 1858 the Arnolds were finally able to settle at a permanent residence in London. His school district was smaller than before, and his financial situation had improved as well. The new residence at 2 Chester Square was near the Wightmans, and Fanny Lucy was pleased to be near her parents, especially since her family continued to grow. A third son, Richard Penrose, was born in November 1855, and a daughter, Lucy, would be born on Christmas Day, 1858. Through the Judge's connections in London society, the Arnolds became more socially active. In the following August and September, Arnold went on a walking tour of Switzerland with his old friend Theodore Walrond. Then in the spring of 1859, Arnold, always eager for opportunities to travel abroad, happily accepted a mission from the Newcastle Commission on elementary education to observe primary schools in France, the French cantons of Switzerland, and Holland.

He was one of several foreign assistant commissioners sent abroad to collect new ideas for extending 'sound and cheap elementary Instruction to all Classes of People' in Britain. This unexpected opportunity turned out to be a major factor in the development of Arnold's literary career. In conjunction with his poetry professorship at Oxford, it propelled him forward in his move towards 'criticism' in the largest sense. It reinforced and opened up the expression of tendencies in Arnold's thinking that had been present from his early years: his cosmopolitan outlook, encouraged by his mother's sympathies for French ideals and his father's interest in German scholarship; his comparative, dialogic habits of mind; his sensitivity to large social and political issues, lately expanded by his involvement in the fledgeling, chaotic educational institutions of his country, and contact with large numbers of people from various backgrounds and social classes. Arnold wrote to Jane, 'I like the thoughts of the Mission more and more' though (as he often insisted) 'I have no special interest in the subject of public education . . . I shall for five months get free from the routine work . . . of which I sometimes get very sick.' Foreign life to him is 'perfectly delightful, and *liberating*' (*SL* 115). Arnold took advantage of this European tour during the period March–August 1859 to meet leading French educationists as well as intellectuals and literary men such as Ernest

Renan, Charles Augustin Sainte-Beuve, François Guizot and Victor Cousin. Arnold was already familiar with these men through their publications, and he had corresponded with Sainte-Beuve. In educational matters Arnold developed a special respect for Guizot, a statesman, political philosopher and historian who had drafted and sponsored the passage of France's first basic law on primary education in 1833. Arnold also made a special effort to visit the boys' college at Sorèze run by the controversial and enigmatic ecclesiastic Lacordaire, famous for reviving the Dominican order in France. Arnold was struck by Lacordaire's commitment to a sound Christian education for his young men and was reminded of his father. At the same time, this 'great Christian orator of the fourth century, born in the nineteenth' refreshed his old nostalgia for a mediaeval age of faith.

This European experience was intellectually exciting for Arnold and crucial to his development as a writer, but the first two months were full of trials and worries as well. Soon after Arnold's wife and children joined him in Paris, his son Tommy became ill with a 'congestion of the lungs' and nearly died. The whole family was miserable in their cramped hotel rooms, and medical bills soared. Tommy recovered, but then Arnold was shaken by news of the death of his brother William Delafield at Gibraltar, on his way back to England from India, where he was Director of Public Instruction in the Punjab. With characteristic concern about family relationships, Arnold wrote a sober letter to his mother expressing guilt because he had shown his brother inadequate 'tenderness', and he worried about Willy's four orphaned children, whose mother had died earlier (*SL* 118). (They were adopted by Jane Forster and her husband.) With a heavy heart, Arnold wrote an elegy on his brother entitled 'A Southern Night', which expresses his recurring fear that one can never know his true soul or self: 'We who pursue/Our business with unslackening stride ... never once possess our soul/Before we die.'

Arnold submitted his official report to the Newcastle Commission in the spring of 1860; about one year later, Longman published it as *The Popular Education of France with Notices of Holland and Switzerland*. Arnold would later reprint the preface as a separate essay entitled 'Democracy' and use it as one of his principal lectures in his American tour of 1883–4. The book sold so poorly that Arnold lost a great deal of money on it, but it represents important developments in Arnold's vision as a social critic. He begins with the assumption that democracy is both desirable and inevitable, and he emphasizes his commitment to the ideal of equality. In arguing for a comprehensive English school system organized along the lines of the French model, Arnold sharpened his concept of the *State* which he defined, following Edmund Burke, as *'the nation in its collective and corporate character'* (CPW 2:26). Arnold's clarified sense of audience is as important as his evolving social mission: he is speaking primarily to the *middle-class* English, who must shed their narrow and provincial views in order to lead their nation to a more enlightened future.

However, the French report was not the only result of his experience in Europe. While he was in France Arnold became engrossed in the conflict between Napoleon III and Austria's Franz Joseph over the status of Sardinia. After five bloody battles won by the French and her ally Sardinia, a peace settlement was signed at Villafranca in mid-July 1859. In his pamphlet *England and the Italian Question*, published by Longman in late July but written before Villafranca, Arnold urged English involvement and voiced his strong support for the French. Even before his pamphlet was published, Arnold saw with disappointment that Austria would remain a presence in Italy after the settlement. Nevertheless, the pamphlet is significant because it shows his increasing interest in political issues (however naive he may have been in practical politics) and it expresses his still intact idealism about French *liberté* and his admiration for the 'idea-moved masses' of France in contrast to the 'insensible masses' of England. And although the *Italian Question* pamphlet had little practical influence, it served to strengthen his relationship with Sainte-Beuve and other French acquaintances who read it. Arnold would mine his 1859 experiences in France yet again when he drew on his meeting with Lacordaire in writing his essays on secondary education which made up the book *A French Eton* (1864). Sorèze is a model for middle-class education as it might be developed in England through the authority of the State.

In November 1860, Arnold gave an Oxford lecture entitled 'On Translating Homer', and what was intended to be one grew into a series of three lectures, the last of which was presented in late January 1861. The new perspective provided by his stay in Europe made Arnold more confident of his role as an *English* critic, and he returned to his beloved old subject of classical literature with renewed vigour. The Homer lectures went much better than his previous ones and opened up new horizons for Arnold; they are the bridge to the major essays in which he would fashion a new critical tradition in English.

In his essay 'What is Poetry?' John Stuart Mill makes a distinction between eloquence, which is *heard*, and poetry, which is *overheard*. Echoing a typical Romantic concept of poetry, Mill associates the poet with solitude and unconsciousness of an immediate audience. Arnold also inherited this Romantic tradition of the solitary poet, and he reinforced it with the stoicism he found in classical literature. Arnold as poet speaks from his own mind or soul although he hopes and expects to be overheard, sometimes by an audience of close friends and relatives, before his words take on a finished form that is alienated from him by publication. When Arnold came to believe that as a lyric poet he could not transcend the mere 'dialogue of the mind with itself', he turned to 'timeless' narrative and dramatic modes that were meant to engage his readers more directly and powerfully, that would 'animate' and 'ennoble' them. As he reached an impasse in his efforts to produce successful original works of this kind, intended to 'translate' the classic world of Lucretius and Empedocles into that of nineteenth-century England, it is no wonder that the issue of literally *translating* the great classical works so that they might live again for modern readers acquired an ever greater significance for him.

Any successful translation of Homer, the greatest classical writer, would have to capture his special qualities of language: his rapidity, plainness, and directness in thought; his plainness and directness in substance, and his nobility. Arnold was not prepared to take on the enormous work of translation himself – beyond a few experiments in English hexameters – but Francis W. Newman's recent translation of the *Iliad* fortuitously provided him with a wonderfully negative example around which to organize his thoughts. In attacking Newman's inept translation, Arnold found his critical voice; it was one that was heard, not overheard. One lecture led to another, and his Oxford audience responded with increasing enthusiasm. *On Translating Homer: Three Lectures* was published by Longman in January of 1861 (before Arnold's French report appeared in book form). Reviewers responded favourably to Arnold's attempt to rescue Homer from the realm of pedantry but chastised him for what they saw as dogmatic pronouncements. James Fitzjames Stephen (an influential lawyer and Virgina Woolf's uncle) referred to Arnold's 'outrageous self-conceit' in an unsigned article in the *Saturday Review* (*MAPW* 90–7). When Newman responded with a long pamphlet entitled *Homeric Translation in Theory and Practice: A Reply to Matthew Arnold, Esq.,* Arnold responded in turn with still another lecture, 'On Translating Homer: Last Words'. In this lecture, which was itself published in 1862, Arnold continued to refine his critical ideas and prepare himself for the works which would become *Essays in Criticism.*

Arnold's increasing success in engaging his audience directly and immediately through his lectures invigorated him. He made great efforts to find time for study and writing amidst his considerable professional duties and active family life. He hoped that his poetry would stand, but his literary ambitions had been redirected. He knew he was beginning to acquire a certain public presence that would allow him to be *heard* and perhaps even to make a difference in the development of intellectual life in England. But what of the intense inner life that had generated such powerful lyrics of the individual's personal search for truth? Its expression was rechannelled: although he necessarily engaged in controversy, Arnold as a critic does not use his public forum primarily to argue for and against particular issues or even particular doctrines or systems of thought. Instead he attempts to express a certain way of looking at things that represents his true or best self and at least potentially appeals to the true or best selves of his audience.

However, this is to take an overview of Arnold's critical productions and to state the matter in abstract terms. Although he was determined not to adopt the harsh, heavy-handed manner of the English literary reviewers of his day, he would not enter the noisy and contentious discourse without his own verbal weapons. Arnold told his friends and family that he wanted to be unpolemical in his presentations but, in the Homer lectures, he was developing a devastatingly witty, ironic manner of dealing with his opponents that they sometimes found to be insulting. Much of Arnold's prose is in fact polemical in its origin and, despite its characteristic 'urbanity' and 'elegance', controversial in its nature. The most basic problem faced by Arnold as a critic was that he had no really appropriate model for handling the wide range of topics that he proposed to deal with. In the Homer lectures he began to develop the critical language which culminates a decade later in *Culture and Anarchy*, combining elements of social satire, journalism, religious sermons, philosophical dialogues and literary lectures.

Arnold already held an unfavourable impression of Francis Newman, a clergyman and classics professor whose religious book *Phases of Faith* he had described to Clough some fourteen years earlier as 'a display of the theological mind . . . One would think to read him that enquiries into articles, biblical inspiration, &c &c were as much the natural functions of a man as to eat & copulate' (*SL* 61). Now the same man had produced a pedantic translation of the *Iliad* that badly failed to capture the spirit of the original. Arnold took advantage of the situation: Newman's was one of several contemporary translations of Homer, and the audience at Oxford would be familiar with current academic controversies over the exact nature of Homer's metre and Friedrich Wolf's theory that the Homeric poems had been written by multiple authors. One of Arnold's strongest convictions was that the great classical literatures did not originate in folk ballad. This belief is related to his distaste for the ballad-like qualities of Alexander Smith's poetry (and some of Clough's as well), poetry that was supposed to appeal to ordinary people. To Arnold, the high art of the true classic should be the only standard for poetry, even in a democracy (whether ancient Athenian or nineteenth-century English).

In his lectures Arnold quotes exceedingly awkward passages from Newman's translation to show how his words elicit in the reader a feeling 'totally different' from that conveyed by the Greek original. Newman's angry retort in his pamphlet was in the long run fortunate for Arnold, because in attempting to answer as well as soothe the feelings of his antagonist, Arnold focused on the role of the critic:

> The 'thing itself' with which one is here dealing, – the critical perception of poetic truth, – is of all things the most volatile, elusive, and evanescent; by even pressing too impetuously after it, one runs the risk of losing it. The critic of poetry should have the finest tact, the nicest moderation, the most free, flexible, and elastic spirit imaginable. (*CPW* 1:174)

This is recognizably the Arnold of *Essays in Criticism* and *Culture and Anarchy*, the prose classics of the 1860s that many modern critics believe are his most important literary productions. These critics tend to emphasize the significance of his literary persona, his tone, his *voice*. John Holloway articulated well the subtle qualities of the Arnoldian style when he wrote that 'his work inculcates not a set of ultimate beliefs ... but ... a certain temper of mind'.[2] 'Attitudes', 'habits', a 'frame' or 'temper' of mind, rather than a precise philosophy or set of doctrines, are said to inform Arnold's prose writings. For some critics, 'flexibility' is the key term.[3] Stefan Collini describes the elusive Arnoldian qualities in this way: 'a cast of mind, but of more than a mind – a temper, a way, at once emotional, intellectual, and psychological, of possessing one's experience and conducting one's life'.[4] As a poet, Arnold had been anxious about the apparent failure of his poems to *charm* their readers; as an essayist, he frequently comments on his special efforts to *persuade* and *charm*. Of course, even his modern admirers might admit – as some of Arnold's contemporaries thought – that Arnold's persona can be occasionally priggish and irritating as well as witty and urbane, but the critical voice of Arnold is one of the most significant innovations in nineteenth-century English letters.

Arnold's correspondence in the early 1860s suggests that he was very conscious of this as a crucial time in his literary career. Always sensitive to the passing of time and his own mortality – 'I am past thirty, and three parts iced over' he writes to Clough in February, 1853 (*SL* 79) – Arnold seemed to be more optimistic than ever before about his chance to make a lasting contribution to English literature. As he approached his thirty-eighth birthday at the end of 1860, he felt positive about prospects for both his health and his career, and he wrote to his mother, '[I]f I live and do well from now to 50 (only 12 years!) I will get something out of myself' (*SL* 135). The sudden death of Clough in November of 1861 came as a shocking reminder to Arnold that he was no longer a young man. Perhaps Arnold's concentrated effort in 'Last Words', written soon afterwards, was in part a reaction to Clough's death. He incorporated into his lecture references to Clough's attempts to translate Homer and later sent a copy of the published essay to Emerson in America, enclosing a letter that called attention to the mention of their mutual friend.

Arnold could not bring himself to write about Clough for the newspapers. For complex reasons, he was uneasy and troubled about his friend's death. It was tragic for Clough to die at the age of forty-two, and beyond that it was unfortunate that he had never fulfilled the promise of his brilliant youth. It seemed to Arnold that Clough had never really recovered from his self-exile from Oxford in 1848, when he resigned his Oriel fellowship because of conscientious difficulties about religious subscription. His sojourn in America, while interesting because of his association with Emerson and other American intellectuals, had not resulted in permanent employment. Back in England, he had obtained – with Arnold's help – a position at the Education Office. But for Arnold the story of Clough's disappointing career was entangled with the story of the troubled relationship between the two men. Arnold's harsh criticism of Clough's long poem, *The Bothie of Toper-na-Fousich*, and of his collection, *Ambarvalia*, helps to account for a growing distance between them. In addition, Clough did not get along well with Fanny Lucy, and he felt that Arnold's marriage made him more aloof from his old friend. Nevertheless, as Clough had grown increasingly cool towards Arnold in the winter and spring of 1853, Arnold had written sympathetic letters to him, making a determined attempt to revive and strengthen the friendship. Just as Arnold cherished memories of childhood and persistently kept in contact with his mother and his favourite siblings, he was in his 'emotional conservatism' reluctant to separate himself from the man he most closely associated with the special kind of scholarly bachelorhood at Oxford that had meant so much to him but was gone forever. There is no evidence that Arnold was seriously disappointed or unhappy in his marriage – on the contrary, he and Fanny Lucy apparently developed a strong relationship based on mutual respect and friendship – but he nonetheless felt the loss of a certain kind of male companionship (not necessarily 'homoerotic') with shared intellectual interests and modes of perception. At the same time, Arnold held deeply ambivalent feelings towards Clough that he could not sort out easily. He would finally complete the elegy 'Thyrsis' over four years after Clough's death.

Meanwhile, Arnold faced more immediate and material problems in his life. His habit of complaining and joking about his duties of school inspecting cannot obscure the seriousness and intensity of his interest in educational issues and commitment to professional duties. On frequent occasions later in his literary career Arnold would demonstrate his willingness to address a potentially hostile audience with outspoken and controversial ideas. However, his essay 'The Twice Revised Code' in the March 1862 issue of *Fraser's Magazine,* highly critical of his professional superiors, is probably the most courageous piece he ever published. During the period 1860–2 the various regulations affecting elementary education had been reformed and codified. As part of this process the Newcastle Commission (on whose behalf Arnold had travelled to the Continent) proposed a rigorous examination of every pupil in the fundamentals of reading, writing, and arithmetic. Robert Lowe, then Vice-President of the Committee of Council on Education and Arnold's highest superior at the Education Office, with the cooperation of Ralph Lingen, an old Balliol tutor who was Secretary of the Council Office and Arnold's immediate supervisor, incorporated the Commission's recommendations into a Code which would require Her Majesty's Inspectors to examine every child in every school they inspected. Most importantly, school funding would depend on the students' performance. A certain amount would be deducted from a school's grant for each pupil who either could not answer his question or was absent from school (for any reason) on the day of the examination. The 'payment by results' principle, as it was called, was controversial for several obvious reasons. Not only would the inspectors (who, like the teachers, overwhelmingly opposed it) have to work much harder than before, but one obvious result would be to take away sorely needed funds from the poorer, marginal schools in working-class areas.

Arnold's chief objection was that the new policy grew out of a mechanical, overly bureaucratic approach to education that ignored the humanistic basis of learning and the overall quality of a school. In his article he adopts an angrier tone than he permits himself in his literary and social criticism and scolds the 'numerous, resolute, and powerful' friends of the Revised Code, including Lowe himself, *The Times* and *Daily News,* the 'extreme Dissenters', the 'friends of economy at any price', the 'selfish vulgar of the upper classes', the 'clever and fastidious'. All of these 'will be gratified by the triumph of the Revised Code . . . [a]nd there will be only one sufferer; – *the education of the people* (*CPW* 2:243). James Kay, former holder of Lingen's position and an opponent of the Code, sent a copy of Arnold's article to every member of the House of Commons. However, Parliament approved a slightly amended version of Lowe's Revised Code in 1862, and the 'payment by results' principle endured throughout Arnold's lifetime, though certain reforms, including the creation of local school boards, were introduced by the Education Bill of 1870, sponsored by Arnold's brother-in-law William Forster, who was then Vice-President of the Committee.

Arnold was not fired from his post, but his working relationship with the Education Office became less pleasant, and his perceived impertinence at this stage in his career, along with the controversial ideas about increased State support for (and intervention in) education that he put forward in his reports on foreign schools, helps to account for the slow pace of his professional advancement in the following years. Arnold could not be described as 'disgruntled', although – spurred by his wife's attention to his lack of timely promotions – he would apply for other positions later in the 1860s. His actual working conditions improved somewhat soon after the Revised Code debate, when he obtained the services of an assistant, Thomas Healing, who took over some of his duties. In the long run Arnold resigned himself to a position that allowed him nearly complete freedom of expression in literary and cultural matters, and in general he did not desire the kind of direct involvement in politics that would have conflicted with his government post. (In 1862 he was quietly elected to his second five-year term as poetry professor at Oxford.) In addition to providing the broad cultural experience that he found useful in his criticism and occasional opportunities for the foreign travel that he loved, his work brought him into contact with a few exceptional individuals who became important in his life. The most notable of these was Louisa de Rothschild, wife of Anthony de Rothschild, who was a grandson of the famous Frankfurt banker. After the children's school founded by Lady de Rothschild on her Aston Clinton estate was inspected by Arnold in 1858, they became friends. She was an intellectual who shared Arnold's interest in Heine and introduced him to aspects of Judaism. Arnold 'flirted lightly' with her (*MAAL* 110) and visited Aston Clinton frequently. It was there he met Disraeli in 1864. Although she could never displace Jane Forster, who had been the 'first reader (or hearer)' of his poems, in the coming years Arnold repeatedly mentions in his letters to Lady de Rothschild that he has her in mind as he writes his essays for publication. (Although there is ample evidence of Arnold's continuing love and respect for his wife, Fanny Lucy – who made a point of reading his publications and sometimes offered advice on his controversial topics – did not always share his intellectual interests.)

In the seventies even Arnold's working relations with his superiors would become more cordial, but he maintained his strong ideological opposition to 'payment by results' and dissatisfaction with the education establishment in general until the end of his life.

4

Essays in Criticism (1865), *New Poems* (1867)

Although there is evidence that Arnold had plans from the beginning to publish his Oxford lectures, the ones on Homer were the first to see print. From that point on, nearly all of them were published, initially as essays in journals. As Arnold became increasingly accustomed to journal publication, he supplemented these essays with other original articles as suitable subjects presented themselves. Many of the journal articles were in turn revised and collected in book form. Arnold followed this pattern with the pieces that eventually made up *Essays in Criticism*, one of the most important books of his career.

Arnold's strategy of literary production helped him to become surprisingly prolific as a writer, given the pressures of his personal and professional life. Beginning with the Homer lectures, Arnold was motivated by his increasing success in reaching a public audience and ever more confident that he had important things to say. Lecturing commitments and publication deadlines compelled him to complete his projects when he was tempted to procrastinate. Continually faced with the grind of his school inspection duties, Arnold arranged his schedule to create the blocks of time he needed for reading and writing. Through the influence of his brother-in-law, William Forster, he was elected to the prestigious Athenaeum Club in 1856. In the 1860s, Arnold, now conveniently settled in London, often spent portions of his week-day afternoons at the club and did much of his writing there. (As his literary reputation increased, however, he was interrupted in his work more often and he found the club less useful as a haven.) He also often used the North Library of the British Museum (*MAAL* 316). At times he was able to work on his essays nearly steadily from about two until six in the afternoon and return home by seven, after a workday that began when he arose at six in the morning. At other times, school inspecting kept him busy all day and into the night. At his most ambitious stage, he set himself the goal of publishing one article a month for seven months. Nevertheless, he sometimes had difficulty in completing his lectures and essays on time and was forced to write feverishly on trains between official assignments or work late into the night, and he was not always satisfied with the results.

In May of 1862, Arnold lectured on 'Dante and Beatrice'. The lecture was later published in *Fraser's* but it would not be included in *Essays*. The first lecture destined for that collection was 'A Modern French Poet' (renamed 'Maurice de Guérin' for the book), delivered in November of the same year and published in *Fraser's* in January 1863. Guérin was a French poet who had died in 1839, relatively unknown and unappreciated, at the age of 28. Arnold's lecture was occasioned by the publication in 1860 of the poet's collected works, with an introduction by Sainte-Beuve, whom Arnold now flatteringly described as 'the first of living critics'. Arnold made Guérin representative of the artistic temperament, and he generalized about two formations of that temperament: 'Poetry is the interpretress of the natural world, and she is the interpretress of the moral world; it was as the interpretress of the natural world that she had Guérin for her mouthpiece' (*CPW* 3:30). Arnold quoted extracts from Guérin's prose poem 'The Centaur' to illustrate the 'natural magic' of the Frenchman.

The publication of Arnold's essay elicited not only a 'long and charming' letter from Sainte-Beuve, but the gift of a printed journal by Eugénie, Guérin's sister, from their surviving sister Marie de Guérin. Arnold decided to write on Eugénie de Guérin as well, and his essay by that name was published in the *Cornhill* of June 1863.

In the meantime, however, Arnold had become engaged in a controversial public issue that energized him much as the Homer translations had done. By November 1862, he had decided to write an article on the seventeenth-century Jewish Dutch philosopher Baruch Spinoza, whom he had begun to read as early as the late 1840s. In January of 1863 he published in *Macmillan's Magazine* an essay entitled 'The Bishop and the Philosopher', comparing the religious ideas of Spinoza with those of John William Colenso, the Anglican Bishop of Natal, who had recently returned from Africa to publish a book in which he pointed out numerous factual and logical errors in a literal reading of the Pentateuch. One of the ludicrous examples cited by Arnold: 'For Deuteronomy, take the number of lambs slain at the Sanctuary, as compared with the space for slaying them: *'In an area of 1,692 square yards, how many lambs per minute can 150,000 persons kill in two hours?'* Certainly not 1,250, the number required' (*CPW* 3:48). Colenso, although he had his defenders (who thought that the English had finally produced a scholar to compete with the German practitioners of Higher Criticism), had already been ridiculed by critics for his obvious failure to appreciate the mythical significance of the Bible. However, Arnold says that he will consider his book from a general literary rather than a theological point of view: 'Religious books come within the jurisdiction of literary criticism so far as they affect general culture' (*CPW* 3:41). The question to be asked was whether Colenso *enlightened intellectually*; the answer for Arnold was obviously no, Colenso failed to edify the many or inform the few, and failed to advance the culture of England. On the other hand, Spinoza, considered to be a heretic by most English readers, acknowledges the contradictions in Scripture and then 'attempts to answer the crucial question, *'What then?'* and by the attempt, successful or unsuccessful, he interests the higher culture of Europe' (*CPW* 3:52–3). Arnold was attracted by Spinoza's apparent attempt to deal with the Bible metaphorically, *as literature*, and to conceptualize God as coextensive with the universe and yet capable of being worshipped. God could be understood in terms of universal law, but not in terms of human nature (*MAAL* 322–3).

Thus Arnold's work on Spinoza in the 1860s extends the inquiring spirit of certain early poems like 'Quiet Work' and 'In Harmony with Nature' which question the relationship between man and nature, and it looks forward to the Biblical criticism of the 1870s. But Arnold was by no means finished with Spinoza. Even before his first essay was published, the first English translation of Spinoza's *Tractatus Theologico-Politicus* came out, and Arnold, although disappointed with the translator's work, quickly reviewed the book for the *London Review*. He replied to criticisms of his January Spinoza article in *Macmillan's* with 'Dr Stanley's Lectures on the Jewish Church' in the February issue of the same journal, using the occasion of lectures published by A. P. Stanley to show how a contemporary churchman could edify the public without being false. 'A Word More about Spinoza' in the December *Macmillan's* completed the series of journal articles. Arnold would reprint 'A Word' under the shortened title 'Spinoza' in *Essays* but, for the second edition of the book, revised the essay as 'Spinoza and the Bible', incorporating passages from the old 'Bishop and Philosopher' essay but avoiding specific reference to the Colenso controversy. Arnold continued his practice of revising his essays in response to contemporary criticism, already begun in the Homer lectures, throughout his career as a prose writer.

His Oxford lecture on Heinrich Heine, another longstanding interest of his, was given in June 1863 and published the following August in the *Cornhill*. An essay on Marcus Aurelius, published in the November 1863 issue of *Victorian Magazine*, recalls the Stoic strain in Arnold's early poetry. Arnold brought another obscure French writer to the attention of the English public in his lecture on Joseph Joubert, whom he called 'A French Coleridge', also in November 1863. The essay version came out in the *National Review* of January 1864. 'Pagan and Christian Religious Sentiment', a lecture of March 1864 in which Arnold introduces the concept of an 'imaginative reason' that appeals both to intellect and a religious sense, was published under a slightly different title in the April *Cornhill*. In June, Arnold lectured on 'The Influence of Academies on National Spirit and Literature', a subject suggested by an essay Renan wrote on the French Academy, and a revised version appeared in the *Cornhill*. Finally, Arnold lectured on 'The Functions of Criticism at the present Time' (later entitled 'The Function . . .') in October and the essay version published in *The National Review* the next month was the last one destined for the 1865 *Essays*, serving as its introduction.

In late 1863 and early 1864 Arnold was also finally writing his long-planned essay *A French Eton; or, Middle-Class Education and the State*, based on his 1859 visit to France for the Newcastle Commission. Although his lively and colourful account of Lacordaire's Sorèze is a high point of the work, Arnold's main purpose was to promote State involvement in education at home. *A French Eton* incorporates a discussion of the three classes – aristocracy, middle class, and populace – that anticipates his landmark lecture on 'Culture and its Enemies' three years later. *A French Eton* was published in three parts in the *Macmillan's* of September 1863 and February and May 1864. The following summer Macmillan brought out the whole thing in pamphlet form.

This account of Arnold's publishing activities in the early-to mid-1860s shows that he quickly worked his way into the expanding world of literary journalism. Avoiding the well-established and predictable journals such as the *Quarterly* and *Edinburgh*, he concentrated on new or renovated journals that were reaching out to new audiences more open to intellectual change. This expanding 'higher journalism' was helping to bridge the distance between the discourse of *cognoscenti* and that of the popular press. Especially important for Arnold were the recently reorganized *Fraser's Magazine*, under the editorship of Arnold's old Oxford acquaintance J. A. Froude, and *Macmillan's Magazine* and *Cornhill Magazine*, both of which had been launched in 1859. Through the years Arnold developed friendly relationships with both Alexander Macmillan and George Smith, publishers of the two journals, respectively, and they came to publish his books as well. Macmillan, who would soon begin to publish editions of Arnold's poetry, took a serious interest in Arnold as an author, an interest that went beyond financial considerations. Smith showed less intellectual or aesthetic appreciation of Arnold's work but became a personal friend with whom Arnold lunched and played billiards (and from whom he borrowed money on more than one occasion).

When Arnold's book *The Popular Education of France* failed to meet its production costs in 1861, he had to pay Longman over £80, more than the total sum he had earned from all his publications up to that point. But now the situation was improving. Arnold's new career in literary journalism did not of course make him a wealthy man, but the fairly steady income from his articles (and from the books into which they would be collected) was not inconsequential. For example, he earned £11.5s from *Fraser's* for 'Maurice de Guérin', and from *Macmillan's* he earned £16 for 'The Bishop and the Philosopher', £10 for 'Dr. Stanley's Lectures', and 10 guineas, 12 guineas, and £14, respectively, for the three *French Eton* articles. (In pamphlet form, however, this last work was unsuccessful, and Arnold eventually found himself dividing losses with the publisher.) From the *Cornhill*, which usually paid somewhat better than the others, he earned £21 for 'Eugénie de Guérin', £21 for 'Heinrich Heine', and £25 for 'The Literary Influence of Academies'. Walter Bagehot's new *National Review* paid at about the same rate as the *Cornhill*. It must not be forgotten that apart from Arnold's genuine engagement in his literary work, earning extra money to pay for governesses, schools, and other expenses was a constant motive.

Arnold deplored the level of discourse in the English literary journals of his day, but he realized that they had become the chief source of intellectual influence in England. The development of his critical prose can be understood only in the context of the reviews and periodicals that were a major force in shaping popular taste and ideas, even on the higher levels of literary culture. It is difficult to imagine how Arnold would have developed his critical talents without them. He thought and composed in terms of essays, not books. Though Arnold was persistent in his core ideas, his books emerged from the give and take of critical dialogue in the journals. He was pleased by the comments of Henry Lancaster (though he was a 'Scotchman') in *The North British Review* when he wrote in reference to Arnold that 'men of the greatest ability ... do not now think it unworthy of them to write ... in magazines'.[1]

By mid-summer in 1864 Arnold was making definite plans to collect his essays for a book, and Macmillan brought out *Essays in Criticism* early in 1865. In deciding on the title, Arnold was thinking of the original meaning of 'essay' as 'attempt' or 'specimen' (*MAB* 67). The first edition contained a Preface, 'The Function of Criticism at the Present Time', 'The Literary Influence of Academies', 'Maurice de Guérin', 'Eugénie de Guérin', 'Heinrich Heine', 'Pagan and Mediaeval Religious Sentiment', 'Joubert', 'Spinoza' and 'Marcus Aurelius'. Macmillan agreed to Arnold's proposal to issue the book in yellow paper (on the French model) rather than cloth boards and to charge 6s (30p) a copy (the same as Tennyson's recent *Enoch Arden*). Arnold wrote his publisher that he intended to retire to a monastery if the volume did not pay its expenses (*MAB* 67), but in fact it was a solid if modest financial success and the next summer was reprinted in America by Ticknor & Fields in an edition that added *A French Eton* and *On Translating Homer*.

Although the individual essays had been written over a period of five years on various topics, the book has a surprising unity that is achieved by Arnold's distinctive personal voice and his consistent methods and goals as an English critic. The most essential essays in defining the Arnoldian critic at this stage of development are those on Heine and literary academies as well as the introductory 'Function of Criticism'. For Arnold, Heine carried on Goethe's most important line of activity as 'a soldier in the war of liberation of humanity' (*CPW* 3:108). Like his greater precursor, Heine embodied the modern spirit, and Arnold admires his 'life and death battle' with *Philistinism*. With this key term provided by Heine, Arnold calls his own English enemies the 'narrow' Philistines who value 'practical conveniences' over ideas and reason, and he will make great use of this satirical nickname for the English middle class.

Goethe and Heine had rejected 'routine' thinking by placing the standard for judgment 'inside every man instead of outside him' (*CPW* 3:110). The essay on academies seems to be arguing for the value of a central authority like that of the Académie Française in establishing high standards of British literary taste – especially in prose – but Arnold is finally interested in the articulation of a common culture, not a formal institution. The real authority will emerge from a social bond developed collectively by individuals who transcend their provincialism and 'the two great banes of humanity', 'self-conceit and the laziness coming from self-conceit' (*CPW* 3:232). This idea clearly anticipates Arnold's argument for *culture* as authority in *Culture and Anarchy*.

'The Function of Criticism' is by far the most important essay in Arnold's 1865 volume and perhaps the single most important essay of its kind in Victorian literature. In this remarkably suggestive piece for which he drew on his own powerful impressions of the *secular* side of J. H. Newman's legacy – the ideal of knowledge for its own sake – Arnold in turn helped to lay the groundwork for disparate future developments such as late nineteenth-century Paterian aestheticism, early twentieth-century liberal humanism, and the late twentieth-century ascendancy of 'criticism' over 'literature' in academia. Like the volume as a whole, 'Function' relies heavily on Arnold's adaptation of French sources (especially Renan and Sainte-Beuve). Renan is surely one of Arnold's models for the ideal critic, though Arnold believed his own primary purpose of inculcating intelligence, as contrasted with Renan's purpose of inculcating morality, corresponded to the contrasting needs and deficiencies of the English and French readers of the day. From Sainte-Beuve Arnold adapted his central idea of disinterestedness. Characteristically, when Arnold finally gives his 'definition' of criticism late in the essay, it is a very broad and inclusive one: '*a disinterested endeavour to learn and propagate the best that is known and thought in the world*' (*CPW* 3:283).

Of course, in formulating this somewhat idealistic quest Arnold is also defending and elevating the importance of his own position as an already established poet who is marking out an important new position for himself in contemporary English literature and culture. As in some of the other essays, Arnold risks being seen as self-congratulatory and pompous if he is not successful in charming the reader into identifying with the critical point of view he is advocating. In his short Preface Arnold attempted to give an enhanced ironic and satirical edge to his endeavour. Referring to his own excessive 'vivacity' in criticizing an English translation of the *Iliad* (one by I. C. Wright, not the one by Francis Newman) in his Homer lectures, Arnold jokingly prophesied:

> My vivacity is but the last sparkle of flame before we are all in the dark ... Yes, the world will soon be the Philistines'! and then ... the whole earth filled and ennobled every morning by the magnificent roaring of the young lions of the *Daily Telegraph*, we shall all yawn in one another's faces with the dismallest, the most unimpeachable gravity. (*CPW* 3:287)

Even Arnold's mother did not approve of his 'vivacity', however. 'I felt sure that the preface would not exactly suit you or any member of my own family', he wrote to her (*SL* 168). The *Daily Telegraph*, the most important of the cheap new newspapers that sprang into existence after the repeal of the penny stamp duty in 1855, had introduced a less serious, less formal style of writing in the 1860s that gave a stimulus to popular journalism. This newspaper – and especially George Augustus Sala, one of its leading writers – became persistent adversaries of Arnold in the years ahead. Arnold, who knew he was considered an intellectual snob by these journalists (whom he considered vulgar), thought that 'vivacity' would be the most effective weapon to use against them.

Essays in Criticism was widely reviewed, at least partially because most of the individual essays – or earlier versions of them – had already been commented on in print, and Arnold had opened up a debate with his critics. For example, in a December 1864 article entitled 'Mr. Matthew Arnold and His Countrymen', the *Saturday Review*'s James Fitzjames Stephen – who had already commented negatively on Arnold's Italian pamphlet and Homer lectures – complained about Arnold's elitism in his 'Function of

Criticism' essay. Stephen deplored Arnold's tendency to make sweeping indictments of the English while praising foreign or classical sources of enlightenment that are available only to the privileged few (*MAPW* 117–27), a position that anticipates many of Arnold's later critics. Stephen did not sign his article, but Arnold knew who had written it. By this time, of course, he already thought of the *Saturday Review* as his 'old adversary' and Stephen as one whose ideas were 'naturally very antagonistic to mine' (*SL* 166).

In contrast to Stephen, S. H. Reynolds, writing in the *Westminster Review* of October 1863, over a year before the collected *Essays* were published, praised Arnold's criticism so strongly that Arnold wrote his friend Lady de Rothschild that 'you must have thought I wrote it myself, except that I should hardly have called myself by the hideous title of "Professor"' (*LMA* 1:231–2). Most reviewers were less condemnatory than Stephen, yet less admiring than Reynolds.

The comment on Arnold's *literary* criticism *per se*, the essays on the Guérins and Joubert, was almost universally positive. On the other hand, many reviewers, while not as censorious as Stephen, were unhappy with the *social* criticism; such as Arnold's assaults on English complacency and his ridicule of figures like Sir Charles Adderly and J. A. Roebuck, who celebrated 'Our old Anglo-Saxon breed, the best in the whole world!' In order to demonstrate 'how much that is harsh and ill-favoured there is in this best', Arnold juxtaposes this claim with a recent newspaper account of 'a shocking child murder' by a 'girl named Wragg'. Then he goes on to ridicule 'hideous' English names such as 'Higginbottom, Stiggins, Bugg!' (*CPW* 3:273). Arnold meant to jolt his readers out of their complacency but risked alienating them by being harsh and unfair. Indeed his apparent linking of the unaesthetic qualities of 'Wragg' and the other names with the ethical issues involved seems to stretch the idea of 'critical taste' rather far.

His critics wondered why Arnold had to be so negative about English society and why he had not confined himself to literary matters, where his knowledge and authority were obvious. The situation was similar to that of another Victorian sage: John Ruskin, an acknowledged authority on art and architecture, found little sympathy for his views on political economy. Arnold knew what he was trying to do, however, and social criticism was not peripheral but central to his critical project. Arnold did not limit his subject to taste; his concern was with the totality of human experience as it was interpreted by a national culture. An aesthetic sense was important not primarily in itself but rather in its relation to knowledge and to religion. He did not ignore his critics – he tried to answer them – but he only intensified his attack on the Philistines in the work-in-progress that was eventually published as *Culture and Anarchy* in 1869. The first instalment of that project would be an essay entitled 'My Countrymen', written, as the title suggests, as an answer to Stephen's article. And yet, as 'Function' illustrates, Arnold's prose style is not always consistent with his aim to 'charm the wild beast of Philistinism while I am trying to convert him', as he put it in a November 1863 letter to Jane (*SL* 155).

Overall, Arnold was pleased with the reception of *Essays in Criticism*. Although he was fond of describing himself as an 'unpopular author' he knew that he was now a literary figure to be reckoned with. He was injecting a much-needed stream of cosmopolitan ideas into public discussion, ideas associated with controversial philosophers and poets, with Jewish and French Catholic sensibilities, and at the same time he considered himself to be advancing the work of his more conventionally religious but reform-minded father.

During his tour of French elementary schools in 1859 Arnold had found time to visit a few secondary schools as well, and his *French Eton* suggests the need for a comparative study of English and European secondary schools. After the Newcastle Commission (1858–61) had reported on the elementary education of the poor and the Clarendon Commission (1861–4) had reported on the secondary education of the aristocracy, Arnold assumed that a royal commission would soon be appointed to study the secondary education of the English middle class, and he was determined to take part in any new review of foreign schools undertaken. Arnold in fact was considered for appointment to the commission itself but his controversial views in favour of State support of education were well known, and even his old friend Frederick Temple, who was now headmaster at Rugby, did not support him. Arnold scrupulously avoided asking for favours from his brother-in-law, William Forster – who, like Temple, was appointed to the commission by Lord Granville (Lord

President of the Privy Council) – but the Taunton Commission, as it was now called, approved Arnold's foreign mission anyway. Arnold was content to serve as an observer and reporter rather than a commissioner; he wrote to his mother that he had turned away 'from the thought of any attempt at direct practical and political action' and had fixed 'all my care upon a spiritual action, to tell upon people's minds, which after all is the great thing, hard as it is to make oneself fully believe it so'.[2]

During the period April-November 1865, Arnold toured the secondary schools of France, Italy and Prussia, as well as other German states, but after a good start in Paris, where he renewed his acquaintance with Guizot and others, he was hampered by logistical problems and bureaucratic confusion. In many cases he did not have reliable information about the schedules of the schools he wished to see, and time after time he found them closed. Nevertheless, he collected a great deal of information and took the opportunity to study the language of each country he visited.

Back in England, he was immediately faced with the resumption of his regular inspection duties and the prospect of producing a coherent report out of the 'ocean of documents' he had collected in Europe. Still unhappy about the changes in school inspection brought on by the Revised Code, Arnold was restless in his position. In the spring of 1866 he would apply for an appointment as a Charity Commissioner, in 1867 as Librarian of the House of Commons, and in 1869 as one of three commissioners under the Endowed Schools Act, unsuccessfully in all three cases. Now in late 1865 the preparation of his official report to the Taunton Commission promised to be a long and frustrating task. Nevertheless, he was obligated to resume his Oxford lectures (he was threatened with a fine for the long interruption), and he agreed to lecture on two successive days in December 1865 on 'The Study of Celtic Literature'.

The subject had been on his mind for several years. While visiting Brittany in 1859 as part of his first official tour of Europe, the Celtic names and features of the people there reminded him of the Cornish origins of his mother. His interest was heightened by reading Renan's essays on the Celts, although he felt that Renan had gone too far in glorifying them. On Christmas Eve, his birthday, Arnold wrote to his sister Jane:

I have long felt that we owed far more, spiritually and artistically, to the Celtic races than the somewhat coarse Germanic intelligence readily perceived, and been increasingly satisfied at our own semi-celtic origin, which, as I fancy, gives us the power, if we will use it, of comprehending the nature of both races. (*SL* 131)

Arnold delivered the two lectures on the Celts as part of his continuing series on 'The Modern Element in Literature', one before and one after the Homer lectures, but he did not publish them, and he turned his attention to other subjects. Then in the summer of 1864, he took his family on a holiday to Llandudno, a popular resort in Wales, and the 'charm' of the country there reawakened his interest in Celtic traditions. Arnold was especially impressed by the annual assembly of Welsh poets and musicians known as the Eisteddfod, which was held during his stay. Soon afterwards, he made an expedition to the Scottish Highlands. Arnold had originally intended to lecture on Celtic literature in March, before leaving on his European tour, but the date of his proposed lecture coincided with United University Sports day, when much of his potential audience would be at Cambridge, so he had postponed this new series until his return later in the year. A statement Arnold made in a letter to his mother in January 1865 suggests how Celtic Studies fits into his overall critical enterprise: 'I hate all over-preponderance of single elements, and all my efforts are directed to enlarge and complete us by bringing in as much as possible of Greek, Latin, Celtic cultures; more and more I see hopes of fruit by steadily working in this direction' (*SL* 168).

After his two Celtic lectures in December 1865, Arnold added another in February 1866 and a final one in May of that year. The four lectures were soon published by George Smith in the *Cornhill*, and Arnold revised them for book publication. Smith's publishing house, Smith, Elder & Co., brought out *On the Study of Celtic Literature* in June 1867. As a whole the book argues that British greatness is produced by a mixture of Celtic, Teutonic and Norman elements, but, as Honan notes, Arnold is also using these ethnographic terms to define aspects of himself (*MAAL* 334).

Arnold's great difficulty was that in spite of his genuine interest in and appreciation for his subject, he was by no means an accomplished scholar of Celtic literature. The situation was quite different from the one he had faced when he took on the subject of Homer. From the beginning of the project, Arnold was keenly aware of his limitations, and even after his lectures and publications had some limited success in stirring up interest in the Celtic heritage (a chair of Celtic Studies eventually was established at Oxford as a result of his efforts), he was reluctant to represent himself as an authority on the subject. Although he came out of this experience with a deeper understanding of the Irish Question and related issues, he did not allow himself to become identified as a public spokesman for Celtic interests.

Arnold was attracted to the 'melancholy and unprogressiveness' of the Celts (*SL* 165) and associated them with Oxford, that home of 'lost causes, and forsaken beliefs, and unpopular names, and impossible loyalties' as he describes it in the Preface to *Essays in Criticism*, and fundamentally opposed to the spirit of Benthamism and the Philistines. Arnold was not surprised when his Celtic essays received negative comment from the Philistine press at *The Times* and the *Daily Telegraph*, but he was pleased to see, as the *Athenaeum* acknowledged, that he was having some effect in increasing public awareness of the Celts.

While he fussed over troublesome etymological and other 'technical' problems in the revision of his Celtic essays and continued to toil away at his massive European report, Arnold was preparing his last important volume of new poetry. It was published by Macmillan in July 1867, one month after Arnold's Celtic book. Not all of the poems included in *New Poems* were in fact new: most strikingly, *Empedocles on Etna* stood in the initial position, reprinted for the first time since 1852. Six other poems or parts of poems from the 1852 volume were also included. 'Dover Beach' was published for the first time, but probably had been written in the summer of 1851. 'Fragment of Chorus of a "Dejaneira"' was an even earlier effort, dating from 1847–8. Four of the poems had been previously published in journals, including 'Stanzas from the Grande Chartreuse' in *Fraser's* (April 1855), 'Saint Brandan' in *Fraser's* (July 1860), 'A Southern Night' (the elegy on William Arnold) in *The Victoria Regia* (1861), and most recently, 'Thyrsis', Arnold's elegy on Clough, in the *Macmillan's Magazine* of April 1866. 'Stanzas composed at Carnac' is another elegy on Arnold's brother, written slightly earlier than 'Southern Night' during Arnold's European tour of 1859 but not previously published. The idea for 'The Terrace at Berne' also dates from 1859, though Arnold wrote the poem four years later.

Among several recent sonnets were a series of three entitled 'Rachel' (referring to the French actress) and a pair entitled 'East London' and 'West London', all of them composed in the midst of the critical work of 1863. 'Austerity of Poetry', 'Monica's Last Prayer', 'Immortality' and other sonnets were also written during the period 1863–5. Arnold's 'Rugby Chapel', celebrating his father, was begun in late 1857, and 'Heine's Grave' probably in 1858, but 'Growing Old' and 'Epilogue to Lessing's Laocoön' date from 1864 or later, and 'Obermann Once More' was completed in the spring of 1867.

New Poems is thus an interesting amalgamation of old and new materials. Although some of the new poems – especially 'Thyrsis' – were recognized as being of substantial quality, even many sympathetic reviewers recognized that Arnold as a poet had reached the end of the line. His short verse preface (later entitled 'Persistency of Poetry') may have encouraged this view:

> Though the Muse be gone away,
> Though she move not earth to-day,
> Souls, erewhile who caught her word,
> Ah! still harp on what they heard.

These lines recall Arnold's familiar idea of living in an unpoetic age, but they also suggest resignation to the withdrawal of his own Muse: his production of poetry is now in the past but his works will endure.

The first poem in Arnold's first volume of poetry is 'Quiet Work', in which the poet, then in his mid-twenties, asks Nature that he be allowed to learn 'One lesson of two duties kept at one/Though the loud world proclaim their enmity – /Of toil unsevered from tranquillity!/Of labour, that in lasting fruit out-grows/Far noisier schemes, accomplished in repose'. At the age of forty-five, Arnold is engaged in the noisy world, both in his life and his art, and though he still strives for *disinterestedness* in his critical prose, he has given up his search for the calm and repose that he associates with the greatest poetry. In a note Arnold explained his rehabilitation of *Empedocles* in *New Poems* by say-ing he acted at the request of Robert Browning, but in doing so, Arnold finally conceded the failure of his 1853 initiative. Disap-

pointed by the reception of *Merope* and worn down by professional duties, he had used his concept of 'modern' classicism as
a bridge to a new mode of expression and a different literary
vocation. Between *Merope* in 1858 and *New Poems* in 1867, Arnold
had published a total of four poems, all in journals. *Empedocles*
could now be seen, retrospectively, as representing a stage in
the development of a poet who had had his say.

'Dover Beach', on the other hand, was a jewel that Arnold
had (uncharacteristically) kept to himself since the beginning of
his married life. Although it was not immediately appreciated
by Victorian readers, it was destined to be read by later generations of readers as an important poem in its own right and representative of Victorian consciousness.[3] The poem also illustrates
how Arnold's deepest structures of feeling, throughout his literary career, are grounded in his religious heritage. At the emotional climax of the poem, the speaker addresses his companion:
'Ah, love, let us be true/To one another! for', and it goes on to
describe the senseless violence of the world that underlies its
seeming beauty. This is an echo of 1 John 4:7–10, which reads
'Beloved, let us love one another: for love is of God.' Arnold's
lines constitute a profound secularization of the Biblical passage
but remind us how his language is saturated with conscious and
unconscious references to the Bible. Arnold would devote much
of his critical effort in the 1870s to reading Biblical texts and
defending the Bible as literature.

'The Terrace at Berne' is not a major poem in itself but in
future editions of Arnold's poems, it would take its place as the
eighth and concluding poem in the 'Switzerland' series. It provides closure by describing the speaker's visit to Berne ten years
after his final meeting with Marguerite:

> I knew it when my life was young;
> I feel it still, now youth is o'er
> – The mists are on the mountain hung,
> And Marguerite I shall see no more.
>
> (ll. 49–52)

This poem, conceived during Arnold's visit to Switzerland as
part of his European tour in the summer of 1859, reinforces the
sense of limitations and conclusions, of looking backwards, that
pervades the 1867 volume.

'Growing Old' is probably meant to answer Browning's 'Rabbi Ben Ezra', first published in 1864 ('Grow old along with me/ The best is yet to be'). After listing the pains and disappointments of old age, Arnold's speaker concludes with the last stage of decline: 'To hear the world applaud the hollow ghost/Which blamed the living man'. Arnold, whose habit of anticipating old age had been noticed by some of his critics, was thinking realistically not only about the ageing process but also about the ironies associated with public reputations.

'Thyrsis' is the most important elegy in this elegiac volume. Arnold's contemporaries singled out the poem for praise, and Swinburne (perhaps the most elegiac English poet of all) wrote most extravagantly in the *Fortnightly Review* that the poem, along with Milton's 'Lycidas' and Shelley's 'Adonais', is one of the three English elegies 'so great that they eclipse and efface all the elegiac poetry we know; all of Italian, all of Greek' (*MAP* 162). As discussed earlier, Arnold held deeply conflictive feelings about his old friend who had died too young, but he finally finished the poem some four-and-a-half years after Clough's death. There is no doubt that Arnold was nostalgic about the Oxford years spent with his friend and that he continued to feel genuine affection for Clough. Nevertheless, while working on the elegy in 1865, Arnold read Clough's *Letters and Remains* and was troubled by evidence he found of emotional instability and overdependence on Dr Arnold.[4]

In 1837 Arnold had entered the fifth form at Rugby only one month before Clough went up to Oxford, so Arnold had little direct contact with Clough during his Rugby years; however, Clough's close relationship with Dr Arnold made him something like a surrogate older brother. If there had been a latent 'sibling rivalry' in Arnold's mind, his reading of *Letters and Remains* brought it to consciousness. For the first time, Arnold understood from certain passages in Clough's juvenile letters how intense the young man's attachment to the headmaster had been, and the extent to which Clough considered himself to be a channel for the continuing of Dr Arnold's work. 'Clough appears to have felt him *too much*', Arnold wrote to his mother, and he associated this aspect of Clough with the 'overtaxed religiousness of his early life'.[5] Arnold's enhanced impression that there was a 'screw loose' in Clough's 'whole organization' undoubtedly contributed to the curiously one-sided view of the poet given in 'Thyrsis'. Arnold effectively adapted the pastoral imagery and the associations with the Cumnor countryside from 'The Scholar-Gypsy' to explore his theme of the truth-quest in relation to Clough. However, as several twentieth-century critics have pointed out, Arnold oversimplified his portrait of Clough, stressing Clough's single-minded love of Truth and labelling him as a troubled poet who failed to live up to his potential.[6] Keeping in mind Harold Bloom's contention that the great elegies centre on the creative anxieties of the poet rather than on his grief, it is easy to see how Arnold's anxieties about his own accomplishments and his future reputation as a poet are reflected in the poem. When Clough was alive, he and Arnold argued about the nature of poetry and competed as contemporary active poets. After Clough's death, as Arnold contemplated the elegy, he increasingly associated his old companion with the mythic wanderer figure of the 'Scholar-Gipsy', the long Keatsian poem whose presence in the pivotal 1853 volume, along with many of the shorter lyrics, offers a subtle counter force to the Preface and its model poem 'Sohrab and Rustum'.

Particularly revealing is an epigraph to 'Thyrsis' that appears in the 1867 volume (and in the second edition in 1868) but was deleted in later collections. The short stanza appropriately refers to the 'hustling' passage of time but has no special application to Clough. Arnold identifies it as being '*From* Lucretius, *an unpublished tragedy*'. This is of course a reference to Arnold's old work-in-progress that had frustrated him since the first stage of his mature poetry in the mid- to late 1840s. Even after the failure of *Merope* and the poetics of 1853 (tacitly acknowledged by his reinstatement of *Empedocles*), Arnold doggedly clung to the hope of one day completing his long poem on Lucretius. His letter of 17 March 1866 to his mother helps to explain why he used this fragment in this way. He writes:

> I am rather troubled to find that Tennyson is at work on a subject, the story of the Latin poet Lucretius, which I have been occupied with for some 20 years; I was going to make a tragedy out of it; and the worst of it is that everyone, except the few friends who have known that I had it in hand will think I borrowed the subject from him. (*SL* 191)

Arnold goes on to speculate that the subject was 'put into [Tennyson's] head' by their mutual acquaintance Francis Palgrave, the poet and editor who had been with Arnold at Oxford, but he is probably mistaken (see *SL* 318–19). Arnold wanted to assert a prior claim to Lucretius as poetic subject because, as he told his mother, 'I shall probably go on', but he never completed his grand project. Tennyson's 'Lucretius' first appeared in the *Macmillan's* of May 1868. As Arnold's poetic career approached a premature end, the loss of his pet subject to his great rival was an added torment. Significantly, in the same letter, Arnold complains to his mother (in an uncharacteristically brusque tone) about the tedious work of completing his report for the Taunton Commission.

Arnold was moved to write 'Rugby Chapel', his elegy on his father, after reading *Tom Brown's Schooldays*, Tom Hughes's novel about Dr Arnold's Rugby, and, soon afterwards, a review of the book by James Fitzjames Stephen. Hughes portrayed Dr Arnold as a Carlylean hero, but Stephen made unflattering remarks about the celebrated headmaster. Although Stephen's review was the immediate occasion for beginning this poem fifteen years after Dr Arnold's death, Arnold had deeper motives. Always haunted by the memory of his father and sensitive to the reputation of the Arnold name, he felt that in his newly developing role as social critic he was closer than ever to the work of his father, who in addition to his histories and sermons had published *Thirteen Letters on Our Social Condition* (1832) during a time of political crisis in England. In June 1868, Arnold writes to his mother:

> The nearer I get to accomplishing the term of years which was papa's, the more I am struck with admiration at what he did in them. It is impossible to conceive him exactly as living now, amidst our present ideas, because those ideas he himself would have so much influenced ... Still, on the whole, I think of the main part of what I have done, and am doing, as work which he would have approved and seen to be indispensable. (*LMA* 1:455)

Nevertheless, as many commentators have noted, 'Rugby Chapel' is atypical of Arnold's poems. It is as though Arnold had adopted the confident, forceful voice of his father while describing him as a kind of Moses leading his people 'On, to the City of God'. However, as Kenneth Allott has pointed out, in Arnold's later religious prose, the phrase 'City of God' is used as a poetical way of saying 'righteousness' (*P* 490). The pronounced 'marching' cadence of the poem may have been influenced by Arnold's experience as a volunteer in the Westminster Rifle Volunteers in 1857 when he was planning the poem. During a crisis in British relations with France, he marched with the militia twice a week, and he found the experience stimulating.

Among the 1867 sonnets, the three on Rachel commemorate the French actress who had fascinated the young Arnold for the first time in 1846 and had died in 1858 at the age of 36. 'East London' and 'West London' draw on his experiences as a school inspector but they also, as Honan suggests, comment on Wordsworth's London sonnets by picturing urban poverty and misery (*MAAL* 336).

Arnold developed his idea for 'Heine's Grave' while writing his Oxford lecture on the German poet, but his treatment of Heine's 'Mocking laughter' in this dark and brooding poem contrasts with his playful celebration of ironic wit in the lecture. The contrast between the Arnoldian voice of the critic and the voice of the poet is powerfully displayed in the juxtaposition of these two texts. For Arnold the poet, Heine was deficient because he lacked a genuine love for humankind. Arnold the critic suspends judgment of Heine and celebrates his free play of mind.

'Obermann Once More' is the final poem in the 1867 volume and probably was written last. In fact, it is Arnold's last major poem. He had visited Vevey during his European tour of 1865 and the Swiss Alpine scenery refreshed his old feeling for Senancour's novel. Twenty years earlier, he had taken refuge in *Obermann* to escape the *Zeitgeist* of Clough and his friends, and in his 1852 poem on Senancour's protagonist he had located 'two desires' that 'toss about/The poet's feverish blood./One drives him to the world without,/And one to solitude' (ll. 93–6). Now Arnold's speaker has a vision of Obermann who, in a long monologue, reinterprets the story of his retreat from the outside world, advising his listener 'Despair not thou as I despaired,/Nor be cold gloom thy prison! (ll. 281–2), and ending on a much more optimistic note:

> The world's great order dawns in sheen,
> After long darkness rude,
> Divinelier imaged, clearer seen,
> With happier zeal pursued.   (ll. 293–6)

In this poem Arnold finally rejects Romantic melancholy, which has been one of the great driving forces behind his poetry, and acknowledges humankind's profound need for a 'joy whose grounds are true'. 'Obermann Once More' is not a great poem, but it is a benchmark in Arnold's literary life. Nevertheless, Arnold had hardly turned to an easy optimism. He wrote and published this poem at a time when he was entering into the cultural debate that would produce *Culture and Anarchy*, which holds up the ideal of culture but expresses deep fears of class warfare; hardly a cheerful appraisal of the condition of England. His last Obermann poem does anticipate, however, his religious criticism of the 1870s. Like the early lectures on the 'Modern Element in Literature', the poem invokes the parallel between the late Roman world and the modern one: as in the Roman world, humankind once again is without its comforting illusions and greatly in need of genuine religious feeling.

By the time Arnold published *New Poems* in 1867, his reputation as a poet had sunk low. He was better known to the public than ever before, but nearly all the attention was focused on his criticism. It had been nearly a decade since the disappointing *Merope*. However, Arnold's new book was eagerly reviewed. Most of the reviewers found positive things to say about the volume, but most of them recognized that they were dealing with a poet who unfortunately had more or less completed his oeuvre (*MAP* 20). It could hardly have been otherwise in the light of all the internal clues in *New Poems*, though none of the reviewers could have known the full implications of details such the epigraph to 'Thyrsis'. Of the three largest weekly reviews, the *Athenaeum* was less favourable than either the *Saturday Review* or the *Spectator*. The *Athenaeum* reviewer concluded that 'The poet is dead', yet his lament that 'We have lost a poet' implies a certain appreciation for Arnold's works, especially his earlier poetry. His evaluation of the restored *Empedocles* as the finest of Arnold's poems was typical of current opinion and also in line with critical views even today.[7] Writing for the *Saturday Review*, the most influential of the weeklies at this time, the reviewer (probably Leslie Stephen, whose brother was one of Arnold's most persistent critics) disagreed about *Empedocles* and instead championed 'Sohrab and Rustum' among Arnold's former poems, but he, too, complained about the overpowering sense of loss in the 1867 volume, and made the already familiar charge that Arnold as a poet lacks spontaneity and 'overweights his poetry with thought' (*MAP* 157–62). Like Arnold himself, he concludes that the age itself is unpoetic. The *Fortnightly* review by Swinburne – who later repudiated him – is a personal appreciation of Arnold's greatness as a poet. In praising Arnold's poetry over his prose, Swinburne anticipated the consensus of critical opinion about Arnold towards the end of the century.

Ironically, the idea of finality associated with *New Poems* and the accompanying sense that Arnold's poetic career had reached a premature end seemed to enhance his reputation as a poet. Arnold gradually began to be seen as the poet of an earlier generation, and of considerable importance, even if his poetic range was limited. Macmillan published a second edition of *New Poems* in 1868, and in 1869 Arnold's first collected edition of poems, in two volumes.

The 1869 *Poems*, which received major reviews by Alfred Austin, John Skelton, R. H. Hutton, Henry Hewlett and others, helped to solidify Arnold's critical reputation and increased his popularity with readers. In spite of the retrospective function of this edition, with the 'Faded Leaves' and 'Switzerland' sequences in nearly final form ('A Memory Picture' was later taken out of 'Switzerland'), Arnold did not choose an order of poems that would reflect the overall pattern of his creative development. The first volume begins with the 1853 'Sohrab and Rustum', which Arnold continued to regard most highly, the second volume with the 1852 *Empedocles*. Poems of 1849 are interspersed with those of 1852 and 1853. Among a handful of previously published poems omitted in 1869 is 'A Dream', the 1853 Marguerite poem, perhaps a genuine dream-fragment (*MAAL* 167) that had been displaced from the 'Switzerland' sequence. 'Obermann Once More' is now the penultimate poem of volume two, followed by 'The Future', an 1852 poem which is his most straightforward exposition of a favourite image: the 'river of Time' that flows to the 'infinite sea'. In choosing this arrangement, Arnold may have been thinking of the parallel image at the end of 'Sohrab and Rustum' of the Oxus flowing into the 'luminous' Aral Sea. Though he completed no major poems after 1867, Arnold was very much aware of the evolving contours of his poetic reputation, and he monitored reviews carefully, occasionally taking the advice of critics in revising individual poems.

On the day after his 1869 collection came out, Arnold wrote

an especially interesting letter to his mother. Following a remark about his cheque from Macmillan for £200 (which brought his earnings from his poetry to £500 for the previous two years), Arnold offered his best-known overall assessment of his own poetry:

> My poems represent, on the whole, the main movement of mind of the last quarter of a century, and thus they will probably have their day as people become conscious to themselves of what that movement of mind is, and interested in the literary productions which reflect it. It might be fairly urged that I have less poetical sentiment than Tennyson and less intellectual vigour and abundance than Browning; yet because I have perhaps more of a fusion of the two than either of them, and have more regularly applied that fusion to the main line of modern development, I am likely enough to have my turn as they have had theirs. (*SL* 217)

He then refers to recent articles in *Temple Bar* on Tennyson and Browning that illustrate the 'more clearly conceived demands' now being made on modern poets (*SL* 217). Arnold's assumptions here about the poet are a far cry from those of the 1853 Preface, where he had declared that true poets 'do not talk of their mission, nor of interpreting their age' (*CPW* 1:13), but they are in line with the historical contextualization of poets and poetry that he had discussed in 'The Function of Criticism'.

Though Arnold had made the decisive turn to prose long before he published *New Poems* in 1867, that book was a landmark in his literary career and a prelude to the collected *Poems* of June 1869. The fact that Arnold published *Culture and Anarchy*, his most influential book of social criticism, about six months earlier, in January 1869, lends a neat symmetry to the outline of his career as an active writer. Although nearly all of his important poems were now behind him, however, Arnold's reputation as a poet would grow during the final two decades of his life.

5

Culture and Anarchy (1869), *Friendship's Garland* (1871)

After publishing *Essays in Criticism* in 1865, Arnold not only curtailed his composition of poetry, he even abandoned literary criticism *per se* for an entire decade. Most of his contemporary critics encouraged him to publish more essays on poets and poetry, but the introductory 'Function of Criticism' in *Essays* clearly signalled the direction of his development. Arnold's expansive concept of *criticism* in that essay anticipates that of *culture* in *Culture and Anarchy*, and the thematic continuity is acknowledged in modern criticism of Arnold, which refers to these titles more often than to any of his other works. There is also an obviously close connection between these two texts in the history of Arnold's polemics. In the mid-1860s, he did not waste his creative energy in worrying about the poetic vocation that was slipping away from him. Soon after reading Stephen's attack on 'Function' in December 1864, Arnold wrote to his mother that:

[the critic's] complaint that I do not argue reminds me of dear old [brother] Edward, who always says when any of his family do not go his way, that they do not reason. However my sinuous, easy unpolemical mode of proceeding has been adopted by me first, because I really think it the best way of proceeding if one wants to get at, and keep with, truth; secondly because I am convinced only by a literary form of this kind being given to them can ideas such as mine ever gain any access in a country such as ours. So from anything like a direct answer, or direct controversy I shall religiously abstain; but here and there I shall take an opportunity of putting back this and that matter into its true light, if I think he has pulled them out of it; and I have the idea of a paper for the Cornhill, about March, to be called 'My Countrymen' and in which I may be able to say a

number of things I want to say, about the course of this Middle
Class Education matter amongst others. (*SL* 166–7)

Arnold began to collect relevant quotations from current newspaper articles to use in his essay, but his European tour and
other obligations and more urgent writing projects made it
impossible to carry out his intention for some time. The *Cornhill*
article finally appeared in February 1866 and pleased Arnold by
generating a great deal of attention. By this time, he was in the
midst of his Celtic lectures, but 'My Countrymen' signalled
Arnold's commitment to political commentary. Rather than being
primarily a reminder of the debate over *Essays*, it was a bridge
from the social and political side of that book to a more thoroughly political one. But it is important to remember that Arnold
thinks of his 'easy unpolemical mode of proceeding' as a *literary*, not a polemical, form.

For Arnold, Britain's failure to provide the kind of strong, unified
school systems he saw in Prussia and France was only part of a
much larger and more comprehensive cultural and political problem, but his European tour and continuing work on his report
served to strengthen his opinion that his own country was badly
in need of educational reform. In the spring of 1867, he worked
determinedly to complete his official, comprehensive report to
the Taunton Commission. His task was all the more difficult
because he had to refer to piles of documents he had stored at
home and so he could not use his customary writer's retreat at
the Athenaeum Club. The full report – replete with statistical
tables showing the number and population of French, Italian,
and Prussian secondary schools and universities, the educational
budget for all of France in the year 1865, detailed description of
curricula in French and German schools, and various other related
facts – was finally presented to the Commission in December.

Macmillan published the report, along with a Preface by Arnold,
in March 1868, as *Schools and Universities on the Continent*. Re-
membering his monetary loss on *The Popular Education of France*,
which had sold only about 300 copies, Arnold was gratified by
Macmillan's decision to publish the book at its own expense. In
fact, the new book sold an entire edition of 750, and the German
chapters would later be published separately in much larger
editions. Arnold's 1861 report had dealt primarily with elementary education, truly *popular* education, but his new report was

concerned with levels of education unavailable to the majority of Englishmen. This consideration led Arnold into the area of class distinctions, adding to the controversy surrounding his ideas about the role of the State in education. As a result of his 1865 tour, Arnold's respect for the intelligence and administrative skills of the German people had increased markedly, and he regarded the German part of his report as the most useful. At this time, of course, Bismarck was on the verge of uniting the German states to form a powerful new nation. Arnold never developed the affection for Germans that he felt for the French, but while writing his report he was also creating the character of Arminius, the fictional German visitor he used to satirize British society in *Friendship's Garland*.

Arnold's foreign tours supplemented the ordinary work as a school inspector that permitted him to construct a comprehensive view of British society. As Honan puts it, Arnold had been for sixteen years 'an empirical observer of the English people in scores of communities and had talked with farmers and engineers, clergymen and businessmen, working-class trainees and children, day in and out' (*MAAL* 339). Arnold saw that the working class lacked political power and that the aristocracy was largely ineffectual and was losing its power to the middle class. Unfortunately, in Arnold's view, the English middle class, as he later summed it up, had 'a defective type of religion, a narrow range of intellect and knowledge, a stunted sense of beauty' (*CPW* 9:276) and was largely unaware of its deficiencies. It was up to men like Arnold to make these people aware, so that they could improve themselves and provide proper leadership for the nation.

Schools and Universities on the Continent, however, like most of Arnold's writing on education, is more than a study of governmental policies, institutions and curricula. Often passages which seem only marginally relevant to his main points reflect his evolving concepts of culture and the role of the critic. One such apparent digression in the 1868 volume occurs in his discussion of Italian schools. In a section which places Italian Catholic schools in a very favourable light, Arnold makes admiring references to the Averroists, Italian followers of the twelfth-century Muslim philosopher known in the West as Averroes (*CPW* 4:144). This subject has very little to do with nineteenth-century Italian schools, but in the midst of the Italian part of his 1865 tour, Arnold had been distracted and disorganized in his note-taking (*MAAL* 332–3), and later he was pressed for time while completing his manuscript. However, Arnold's comments on the Averroists are interesting for the light they cast on his thinking about Christianity and the Bible, the subjects that would dominate his critical prose in the 1870s. Averroes, whom Arnold had learned about from Renan, had devoted his life to the study of Aristotelian philosophy while living in an Islamic theocracy. To protect himself from being punished as a heretic, Averroes had to manipulate the religious language of the Koran so that it did not appear to contradict the teachings of Aristotle, and he relied on the understanding of a small group of like-minded scholars to recognize the subterfuge. Renan was attracted to Averroes because the French critic, in a similar way, believed that only a small minority of elitist intellectuals dedicated to 'science' were capable of seeing through the foggy theological thinking of his own day. In the mid-1860s, Arnold, in turn, saw parallels between the position of the medieval Averroes as well as that of his contemporary Renan, and his own ideas about the critic and the enlightened 'alien' who would shortly appear in his lectures on culture. However, it is misleading to assume, as some scholars do today, that Arnold believed there is no 'reality beyond linguistic constructions' and that 'the referent of the expression is not a matter of common trust among the speakers of a language' but only 'a political agreement made with a certain class for the sake of social control'.[1] Certainly Arnold's critical prose is political, and he does reject the idea of finding 'absolute truth' in this world, but even if we see Arnold as naive as well as inconsistent, we should not ignore his deeply felt and often expressed beliefs in a universal human nature and in disinterestedness and the potential moral capacity of the individual to think and act against his or her own class interests.

After completing his series of lectures on Celtic literature in May 1866, Arnold was expected to deliver about three more lectures before his term as Oxford Professor of Poetry expired in June 1867. But he was 'in bondage' to his report on foreign schools and overwhelmed with work, so he set aside his plans to lecture on the Swiss theologian and critic Alexandre Vinet and the Roman elegiac poet Propertius, instead limiting himself to one final lecture based on an idea he had for another *Cornhill* article. On the afternoon of 7 June he delivered 'Culture and its Enemies' to an enthusiastic audience. Arnold was afraid that he had made the lecture too 'Oxfordesque' for journal publication, but Smith decided to publish it without substantial revisions later in the month. This was the beginning of *Culture and Anarchy*.

In his last lecture at Oxford, Arnold is reluctant to define exactly what he means by 'culture', but it is clear that he does not mean a precise body of knowledge or art but rather a psychological attitude of mental freedom, driven by the motive of intellectual curiosity. Arnold's fundamental egalitarianism is evident here. Culture 'seeks to do away with classes' and 'make the best that has been thought and known in the world current everywhere' (*CPW* 5:113). The 'enemies' of culture are a 'mechanical and material civilisation' that stifles the inner life of the individual, an unsympathetic spirit of competition, and an 'intense energetic absorption' in specialized pursuits. Later renamed 'Sweetness and Light' as the first chapter of *Culture and Anarchy*,[2] 'Culture and its Enemies' adapts Jonathan Swift's metaphor of the bee from *The Battle of the Books*, making sweetness stand for beauty of character and light for intelligence, with the additional connotation of spiritual illumination.

Arnold's part in developing the modern usage of the term 'culture', which has become ubiquitous in literary and socio-political discourse, is one of his most important contributions as a man of letters, and it is intimately tied to his own growth and development as a writer.[3] Use of the term was already fairly common among English writers and intellectuals in the 1850s, but it was closely associated with the German word *Bildung* and its English equivalents, self-development and self-cultivation. That is, 'culture' usually meant 'self-culture', and for many it had negative connotations of amorality, egoism, and an unhealthy aestheticism. The English reputation of Goethe was intimately connected with these ideas and associations. Goethe had been seen as a liberating hero to Arnold and others of his generation in the 1840s. Arnold, in his characteristically comparative manner, found in Goethe an alternative to the Christian orthodoxy of his upbringing, although as he moved toward the new classicism expressed in his 1853 Preface, he selected only certain aspects of Goethe's legacy for his own use. Arnold's version of Goethe as 'physician' and moralist was influenced by Carlyle's early views of Goethe: it informs Arnold's early criticism, notably the essay on Heine. However, by the mid-1860s Goethe's influence on Arnold had waned. Earlier, the probable reference to Goethe as the suffering figure who 'takes dejectedly/His seat upon the intellectual throne' in 'The Scholar-Gipsy' ('This for our wisest!') signalled Arnold's movement from alienation to accommodation with society.

The line of criticism that had classified Arnold's poetry from the beginning as too detached and academic, too lacking in spontaneous passion, was in a sense reacting to that side of Arnold which was closest to the Goethean ideal of self-development and self-culture. Ironically, Swinburne's *positive* assessment of Arnold's poetry following the publication of the 1867 poems turned this judgment on its head and praised the aesthetic element in Arnold at the same time that Arnold himself was broadening his concept of culture to mean something like an individual ideal of enlightenment *within* the totality of socially transmitted behaviour patterns, arts, beliefs, and institutions of a people.

'Culture and its Enemies', Arnold's last lecture at Oxford, was in its published form his first unambiguous essay in social and political criticism. In writing this kind of criticism in the troubled times prior to the Second Reform Bill in 1867 Arnold was following the precedent of Carlyle, whose first social and political essay, 'Signs of the Times', had appeared in the *Edinburgh Review* of June 1829, during the period of social disturbance prior to the First Reform Bill in 1832. Carlyle's critique of the 'Age of Machinery' provided Arnold with one of the basic metaphors of *Culture and Anarchy*, the Englishman's unwarranted faith in (institutional) machinery. Carlyle's reputation in England had long been tarnished by his stylistic excesses and curmudgeonly authoritarianism, and Arnold's early enthusiasm for the great sage had largely faded by 1850. The critical prose style that Arnold developed in the 1860s owed much more to John Henry Newman than to Carlyle. Still, Carlyle had left indelible traces in Arnold's thought, more than Arnold himself cared to acknowledge.[4] When Arnold was formulating his concept of 'anarchy', he must have remembered Carlyle's references to the 'disorganized condition of society' and social forces working in a 'wasteful, chaotic manner' in *Heroes and Hero-Worship* (a series of lectures that was printed as a book in 1841, a model for Arnold's own mode of publication). That the times are in desperate need of change but that potential greatness can be achieved through the transformation of the individual are Carlylean assumptions. But Arnold had his Empedocles reject something like Carlyle's religious philosophy fifteen years before, and now he offers something very different: 'culture'.

On returning the proofs of 'Culture and its Enemies' to Smith, Arnold, following a familiar pattern, announced that he would like to follow up the original article with another, entitled 'Anarchy and Authority', later in the summer; however, the response to the first article was so great that he delayed the second until January 1868, so that he could follow his now routine practice of responding to his critics. Thirteen months later, the total number of articles had grown to six (for which Arnold received £25 apiece). The book was published at the end of January 1869, with the subtitle 'an essay in political and social criticism'.

Arnold substantially revised the journal articles and wrote to his mother that 'in going through them I have much improved their arrangement and expression, and think them now, a well-looking and useful body of doctrine'.[5] Nevertheless, the completed text of *Culture and Anarchy* retained signs of its piecemeal composition: in one chapter Arnold may allude to critical comment on a preceding chapter. It is remarkable that a text so intimately tied to its historical context has become a classic that is still seriously discussed and cited in cultural debates in Britain and, especially, in the United States over 125 years later.[6] Arnold wrote at a time of social disturbances and general unrest. In March of 1866, Gladstone, in Earl Russell's Whig ministry, introduced a moderate franchise measure; however, it was opposed even by members of his own party, led by Robert Lowe. Soon the Whig government was defeated, and Lord Derby formed a Tory ministry with Disraeli as a leading figure. The Hyde Park riots of 23 July broke out when supporters of the Reform League, refused the use of the Park, smashed the railings that surrounded it. Later in the evening, Arnold and his wife watched from their balcony as rioters stoned the windows of their neighbour, Richard Mayne, the police commissioner (*SL* 192).

Arnold, like many others, was dismayed at the inability of Spencer Walpole, the Home Secretary, to cope with the situation. Radical leaders such as John Bright organized mass meetings in various parts of England. By the time Parliament convened in February 1867, Disraeli was convinced that reform was inevitable, and he introduced a measure more radical than the previous one of the Whigs. Fenian and trades union disturbances continued through the spring and summer, however, and on 10 June, a minor riot proceeded unchecked in the presence of the Royal London Militia. The Second Reform Bill, increasing the electorate from one-fifth to two-fifths of the adult male population, was passed on 15 August, but civil strife continued. In mid-December, Irish Fenian Nationalists set off an explosion at Clerkenwell prison that killed twelve people and injured many more. In February 1868, Disraeli succeeded Lord Derby as Prime Minister, but in April he was defeated on the Irish Church question. In November a general election under the provisions of the reformed franchise returned a liberal Parliament, and *Culture and Anarchy* was published in January 1869, just before the new Parliament convened in February.

Arnold's second chapter, 'Doing as One Likes', sets the limited ideal of personal liberty – which, if undirected, leads to anarchy – against the interests and authority of the State, the 'nation in its collective and corporate character' (*CPW* 5:111), the Burkean concept that had taken shape largely in relation to his observations about education. Already responding to critics of his 'religion of culture', Arnold argues that 'if I can show what my opponents call rough or coarse action, but what I would rather call random and ill-regulated action, – action with insufficient light . . . a practical mischief and dangerous to us, then I have found a practical use for light in correcting this state of things' (*CPW* 5:116). Just as J. H. Newman had argued for the fundamental *usefulness* of knowledge for its own sake in the healthy development of the individual's mind, Arnold argues for intellectual enlightenment as a fundamental criterion for the healthy development of society. But how does the individual reach beyond personal and class loyalties to the idea of the 'whole community'? By our 'everyday selves' we are 'separate, personal, at war'. When 'anarchy presents itself . . . we know not where to turn'. According to Arnold, the ideal of culture suggests that beyond his everyday self the individual at least potentially has a *best self*; 'by our *best self* we are united, impersonal, at harmony' (*CPW* 5:134). In the final analysis, this extension of Arnold's earlier idea of critical disinterestedness in 'The Function of Criticism' is still the most intriguing and controversial aspect of Arnold's cultural ideal: that through 'culture' an individual is capable of rising above individual and class interests. In other words, culture is resistant to ideology. This is the idea that has been most savagely attacked by late twentieth-century critics who believe that any appeal to objectivity or disinterestedness is really a device used to conceal motives of domination.[7]

The third chapter develops Arnold's playful tripartite classification of the 'Barbarians, Philistines, Populace' (aristocracy, middle class, and working class) in British society, each with its distinctive qualities. Barbarians have a 'high chivalrous style' but also a 'fierce turn for resistance' and inaccessibility to ideas; Philistines have honesty and energy but also provincialism and narrowness; the Populace is the 'vast residuum' emerging as a force to augment that of the Philistines but still undeveloped, 'marching where it likes, meeting where it likes, bawling what it likes, breaking what it likes' (*CPW* 5:143). Underlying class differences, however, is a common human nature as well as the common English defect of imagining 'happiness to consist in doing what one's ordinary self likes' (*CPW* 5:145). Although Arnold as social critic usually concentrates his energies on the Philistines, the class with the most power and influence, here he looks at society as a whole:

> [I]n each class there are born a certain number of natures with a curiosity about their best self, with a bent for seeing things as they are, for disentangling themselves from machinery, for simply concerning themselves with reason and the will of God, and doing their best to make these prevail; – for the pursuit, in a word, of perfection. (*CPW* 5:145)

I quote this passage not only because it is a good summary of the tag phrases that Arnold associates with culture but also to point out his 'practical' mechanism for the transformation of all classes through culture. He uses the ironical term 'aliens' for those special individuals who come to terms with their best selves in order to be led by a general humane spirit and thus liberate themselves from the blinkers of class ideology, and he believes that the number of aliens 'is capable of being diminished or augmented' (*CPW* 5:146). It is clear that Arnold identifies himself as one of these aliens and that his goal as a social and political critic is to increase the number of independent-minded aliens who like him will dedicate themselves to the 'pursuit of perfection'. As in his earlier 'Academies' essay, Arnold wants to perform in his text the very critical acts he is describing and that he wants his audience to emulate.

In his fourth chapter, 'Hebraism and Hellenism', Arnold asks his reader to join him in probing beneath the habits and practice that prohibit one from understanding the fundamental problem in English society that Arnold has already identified: action with insufficient light, the constant emphasis on doing rather than knowing. From the beginning of his critical career, Arnold had emphasized the need for the British to look to the French for an appreciation of ideas and a needed correction to English provincialism. Later, he suggested that the British should recognize the Celtic elements in British culture that balance those of the Anglo-Germanic. In making easy generalizations about the 'dominant traits' of racial, national and ethnic groups, Arnold was typical of his time, but his comparative, dialogic approach was distinctive. Now in *Culture and Anarchy* he develops his most ambitious and suggestive scheme of bipolar cultural forces that must be balanced in order to achieve a healthy cultural *wholeness*. Both Hellenism and Hebraism aim at the goal of human perfection or salvation, claims Arnold, but 'by very different courses. The uppermost idea with Hellenism is to see things as they really are; the uppermost idea with Hebraism is conduct and obedience' (*CPW* 5:165). Appealing – as he had before – to a cyclical view of history, Arnold argued that both principles play a part in the development of civilization, and 'by alternations of Hebraism and Hellenism, of a man's intellectual and moral impulses . . . the human spirit proceeds' (*CPW* 5:171–2). Early Christianity was the great triumph of Hebraism, the Renaissance was that of Hellenism. However, in England the Hellenic impulse of the Renaissance was 'prematurely' checked by the reactionary cross-current of Puritanism in the seventeenth century. This 'unnatural' state of affairs has impeded progress towards Hellenic 'spontaneity of consciousness' and imposed an overemphasis on 'conscience and conduct', an 'imbalance' toward the moral, Hebraic side.

The 'one thing needful' in the fifth chapter, 'Porro Unum est Necessarium', is of course the Hellenistic corrective to the Puritan moralism dominant in British society. In pointing out what he takes to be the misinterpretation of St Paul's writings by British Puritanism – taking the key terms used by Paul in a 'connected and fluid' way and using them in an 'isolated, fixed, mechanical way, as if they were talismans' – Arnold sets the stage for his first book of religious criticism, *St Paul and Protestantism*.

In the final chapter, 'Our Liberal Practitioners,' Arnold applies his ideas to some 'practical operations' of the day, including the Disestablishment of the Irish Church, the Real Estate Intestacy Bill, and the Deceased Wife's Sister Bill, all of which point out the *mechanical* nature of conventional political thinking. Arnold departs from his elevated, urbane style for a more pointed and heated attack on his targets. Ridiculing the foolish legal debate on the right of a man to marry the sister of his deceased wife, he asks, '[W]ho, that is not manacled and hoodwinked by his Hebraism can believe that, as to love and marriage, our reason and the necessities of our humanity have their true, sufficient, and divine law expressed for them by the voice of any Oriental and polygamous nation like the Hebrews?' (*CPW* 5:208). But his sharpest criticism is reserved for the advocates of the 'talisman of free-trade'. After saluting 'free-trade and its doctors with all respect', Arnold asks:

> whether even here, too, our Liberal friends do not pursue their operations in a mechanical way, without reference to any firm intelligible law of things, to human life as a whole, and human happiness; and whether it is not more for our good . . . if, instead of worshipping free-trade with them Hebraistically, as a kind of fetish, and helping them to pursue it as an end in and for itself, we turn the free stream of our thought upon their treatment of it, and see how this is related to the intelligible law of human life, and to national well-being and happiness. (*CPW* 5:209)

The strength of Arnold's conviction on this issue can be measured by the fact that here his rhetoric comes closest to the characteristic exhortations of Carlyle and Ruskin. Like Ruskin in *Unto This Last* (1862), Arnold reveals the lack of humanity and compassion for the poor inherent in *laissez-faire* political economy, but instead of appealing to traditional Judaeo-Christian morality, he appeals to the right reason of Hellenism. Ruskin had reminded his readers of the wisdom of the 'Jew merchant' Solomon – 'He that oppresseth the poor to increase his riches, shall surely come to want' (Proverbs 22:16) – but in Arnold's scheme it is the narrow-minded free-traders who are 'Hebraistic'.

In his Conclusion to *Culture and Anarchy*, Arnold returns to a higher style and makes his most sweeping claims for culture in stating his conviction that:

the endeavour to reach, through culture, the firm intelligible law of things . . . that the detaching ourselves from our stock notions and habits, that a more free play of consciousness, an increased desire for sweetness and light, and all the bent which we call Hellenising, is the master-impulse even now of the life of our nation and of humanity, – somewhat obscurely perhaps for this actual moment, but decisively and certainly for the immediate future; and that those who work for this are the sovereign educators. (*CPW* 5:229)

'We, indeed, pretend to educate no one', Arnold disarmingly claims, although apparently that is exactly what he is trying to do. However, the relationship between inner enlightenment and social action is always a problematical one, as Arnold's critics were quick to point out.

At the heart of *Culture and Anarchy* is a tension between apolitical individualism and desire for community. Up to the present, Arnold's critics have continued to complain, on the one hand, about the ineffectuality of his privleging 'knowing' above 'doing' in the struggle for human perfection, and, on the other, about his apparent anti-libertarian bias in identifying culture with the State and 'law and order'. This tension in Arnold's cultural ideal results in part from the political dilemmas of Britain in 1867 but also from tendencies in Arnold's thought. What exactly is the epistemological status of the 'best self'? In his poetry Arnold had explored the question of the individual's authentic or true self and had implied that even though we assume it exists, it may be buried or cut off from ordinary consciousness. Now he equates the 'best self' with 'right reason' and cites the positive example of Wilhelm von Humboldt as a man who united the ideal of individual enlightenment with a real programme of social involvement. But can 'beautiful souls' like Humboldt or 'aliens' in touch with their 'best selves' sustain the strong but just State that Arnold has in mind?

In May 1868, when Arnold decided to gather his social and political essays into a single volume, he considered including the essay 'My Countryman', his first unambiguous venture into socio-political criticism, and a series of satirical letters on political and cultural issues which he had been publishing in the *Pall Mall Gazette* since July 1866. However, in order to achieve a more unified structure in a book that threatened to be diverse and shapeless, Arnold limited himself to the 'Culture and Anarchy' lectures. Arnold's first published letter in the *Pall Mall Gazette* series was written in response to two letters signed 'Horace' and dated from Paris which appeared in that journal in March of 1866. The correspondent made reference to Arnold's admiration for French ideas and institutions while he or she expressed the opinion that English freedom was obviously superior to French tyranny under the government of Napoleon III. Arnold defended his views in a letter entitled 'A Courteous Explanation'. Then in July of the same year, he was moved to write a letter to the same journal in response to a letter written by the historian and 'progressive' critic Goldwin Smith on England's position in the Austro-Prussian war. In fact Arnold was on good personal terms with Smith, and they often saw each other at the Athenaeum Club, where they were both members. Two years earlier Arnold had introduced Smith to Emerson during the American's visit to England. However, the two men often disagreed in print. Arnold thought that Smith's opinions in favour of an English alliance with Prussia revealed the blind hatred of France and generally shallow understanding of European matters that was typical of Liberal thought.

Arnold's satiric response to Smith became the first of thirteen 'Arminius' letters to the *Pall Mall Gazette*; Arnold interrupted the series after the seventh letter in the spring of 1867 and resumed it again during the period 1869–71. The Arminius letters would be published along with 'My Countrymen' and 'A Courteous Explanation' in 1871 as *Friendship's Garland*.

In the Arminius letters Arnold writes his most outrageous and funniest satire. Although he had displayed a talent for satire in his treatment of Philistines in some of his lectures and essays, the format of these informal, semi-fictional letters allows him to go much further in developing his verbal humour, revealing the most playful and irreverent side of his wit which had been prominent in his old letters to Clough. Perhaps he found in this project some emotional release from the grief brought on by the death of two sons during the year 1868. But Arnold also drew heavily on the literary precedents of Swift, Voltaire, Heine and Carlyle in composing the Arminius letters, and he offers exaggerated characters that at times seem Dickensian. He used the device of the transparent literary hoax whereby a foreign visitor offers critical comments on English institutions, to the dismay of a naive English friend who attempts to explain their virtues. The visitor in this case is an arrogant young Prussian named Arminius, Baron von Thunder-ten-Tronckh, grandson of the character described by Voltaire in *Candide* ('he was christened Hermann, but I call him Arminius, because it is more in the grand style': *CPW* 5:48). While searching for a living descendent of the optimistic philosopher Dr Pangloss, Arminius visits his English friend Matthew Arnold, a Grub Street hack. Arminius has:

> the true square Teutonic head, a blond and disorderly mass of tow-like hair, a podgy and sanguine countenance, shaven cheeks, and a whity-brown moustache. He wears a rough pilot-coat, and generally smokes away with his hands in the pockets of it, and his light blue eyes fixed on his interlocutor's face. (*CPW* 5:58)

In the first letter (the response to Goldwin Smith), 'Arnold' begins to narrate the Prussian's observations and opinions. In the second letter, Arminius writes in his own voice, and so on. Among later letters is a response by 'My Friend Leo, of the *Daily Telegraph*'. In the book Arnold as the 'Editor' adds notes and commentary. Even more fully than in the 'Culture and Anarchy' essays, Arnold's dialogue with his critics becomes part of the text, but of course Arnold as 'implied author' of the text is in control. Within this framework Arnold builds several layers of irony: with self-deflating humour he pokes fun at his own image as a pretentious intellectual (Mr Matthew 'as a disputant' is 'rather a poor creature', remarks Arminius), and he indulges in a satire of German stereotypes (Arnold himself was not uncritical of German ways of thinking and acting), all the while satirizing a broad range of British life and institutions, with emphasis of course on the Philistines. After all, Arnold had borrowed the term 'Philistines' from the German poet Heine, a severe critic of the English. An adherent of *Geist* (translated as 'intelligence'), Arminius ridicules typical Arnoldian targets such as the Deceased Wife's Sister Bill and the opinions of the 'Young Lions' at the *Daily Telegraph*, which Arnold had already singled out for satire in the Preface of *Essays in Criticism*. (In attacking the *Daily Telegraph*, which he calls in a May 1865 letter to his sister Frances the organ of 'the vulgar Liberals' [LMA 1:305], Arnold was in fact aligning himself with the editorial stance of *The Pall Mall Gazette*.)

'Arnold' introduces Arminius to vacuous and complacent types who represent various political and class interests. Most memorable is Bottles, Esq., a millionaire bottle manufacturer, who presents his views on political and social issues; in praising the 'modern' educational system of his teacher Archimedes Silverpump, PhD, at the Lycurgus House Academy, Bottles rhapsodizes: 'None of your antiquated rubbish – all practical work – latest discoveries in science – mind constantly kept excited – lots of interesting experiments – lights of all colours – fizz! fizz! bang! bang! That's what I call forming a man' (*CPW* 5:71).

For a time in the late 1860s Arnold was working concurrently on his foreign education report, his 'Culture and Anarchy' essays, and the Arminius letters, using three separate but interrelated literary modes to express his ideas and opinions. Even more than *Culture and Anarchy, Friendship's Garland* is tied to its historical context, full of topical references to ephemeral issues, and sometimes puzzling to modern readers who are not scholars of the period. The publication history of this most unusual of Arnold's books is interesting for several reasons. After Arnold decided to kill off Arminius before the fortifications of Paris in the letter published 29 November 1870, either he or his publisher George Smith proposed Arnold's 'memorial edition' of Arminius letters which make up the bulk of *Friendship's Garland* (*CPW* 5:357).

Shortly after publishing the final Arminius letter, Arnold visited the Income Tax Commissioners at Edgware, who had assessed his profits from literary publications at £1000 a year (*SL* 227–8). Amused (and flattered) by the commissioners' assumption that he was 'a most distinguished literary man' whose works 'were mentioned everywhere and must have a wide circulation', Arnold assured the men that he was '*an unpopular author*' and convinced them to reduce the annual assessment to £200 (*SL* 227–8).

In early January 1871, Arnold wrote to Smith saying that he was prevented 'from turning to the literary remains of poor dear Arminius' by a large stack of grammar papers he was obliged to look over, but nevertheless he worked very quickly and by February 1 he had already sent back the first sheet of proofs (*MAB* 94). Arnold was particularly concerned with the 'look' or design of his new book. Even after he had pruned some of the more ephemeral, and some of the more insulting, personal references from the letters, Arnold saw that some explanatory notes would be necessary, and of course it would be appropriate to use a witty tone in them, too. Although it was 'fun' to add notes and commentary as the 'Editor', Arnold worried about the appearance of intermixed letters and notes and was afraid it looked 'self-important and *bête*' to place '*Ed.*' after every note (*MAB* 94). In fact Smith thought that Arnold had become carried away with the notes and made too many of them. Arnold reasoned 'that though the public may not much like notes, it still less likes being puzzled and thrown out by allusions it does not know or has forgotten' (suggesting that some references in the book were already obscure to a British audience in 1871: see *CPW* 5:358). Finally, Arnold agreed to omit the numerous notes marked for deletion by Smith. Arnold was sensitive to the curious image he was presenting of himself in the book, to some extent a self-conscious caricature and yet closely associated with the persona in his 'serious' publications. When he saw that the printer had placed his former university titles after his name, Arnold struck them out, saying, 'It would be carrying the joke too far.'

Although its origin is not known, the title may have been a composite of two of the literary annuals that had been fashionable earlier in the century, *Friendship's Offering* and *The Garland* (*CPW* 5:358). Neither Smith nor Arnold was completely satisfied with the original binding: white cloth with a gold-stamped design and a black mourning border, and dark end-papers. Arnold was concerned about 'the jar to the eye from the inside being darker than the outside'. Later copies were bound in reddish brown or dark blue. The only other edition in Arnold's lifetime was printed in Edinburgh and bound with *Culture and Anarchy* for publication in 1883 by Macmillan in New York (*CPW* 5:359).

Just as *Friendship's Garland* was being advertised for sale in *The Times* in late February, Arnold was shocked to learn that one of the targets of his satire in the book had been awarded damages of £500 in a libel suit against the publishing firm of Hodder & Stoughton. The suit involved James Hain Friswell's book *Modern Men of Letters Honestly Criticised*, where George Sala, the editor (and one of the 'Young Lions') of the *Daily Telegraph*, is described as a disreputable drunk who had spent time in prison. Sala and his vulgar *Daily Telegraph* style had been satirized mercilessly in the final Arminius letter. Arnold feared legal proceedings of the same kind from Sala or others mentioned in the book and wrote to Smith to ask his opinion the matter: 'Nothing would compensate me for being mixed up, and having my name mixed up, in a serious legal encounter with such a crew: not if I beat them a thousand times over.'[8] Arnold's fears did not materialize, however, and, after this time, the sparring between Arnold and the 'Young Lions' subsided, as both sides became more restrained. Years later, Sala joked in his *Memoirs* that when Arnold was attacking the 'Young Lions', some of them were already 'middle-aged lions' and others (including Sala himself) were 'rather ancient lions'.[9]

Even though Arnold's criticism was a common topic of public debate when they were published, neither *Culture and Anarchy* nor *Friendship's Garland* were reviewed extensively as books. Arnold's consistent practice of publishing his individual essays first in journals, then in books, helps to explain this curious fact. His essays were a familiar topic in journals such as the *Saturday Review*, the *Spectator*, the *Fortnightly Review*, *Macmillan's Magazine*, the *Quarterly Review* and the *Edinburgh Review*, as well as in *The Times*, the *Daily Telegraph*, the *Daily News* and other newspapers. Even Arnold's opponents tended to show him a grudging respect: for example, a reviewer for the *Nonconformist* (the journal singled out in *Culture and Anarchy* for its unenlightened motto 'The Dissidence of Dissent and the Protestantism of the Protestant religion') wrote that 'Mr. Arnold has a claim to be heard.'[10] Arnold confidently wrote to his mother in June 1869 that *Culture and Anarchy* 'will have a considerable effect in the end' (*SL* 219).

Yet Arnold was not entirely satisfied with the nature of his reputation and influence. The essays that made up *Culture and Anarchy* and *Friendship's Garland* were received more harshly than those collected as *Essays in Criticism*. By the late 1860s his public image had solidified as the 'Apostle of Culture' and, increasingly, both friends and opponents had strong opinions about him. This situation made it more difficult for Arnold to carry out his intention of influencing public opinion in subtle, indirect ways. As Carl Dawson and John Pfordresher point out, 'to some of his critics he had become more a symbol of a point of view than a reforming teacher' (*MAPW* 27). In the coming years, his rather striking physical appearance – large nose and mouth, 'mutton-chop' whiskers, and hair (dark black, even into his later years) parted in the middle – would become a popular subject for caricature in the press.

Most informed readers seem already to have held definite opinions about the contents of *Culture and Anarchy* and *Friendship's*

Garland by the time they were published, so publication of the books themselves did not make a great impact. Entrenched negative opinions were typical of certain groups, and lines of opposition were clearly drawn. Most obviously, influential Congregationalist leaders such as Edward Baines and, in particular, Edward Miall (the editor of the *Nonconformist* to whom Arnold makes multiple references in both *Culture and Anarchy* and *Friendship's Garland*) strongly disagreed with Arnold's analysis of 'Puritanism' as a negative force in British society, among other issues. Both Baines and Miall were Members of Parliament, as was the Benthamite J. A. Roebuck, whom Arnold had ridiculed in 'The Function of Criticism' and again in *Culture and Anarchy* as representative of the mindless optimists who believed in the 'unrivalled happiness' of Britons. Arnold's harsh treatment of Roebuck and other defenders of the status quo naturally made enemies in some quarters, and many Liberal politicians, whether they were Nonconformists or not, scoffed at Arnold's lack of common sense when dealing with political issues.

On a somewhat higher plane of controversy were adversaries such as Henry Sidgwick and Frederic Harrison. Like Leslie Stephen, who later contrasted his own intellectual background with that of Arnold, Sidgwick represented the traditions of Cambridge. (Ironically, Sidgwick was also an old Rugbeian.) As a young philosopher under the influence of John Stuart Mill, Sidgwick published an article entitled 'The Prophet of Culture' in the *Macmillan's* of August 1867. He acknowledged Arnold's growing reputation but thought it was undeserved. To him Arnold was a shallow thinker who lacked a truly disciplined and philosophic mind. Arnold's criticisms of the English Nonconformists, for example, revealed his inadequate understanding of religion and even culture itself. According to Sidney Coulling, Arnold's 'Hebrew and Hellenism' chapter in *Culture and Anarchy* began as a reply to Sidgwick's article, in an attempt to show that his concept of religion and its relation to culture was much more sophisticated than his critic had given him credit for (*MAHC* 275). In the 'Porro Unum Est Necessarium' chapter, Arnold quotes directly from Sidgwick: 'Culture diffuses "sweetness and light." I do not undervalue these blessings, but religion gives fire and strength, and the world wants fire and strength even more than sweetness and light' (*MAPW* 215). Citing the empiricist historian Henry Thomas Buckle, Arnold acknowledges that it is possible to be a fanatical partisan of light and a fanatical enemy of moral conscience, but then returns to his fundamental historical argument that:

> whether at this or that time, and to this or that set of persons, one ought to insist most on the praises of fire and strength, or on the praises of sweetness and light, must depend, one would think, on the circumstances and needs of that particular time and those particular persons.

And a mere 'glance at the world around us' shows that the 'ruling force' is that of Hebraism (*CPW* 5:179).

Harrison is, however, the individual mentioned most often in *Culture and Anarchy* and *Friendship's Garland*. He was a Comtian philosopher – a defender of positivism and an enemy of Arnold's culture – and Arnold focuses on him as an important adversary in the two books. Harrison opposed Arnold in print on several occasions, but it is interesting that his reference to 'culture' as '[p]erhaps the very silliest cant of the day' gained currency in Arnold criticism, largely because Arnold himself incorporated the quotation into the Introduction to *Culture and Anarchy* (*CPW* 5:87). Like the quotation from Sidgwick, this points to Arnold's method of dramatizing debates with his critics in his published works. By incorporating suggestive references to and quotations (sometimes roughly paraphrased or virtually invented) from Harrison and the others into his prose, he can control the tone and what John Holloway calls the 'value frame' in the presentation of their disagreement with him.[11] Sometimes he gives the impression that he is one man up against an army of critics. In the opening section of 'My Countrymen' alone, Arnold refers to the following opponents: the *Saturday Review*, Sir Thomas Bazley (MP for Manchester), Miall, the *Daily Telegraph*, the *Daily News*, Robert Lowe, John Bright, and the *Morning Star*.

Nevertheless, Arnold rarely presents his adversaries as completely wrong about any issue. Instead he implies by tonal modulations that they are too sectarian or partisan, too crude, too provincial, too little discriminating, too muddled or unclear, too impulsive, too easily satisfied by simplistic solutions to problems. Arnold's persona, on the other hand, is consistently open-minded, balanced, urbane, reasonable, patient, clear, and penetrating in his analysis. This persona would be unbearably arrogant if it were not for the pervasive irony in Arnold's prose. He uses irony not only as a weapon to undercut his adversaries but in a self-deprecating manner to establish his own modesty, as in his quotation of cutting comments like that of Harrison's. But of course this very quality of modesty in Arnold's persona strengthens the impression of his openness, his lack of dogmatism. The clear implication is that Arnold's modesty and sweet reasonableness is not shared by his adversaries. About five years after Arnold's death, his one-time antagonist Leslie Stephen published a long retrospective article about him in the *National and English Review*. He acknowledges Arnold's genuine courtesy and sweetness of nature but he says he wishes he had Arnold's gift for making nasty remarks in such a pleasant manner (*MAPW* 408–28).

Arnold's capacity for self-irony was more than a literary device, however. In November of 1867 Harrison published 'Culture: A Dialogue' in the *Fortnightly Review*, a satire in which he purports to have encountered Arnold's Arminius in a visit to the Continent. (This was after Arnold had published the seventh Arminius letter but long before the appearance of *Friendship's Garland*.) Adapting Arnold's own device, Harrison takes on the role of the naive narrator who questions Arminius about his illustrious English acquaintance. The article makes serious charges against Arnold – not only that he is intellectually confused but that he is an elitist who worries about a future of 'culture' while immediate social needs go unfulfilled – but it is also funny. 'Harrison' gushes about the glories of culture while a frustrated Arminius tries to ask serious philosophical questions. At one point Arminius impatiently demands to know how culture is supposed to make moral distinctions and encourage good works, and 'Harrison' answers:

> 'By diffusing an atmosphere of sweetness and light; by broadening the basis of life and intelligence; by the children of Thy spirit making their light shine upon the earth,' said I, with some unction, easily gliding into my old chant when the college service was intoned, and reverentially repeating some beautiful words I had once heard there. (*MAPW* 233).

Arnold generally enjoyed parodies of his work and jokes on himself, and when he read the article, he found it 'so amusing that I laughed till I cried' (*LMA* 1:432–3).

Arnold's consistent refusal to *systematize* his ideas – a quality that irritated the philosopher Harrison and other critics – was at least partially a legacy from Arnold's father, who observed in his Oxford lectures on history 'how little any real history is an exact exemplification of abstract principles.'[12] Nevertheless, several years after Arnold's death, Harrison published an article in which he argued that in spite of Arnold's claim that he has no 'system, principles, or doctrines of any kind', many of his intellectual positions were in the final analysis very close to those of Harrison's own Comtian positivism. Harrison thought that even the language Arnold used to describe the mission of 'Culture' in his conclusion to *Culture and Anarchy* is 'the very language' Comte himself used to describe the mission of Positivism (*MAPW* 432–40).

One early and important instance of the influence of Arnold's cultural criticism was in the Renaissance essays of Walter Pater, the first of which was published in November 1869. But at this point in his career Pater was interested only in the aesthetic dimension of Arnold's thought. According to David DeLaura, 'If there is a "moment" when the Keatsian artist announces an ultimate severance from the hope of affecting nineteenth-century life, it may be in Pater's first essays of the late sixties, as Matthew Arnold's great "critical effort" is systematically reshaped into the catchwords of the new aestheticism.'[13] Like Arnold, Pater was seeking to modify and transform traditional religious categories, but without Arnold's increasing social and ethical motivation. An even more unexpected sign of Arnold's influence came in 1871 with the publication of E. B. Tylor's *Primitive Culture*, a pioneering work in anthropology. Tylor adapted the term that Arnold had popularized for use in a newly developing field of science and applied it in evolutionary and hierarchical senses.[14]

Arnold wrote his seminal essays on culture during a time of personal anguish and grief. His infant son Basil, not yet two years old, died in January 1868, just as Arnold was finishing the second 'Culture and Anarchy' article for the *Cornhill*. Arnold was a dedicated and affectionate father, and the premature death of three of his four sons was the greatest sorrow of his life. In a letter to his sister Jane, Arnold described Basil's death:

I sat up with him till 4 this morning, looking over my papers, that Flu & Mrs. Tuffin [the nurse] might get some sleep; & at the end of every second paper I went to him, stroked his poor twitching hand & kissed his soft warm cheek; & though he never slept he seemed easy & hardly moaned at all. This morning about 6, after I had gone to bed, he became more restless – about 11 he had another convulsion – from that time he sank. Flu Mrs. Tuffin & I were all round him as his breathing gradually ceased – then the spasm of death passed over his face: after that the eyes closed, all the features relaxed, & now as he lies with his hands folded & a white camellia Georgina Whiteman brought him lying on his breast, he is the sweetest & most beautiful sight possible . . .

– And so this loss comes to me just after my 45th birthday, with so much other 'suffering in the flesh,' – the departure of youth, cares of many kinds, an almost painful anxiety about public matters, – to remind me that *the time past of our life may suffice us!* – words which have haunted me for the last year or two, – & that we 'should no longer live the rest of our time in the flesh to the lusts of men, but to the will of God.' – However different the interpretation we put on much of the facts & history of Christianity, we may unite in the bond of this call, which is true for all of us, & for me above all, how full of meaning & warning. (*SL* 208–9)

This poignant account of a personal crisis, laced with quotations from 1 Peter, brings to light a felt spiritual need – deeper than the more obvious cultural or political aims – that helped motivate Arnold's religious writings of the 1870s.

Shortly after the death of Basil, the Arnolds moved from their London home to Byron House, Harrow, with their surviving children Thomas (15), Trevenen or 'Budge' (14), Richard (12), Lucy (9) and Eleanor (7). The principal reasons for the move concerned the sons' education. Arnold doted on Budge in particular and was determined that he should receive a strong grounding in the classics like his own. Budge, however, was a poor student and Arnold was disappointed by his performance first at Miss Leech's Day School in London, then at Laleham under his relation Matt Buckland. The headmaster, Frederic Temple, then accepted Budge at Rugby. (Temple was eager to reconcile with Arnold after opposing his appointment to the Taunton Commission – in spite of their old connections – on the grounds of his views on State intervention in education.) Rugby was expensive, however, and again Budge did poorly. Arnold hoped that Harrow School might provide a solution. By moving his family to the area, Arnold could enrol all three of his sons in the school as home boarders, thus saving a great deal of money. At some other schools there was a prejudice against home boarders, but Arnold heard that this was not so at Harrow, and Budge was a sensitive boy who had sorely missed his family when away from home. The school's prestige had been rising in recent years, and headmaster Montagu Butler was an admirer of Arnold's father.

In fact, the arrangement at Harrow seemed to work well. Arnold was satisfied with Butler, Budge's academic performance improved, and the Arnolds even took into their home the young Prince Thomas of Savoy, who had been sent to Harrow by his uncle, the King of Italy. But all did not go well for Arnold's children. During a holiday at Fox How in late October 1868, Tommy Arnold, always frail, fell from the pony he was riding, and his rheumatic condition worsened. A month later, he was dead. Arnold tried to comfort his wife Fanny Lucy, who had devoted her life to the care of her invalid son. Shortly after Tommy was buried beside his infant brother at Laleham, Arnold saw the proofs of *Culture and Anarchy*. Heartbroken, Arnold once again sought refuge from sorrow in his work.

6

St Paul and Protestantism (1870), Literature and Dogma (1873), God and the Bible (1875), Last Essays on Church and Religion (1877)

Arnold's religious and Biblical criticism grows directly out of his writings about culture. His critique of the English Dissenters begins with 'My Countrymen' in 1866, and he refers to St Paul repeatedly in the essays of *Culture and Anarchy*. To Arnold St Paul represents the best of the Christian 'Hebraic' tradition because, up to a point, he incorporated Hellenism, a free flow of consciousness, into his thinking about morality. The English Puritans, however, treated his teachings in a mechanical way, much like the mechanical way that the Jews treated the Mosaic law in Paul's day. Observers who have watched Puritanism 'handle such terms as *grace, faith, election, righteousness*' must feel that these terms 'have for the mind of Puritanism a sense false and misleading' and that 'this sense is the most monstrous and grotesque caricature of the sense of St Paul, and his true meaning is by these worshippers of his words altogether lost' (*CPW* 5:182). In addition, Arnold wanted to challenge the Dissenters' claim to the historical justification of their separation from the English Church. Arnold felt that he was qualified to make these judgments. As he wrote in a letter he sent to Gladstone in April 1869 along with a copy of *Culture and Anarchy*, 'For fifteen years I have seen the Protestant Dissenters close, from inspecting their schools; and have more and more observed how their real need is not more voluntaryism and separation for their religious organizations, but a larger existence and more sense of public responsibility.'[1]

Arnold's line of thought led to *St Paul and Protestantism* (1870), *Literature and Dogma* (1873), *God and the Bible* (1875), and *Last Essays on Church and Religion* (1877). Following his established habits, he assembled all of these books from periodical essays and lectures written between 1869 and 1876. As before, the argument of each book evolved as he responded to his critics.

Of course, Arnold had already written explicitly about religious topics in the early 1860s, attacking Bishop Colenso's book on the Pentateuch from the standpoint of a literary and cultural critic and attempting to explain the more 'adequate' speculations of Spinoza to the English audience. In 'The Bishop and the Philosopher' he had argued that Colenso's ridiculous Biblical criticism should not obscure the real, fundamental questions about the 'place of the Bible ... among books' if 'the old theory of Scriptural Inspiration is to be abandoned' (*CPW* 3:49).

Although not really unpredictable or surprising, Arnold's charge into the fiercely contentious field of Victorian religious controversy in the 1870s was courageous. Clashes between dogmatic believers and sceptics were the order of the day. Shortly after the publication of *St Paul*, Arnold wrote to his mother about the ceremony at Oxford in which he had been presented with the honorary degree of DCL. Arnold was flattered by the remarks made about him by the University Chancellor, Lord Salisbury, but he went on to describe Salisbury's Oxford speeches as being 'full ... of counsels and resolves for retaining and upholding the old ecclesiastical and dogmatic forms of religion' while at the same time championing the 'great future' for physical science:

> From a juxtaposition of this kind nothing but shocks and collisions can come ... All this pressed a good deal upon my mind at Oxford and made me anxious – but I do hope that what influence I have may be of use in the troubled times which I see are before us as a healing and reconciling influence; – and it is this which makes me glad to find – what I find more and more – that I *have* influence. (*SL* 224)

Arnold felt that he had influence and he wanted to use it, but he cannot be accused of pandering to his audience. He had already been roundly attacked for his supposed lack of expertise in religion and for targeting English Dissenters in his critique of English society. To go further in this direction was bound to be unpopular with large segments of the public. Nevertheless Arnold was convinced that he had important things to say about the status of the Christian religion in an age of scientific scepticism.

Arnold attended religious services regularly and defended the Church of England as a national institution. He wanted the Dissenters to come back into the fold. As he suggested in the Preface to *Culture and Anarchy*, being raised in the national Church provides 'a lesson of religious moderation, and a help towards culture and harmonious perfection' (*CPW* 5:239). Furthermore, he thought it was essential to preserve the English Bible as poetry and as the repository of collective wisdom from the past. However, what many of his contemporaries did not seem to understand was that religion cannot remain dogmatically stationary in the face of a great revolution in scientific knowledge and that, in order to remain vital, sacred texts must be interpreted anew by each age. In a way, his critics were right when they pointed out his inadequacies as a theologian, but Arnold intuitively knew that he did have one great qualification for his new project: his abilities as a literary critic. When reviewers of his social and political essays pleaded with Arnold to turn back to *literary* criticism, they of course never intended that he should turn his critical powers towards the sacred text of the Bible, but that is exactly what he did. Arnold's essays on the English Bible *as literature* have never been equalled for the range and power of their critical insights, although at times his language may seem odd or quaint to a modern reader.

Arnold's comments about Salisbury help to explain why he claims in *St Paul* to conduct his argument in the 'sphere of science'. By this Arnold means that in recognizing the poetic or figurative power of St Paul's language, one is also recognizing its 'scientific' validity: that is, its validity in terms of the psychological experience of the reader. Arnold assumes that there is in the flux of things a 'universal order which the intellect feels after as a law and the heart feels after as a benefit' (*CPW* 6:9). He also assumes that there is a '*stream of tendency by which all things seek to fulfil the law of their being*' (*CPW* 6:10). Paul is dealing with this kind of knowledge and feeling, but the reader cannot understand him unless he grasps the essential metaphorical nature of religious language. In his analysis of Paul's figurative language Arnold focuses on the 'three cardinal points' in Paul's theology: '*dying with Christ, resurrection from the dead, growing into Christ*'. By 'resurrection' Paul means 'rising, in this visible earthly existence, from the death of obedience to blind selfish impulse, to the life of obedience to the eternal moral order' (*CPW* 6:56). For Arnold, faith and love spring from human need, independent of the supernatural 'machinery' of Church doctrine.

During the summer of 1869 Arnold developed his ideas for an extended study of Pauline doctrine and its implications for Christianity in the nineteenth century. His principal historical source was Edouard Reuss's *Histoire de la théologie chrétienne au siècle apostolique* (1860), which he took along with him to Fox How for his summer vacation. From the beginning he planned to take advantage of his longstanding relationship with the *Cornhill*, and in early September he contacted George Smith about his plans for a two-part article on 'St Paul and Protestantism'. It appeared in the October and November issues. Arnold was fully aware of the journal's policy of excluding religious debate and asked Smith to inform him if his subject was 'too grave' for the *Cornhill*. He even advised Smith on the placement of his initial article ('last or first in the number') because of its gravity (*MAB* 99).

Arnold had reason to anticipate a strong negative reaction from the Dissenters, for in his article he sought to separate the defective doctrines that the Puritans mistakenly associated with St Paul from the enlightened ones of the *authentic* St Paul. Unlike Renan, who had rejected both Paul and Puritanism, he was apparently seeking to appropriate St Paul for his own version of Christianity and the English Church. Puritans believe in 'a sort of magnified and non-natural man' and have translated Paul's figurative and imaginative language into a kind of unsatisfying, rigid scholasticism. Of course, Arnold had already been identified as a fierce critic of English 'Puritanism' in his prose, and less than a month before the appearance of the first part of the new article, the *Nonconformist* published a review article on his two-volume *Poems* of 1869 that summarized the effect of Arnold's poetry as 'displeasing'. 'These faithless, hopeless, all but loveless poems', according to the reviewer, 'show what we may expect if Christian art should ever become Pagan; not the freshness, the passion, the delight of early Grecian culture, but more than the trouble, the misanthropy, and the self-scorn of its later days' (*MAHC* 221).

The critical response of the Dissenters to his article was large but less hostile than he had anticipated, and Arnold was pleased to see that he was actually reaching 'the special Puritan class' as he had intended. He decided that a third article, 'Puritanism and the Church of England', published in February 1870, would exhaust his ideas on the subject, and quickly made arrangements with Smith for book publication. By the Easter of that year he had completed a Preface, and the book appeared in May. Because sales of *On the Study of Celtic Literature* and *Culture and Anarchy* had been disappointingly low, Arnold proposed that Smith publish *St Paul and Protestantism* on commission, 'as Longman (sensible man) always did with my books' (*MAB* 100), but Smith did not accept Arnold's offer.

The new book sold much better than Arnold had feared, and *St Paul* was the first of his books to reach a second edition within a single year. In addition, the critical response was much more lively than it had been to *Culture and Anarchy* (as a book), even though many of the reviews were ambivalent or negative. In the spring of 1871, J. N. Simpkinson wrote in the *Edinburgh Review* that '[N]ewspapers, journals, magazines, reviews, pamphlets, speeches, have been full of replies to it, ranging from gentle remonstrances and deprecatory apologies to the fiercest and most unsparing retorts.'[2] Early reviews of *St Paul* focused on Arnold's call for Christian unity within the English Church, while later responses tended to concentrate on his apparently radical revisions of Christian theology. In the *Contemporary Review* of July 1870, R. W. Dale, an Independent minister in Birmingham, wrote a restrained but analytical reply to *St Paul* that was later praised by both Arnold's supporters and his opponents. He argued that Puritanism in fact belongs to the mainstream of the Protestant movement. Arnold failed to appreciate that the 'supreme force' of that movement is 'spiritual, not ethical.'[3] Two long, unsigned reviews in the *British Quarterly Review* of July 1870 also argued against Arnold's ideas from the Dissenters' point of view. In 'The Function of Criticism' Arnold had identified this journal as 'an organ of the political Dissenters' (*CPW* 3:270), but it did not represent an extremist position. Implying that Arnold's familiar arguments for 'Hellenism' and 'sweetness and light' are elitist, an anonymous reviewer describes Anglican worship services as 'repressive and indurating, rather than communicative and educational'. In contrast, the 'real character and life' of church members 'finds free and natural expression' in Nonconformist services (*MAPW* 260–6). Even Leslie Stephen would later defend the

Dissenters against Arnold, describing the English Church as 'the relic of an exploded order of things.'[4] To the agnostic Stephen, Arnold's idea of ignoring doctrinal differences within Christianity for the sake of organizational unity was absurd and unprogressive.

On the other hand, R. W. Church, an Anglican cleric sympathetic to Arnold's call for Church unity, anticipated the consensus of later criticism when he expressed alarm at Arnold's willingness to deny the 'real outward facts of history' on which Christianity itself is based (*MAPW* 271–5). In his lectures on 'Culture and Religion' in late 1870, Arnold's old Oxford acquaintance J. C. Shairp expressed worries about Arnold's way of undermining traditional Christian values with his ideal of culture, and he was troubled by Arnold's 'inadequate notion of the evil of the human heart' (*MAPW* 275–80). This anticipates later charges made against Arnold's religious position by numerous critics (including T. S. Eliot) and it recalls the common complaints about Arnold's tendency to elevate thought and contemplation above doing good in the world. Even Harrison, from a philosophical point of view very different from that of Arnold's Christian critics, had argued that Arnold's culture provides no clear and consistent standards of right and wrong.

Even earlier, however, Richard Holt Hutton, one of Arnold's most perceptive critics, had made an observation about Arnold's literary criticism that in a subtle way anticipates Shairp's observations. Hutton, a theologian and a literary critic who wrote from a religious point of view, published nearly 60 essays and reviews about Arnold. He admired Arnold's poetry, despite Arnold's apparent lack of religious faith, and regretted his shift to criticism. However, he was a perceptive reader of Arnold's prose who understood the close connections between Newman and Arnold. In an 1865 review of *Essays in Criticism* for the *Spectator* (*MAPW* 127–34), he discusses Arnold's negative assessment of Shelley's poetry: just as Arnold ignores the 'daemonic' element in his heroes Goethe and Heine, he fails to appreciate it in Shelley, where it is the essence of his poetry. Overall, Hutton's review was favourable – the essays 'are full of brilliant and keen truth' – but Arnold was upset by the reference to the daemonic, and he told his mother that the article:

has Hutton's fault of seeing so very far into a millstone. No one has a stronger and more abiding sense than I have of the 'daemonic' element – as Goethe called it – which underlies and encompasses our life; but I think, as Goethe thought, that the right thing is, while conscious of this element and of all that there is inexplicable round one, to keep pushing on one's posts into the darkness, and to establish no post that is not perfectly in light, and firm. One gains nothing on the darkness by being, like Shelley, as incoherent as the darkness itself. (*SL* 169–70)

Arnold's defensiveness here suggests that he felt the sting of Hutton's criticism more than he was willing to acknowledge. The term 'daemonic' can refer either to a fiendish, evil force or a spiritual force of creative genius. In the case of a poet such as Shelley (a very destructive and blameworthy man from Arnold's point of view), both meanings may apply simultaneously. According to Hutton, Arnold wants all poets to work in a 'clear, intellectual medium'. Although he makes his remarks in a 'secular' context, Hutton's religious grounding helps to explain his insight into Arnold's thought as a whole. Hutton elucidates Shairp's comments about the evil of the human heart and calls to mind a warning from one of Arnold's favourite authors. In *The Idea of a University*, J. H. Newman writes, 'Quarry the granite rock with razors, or moor the vessel with a thread of silk; then may you hope with such keen and delicate instruments as human knowledge and human reason to contend against those giants, the passion and the pride of man.'[5]

There is evidence that Newman was in fact on Arnold's mind as he concentrated his literary efforts on religious subjects. When he published *A Bible-Reading for Schools* in May 1872, he sent a copy to Newman, and Newman responded with a friendly letter. The thin volume, published by Macmillan, contained Arnold's arrangement and edition of Isaiah, Chapters 40–60, intended for 'Young Learners'. Arnold of course held strong opinions about the value of literature in children's education (in the Preface he expresses his 'conviction for the immense importance in education of what is called *letters*') and this project demonstrates his practical commitment to the concept of 'the Bible as literature'. Not surprisingly, Newman – like reviewers of the book – had reservations about using a Biblical text in this way, but he was polite in his response and commented on Arnold's editorial apparatus. Arnold in turn wrote to thank him for his comments and included some telling remarks about his own development as a writer:

> There are four people, in especial, from whom I am conscious of having *learnt* – a very different thing from merely receiving a strong impression – learnt habits, methods, ruling ideas, which are constantly with me; and the four are – Goethe, Wordsworth, Sainte Beuve and yourself. You will smile and say I have made an odd mixture and the result must be a jumble: however that may be as to the whole, I am sure in details you must recognize your own influence often. (*SL* 233)

Arnold knew that Newman himself – like many of Newman's friends and adversaries alike – might well be puzzled by such a claim from a man apparently so far removed from Newman's deepest beliefs and commitments, but, as we have seen, Arnold's habit of looking past conventional ideological categories was deeply ingrained and integral to his critical thought. In an 1863 letter to his mother in which he defended his interest in the religious thought of Spinoza, Arnold reminded her, '[W]hat the English public cannot understand is that a man is a just and fruitful object of contemplation much more by virtue of what spirit he is of than by virtue of what system of doctrine he elaborates' (*LMA* 1:208).

By the time he wrote the letter to Newman, several important events had occurred in Arnold's life. He had cause to be pleased with the recognition afforded by his honorary degree from Oxford in June of 1870, and later in the year he was finally promoted to the position of Senior Inspector of Schools. In 1871 his inspection duties were shifted to the Westminster district of London and three rural Middlesex counties near his home at Harrow, which was a more convenient arrangement. (Also at this time, as one of the effects of the Education Act of 1870, he began to inspect the schools of all denominations, and his experiences in the Catholic schools increased his sympathy for the Irish poor.) In February 1871 Arnold published *Friendship's Garland*, and in August of that year he took a vacation in France and Switzerland with his wife and his son Richard. Arnold insisted that Budge stay in England and study; he was proud of the progress his son had made at Harrow, and he was ambitious for him. (Budge had risen from fortieth to fourteenth in his class [*MAAL* 358].)

But this pleasant time in Arnold's personal life was abruptly ended by yet another death in the family. In February 1872 Budge developed a 'bad cold' the day after he had run a long distance. His condition worsened, and a few days later he was dead at the age of eighteen. Once again Arnold was crushed with grief.

As we look back from a transitional time between the twentieth and twenty-first centuries, Arnold's religious writings of the 1870s may be the most difficult stage of his career to understand. Bereavement upon the death of three beloved sons undoubtedly motivated Arnold's search for spiritual meaning in his own life. His critics berated Arnold for intellectualizing religion, but beyond his quest for a cultural ideal of human perfection, Arnold felt a real emotional need for spiritual consolation in times of personal crisis. In defending his metaphorical reading of the Bible, Arnold could even call on Goethe as 'an unsuspecting witness': '*Stirb und werde!*' ('Die and come to life!') Goethe had cried in the *West-östlicher Divan*. And yet it is clear, as Super has pointed out, that Arnold 'was a match for his dogmatic opponents' in being 'completely at home with his Bible', moving 'freely from the English to the Vulgate and the Greek' (*CPW* 6:421).

Like many of his contemporaries, Arnold in his youth had responded ambivalently to the powerful religious traditions of his home, and religious questioning had figured in his writing from his early poetry. But after decades of absorbing wide-ranging influences from Wordsworth, Goethe and Carlyle, from the *Imitation of Christ* and the *Bhagavad-Gita*, from Spinoza, John Henry Newman, and Renan, Arnold remained an Anglican ritualist who felt he was in a meaningful way continuing the work of his Broad-Church father. It was important to him that his mother approve of his new religious writings in the 1870s and acknowledge that they followed in the progressive tradition of Dr Arnold's work. Probably the aspect of *St Paul* which most closely represents the views of his father is Arnold's argument that all Christian sects should find a home within the Church establishment. Dr Arnold had argued along these lines in his pamphlet *Principles of Church Reform* (1833). But Arnold was anxious that his reading of Paul's theology also be seen as consistent with his father's reformist tendencies. Pleased by his mother's response to his first two essays on St Paul, Arnold writes to her:

I was much interested and touched by your letter, showing your willingness still, as always, to receive and comprehend what is new instead of shutting your mind against it ... It is not man who determines what truths shall present themselves to this or that age or under what aspect; and until the time is come for the new truth or the new aspect, they are presented unsatisfactorily or in vain. In Papa's time the exploding of the old notions of literal inspiration in Scripture, and the introducing of a truer method of interpretation, were the changes for which, here in England, the moment had come; stiff people could not receive this change, and my dear old Methodist friend, Mr. Scott used to say to the day of his death that Papa and Coleridge might be excellent men, but that 'they had found and shown the rat-hole in the temple.' The old notions about justification will undergo a like change, with a like opposition and cry of alarm from stiff people ... Whether I have rendered St Paul's ideas with perfect correctness or not, there is no doubt that the confidence with which these people regarded their conventional rendering of them was quite baseless, made them narrow and intolerant, and prevented all progress. (*SL* 219–20)

One interesting aspect of Arnold's correspondence to his mother as it developed over the years is how little Mrs Arnold as 'implied reader' resembles the stereotypical Victorian female who must be protected from dangerous ideas. Although undoubtedly circumspect in revealing some of his ideas to the family matriarch, Arnold was proud of his mother's flexibility and openness, particularly regarding religious issues.

In the months following the publication of *St Paul*, Arnold reflected on the response to the book and discovered that he had more to say about the Bible and Bible-reading. From his numerous critics he had learned that he would have to concern himself less with the issue of dissent and more with Christian doctrine if he expected his reading of Paul and the New Testament to 'prevail', as he hoped (*MAHC* 229). Other developments also helped to shape his ideas at this time. Although his increasing respect for the German people after his Continental tour of 1865 had already tempered his longstanding admiration for the French, Arnold was shocked by the defeat of France by Germany in the war of 1870–71. He concluded that the 'want of a serious conception of righteousness' had contributed to France's downfall. In a February 1872 review of Renan's *La Réforme intellectuelle et morale de la France*, he criticized the French for their lack of 'moral conscience, self-control, seriousness, steadfastness' (*CPW* 7:45). Arnold was not about to give up his earlier formulations of Hellenism, but clearly he would have to strengthen his emphasis on conduct and Hebraism. In his next book, conduct is said to be 'three-fourths . . . of human life' and its largest concern (*CPW* 6:173).

At first Arnold conceived the idea of writing a pair of essays on 'literature as it regards dogma' as part of a larger project which included essays on literature and science, but instead the essays on dogma grew into a new book: *Literature and Dogma: An Essay Towards a Better Appreciation of the Bible*. Arnold's change of plan is at least partially explained by a shift in his relationship with the *Cornhill*. Following the retirement of Thackeray as editor of the journal in March 1862, the publisher George Smith himself had taken over most of the editorial duties. As we have seen, Arnold had dealt exclusively with Smith at the *Cornhill* and the two men had developed an understanding with one another. In cooperation with Smith, Arnold had fallen into the practice of publishing his works first in the journal, then in a book. But Smith appointed a new editor for the journal in March 1871: Leslie Stephen, who happened to be Thackeray's son-in-law, and who had complained in print about *St Paul* only a few months earlier. At first Stephen cooperated with Arnold, and a two-part article entitled 'Literature and Dogma' appeared in the *Cornhill* in July and October of 1871. Arnold wrote to Smith that he was glad Stephen was willing to accept it, 'but I attribute a great deal to your good natured way of putting it to him' (*MAB* 95). In the conclusion to the October piece, Arnold promised one additional paper to 'finish our defence of literature against dogma'. Arnold intended the concluding essay for the November issue of the journal, but Stephen did not accept it and abruptly terminated the series.

Although he did not openly quarrel with Stephen, and relations between the two men remained cordial in public, this setback jolted Arnold and necessarily altered his long-term position with Smith & Elder as well as his plans for his new book. He decided to drop his projected studies of literature and science and instead produce a book about the Bible in a popular style. Even after the rejection of his article, Arnold remained on good terms with his publisher, and in February 1873, *Literature and*

Dogma, like the three books preceding it, was published by Smith. (A small slip inserted just before the Preface reads '*A small portion of this work has appeared in the 'Cornhill Magazine.'*) In the meantime, 'A Persian Passion Play', a lecture comparing the popular Oberammergau Passion Play with an ancient Persian drama – which he presented to the Birmingham and Midland Institute in the autumn of 1871 – was published in the December *Cornhill*. After this, however, although Arnold continued to refer to his 'old friend the *Cornhill*', he published most of his journal pieces elsewhere.

Reaching a wider audience than any of his other books, Arnold's last substantial, original book of any kind was a 'best seller' in an age of religious controversy. *Literature and Dogma* reached a fourth edition within a year, and in small editions it eventually sold as many as 100 000 copies (*MAAL* 368). It was the first of Arnold's books to be translated, appearing as *La Crise Religieuse* in France (1876). Coverage by the periodical press – in England, America, and Europe – was correspondingly substantial, the most extensive that Arnold had ever received. The number of words written in reply to Arnold 'easily surpassed the book itself' (*MAHC* 235). The book's success may be partially attributed to the unexpected circumstances that made it Arnold's only major prose work composed primarily as a book manuscript rather than a series of articles. Although it did not make him a wealthy man, it brought him his greatest fame among his contemporaries and made him an even more controversial figure than before.

In *Literature and Dogma* Arnold attempts to rescue Christianity from anthropomorphism and other vulgar errors of popular theology. Following Spinoza, he assumes that miracles must be discounted. The language of the Bible is the poetry of old Israel, 'thrown out' to express experience that otherwise could not be expressed. In addition to his Continental influences, Arnold may have found a source for his approach in the works of his father's friends Richard Whately and R. D. Hampden, the 'Oriel Noetics', who made a distinction between the symbolic language of scripture and the explicative language of dogma. Arnold uses the German term *Aberglaube*, 'extra-belief', to describe much Biblical language. Acknowledging the possibility that future Biblical critics may find him wrong, Arnold asks his readers to accept only what can be demonstrated to be valid in a modern, sceptical age. For Arnold the greatest human achievements have been derived from an attempt to know an unknowable ultimate reality. Always speaking as a literary and cultural critic rather than a theologian, Arnold does not attempt a precise or fixed definition of religion, but he does describe it as *'morality touched by emotion'*. '"By the dispensation of Providence to mankind," says Quintilian, "goodness gives men most satisfaction." That is morality. "The path of the just is as the shining light which shineth more and more unto the perfect day." That is morality touched with emotion, or religion' (*CPW* 6:177).

In order to improve morally, one must consult one's conscience. Jesus's message is clearly stated in all four gospels: *'He that loveth his life shall lose it, and he that hateth his life in this world shall keep it unto life eternal'* (*CPW* 6:291). Arnold's term for God is *'the enduring power, not ourselves, which makes for righteousness'* (*CPW* 6:200). We seek right conduct through 'the operation of that mighty *not ourselves* which is in us and around us' (*CPW* 6:373). God is therefore knowable inwardly through conscience and outwardly through a search for human perfection. Hebraism emphasizes righteousness, but Christianity, with greater sweetness and reason, is 'the greatest and happiest stroke ever yet made for human perfection' (*CPW* 6:232–3). Experience verifies that Christianity leads to right conduct, the lack of which caused the fall of Greece and now threatens France. Right conduct leads to joy, and, as he would later assert, 'joy and happiness are the magnets to which human life irresistibly moves' (*CPW* 7:234).

Early in his career, Arnold had used the term *Zeitgeist*, which he picked up from Goethe and Carlyle, to refer to current intellectual fashion or the spirit of the age, as opposed to the universal verities of human experience. As early as 1863 in his essay 'Dr. Stanley's Lectures on the Jewish Church', however, he was using the term in a more positive sense, to refer to the agent of inevitable intellectual change. Now in the mid-1870s, Arnold argued that the *Zeitgeist* had made it impossible for traditional religious belief in miracles, plenary inspiration and a personal God to stand. In order to preserve the Bible as an essential religious guide in the new scientific age, the Biblical critic must interpret it in terms that will allow a 'real experimental basis' for its claims. This project of 'saving' the English Bible represents the culmination of Arnold's religious writings and the most audacious and challenging critical task that he ever set for himself. In spite of his characteristic self-deprecation in print, Arnold is not particularly humble about his supposed achievement in some of his comments to friends and associates. Soon after publication, he wrote to Alexander Macmillan:

> [T]he book is sure to be much attacked and blamed. No one should suffer himself to exaggerate what can be done at one moment by one individual and one book: all I venture to say is that the so-called orthodox position cannot, I think, ever again be precisely the same in England after the publication of this book, that it has hitherto been. (*MAB* 96)

At present, however, Arnold was eager to escape from the stress of religious controversy as well as from the cold of the English winter. The note to Macmillan was mailed from the Continent, where he had retreated with Fanny Lucy and their two daughters to spend a four-month holiday, primarily in Italy, after he had completed his duties with the Christmas Examinations at the schools. *Literature and Dogma* was published about one year after Budge's death, but neither he nor his wife had recovered from the emotional wounds left by the loss of three sons within a four-year span. In addition, Fanny Lucy had lost her mother and a sister in recent months. In the letter to Lord Ripon requesting a leave of absence as school inspector, Arnold also complained of 'recurring attacks of rheumatism' and 'a not very good pulse' which made him 'remember that there is heart complaint in my family' (*SL* 234). Arnold asked that no reviews of the book be sent to him in Europe. The Arnolds were refreshed by their stay abroad, and while in Rome, Arnold attended a party where he met Henry James (*MAAL* 373).

Upon their return to England in May 1873, Arnold rented Pains Hill Cottage in Cobham, Surrey, his home for the rest of his life. He was pleased with the bucolic setting, where he could walk in the surrounding fields with his dachshunds Max and Geist. A nearby railway would take him to the London schools where he worked, and he would adopt the habit of renting a house in London for a time at the beginning of each year so that he and Fanny Lucy could keep up with social life. It was some time before Arnold could fully enjoy the relative serenity of his new home, however, for, at the time he moved in, his new book had already gone into its third printing and he could no longer ignore the sensation it was causing.

The critical response to *Literature and Dogma* ranged from 'blanket condemnation to surprise that Arnold should attempt anything so remarkable as salvaging the Bible' (*MAHC* 235). One of the most perceptive favourable reviews was written by Albert Réville, a French Protestant theologian who, in spite of some reservations about the book, described it as 'penetrated with the great need which the present age feels for a religious renovation that, without breaking with the past, will do justice to the progress accomplished by the general intelligence' (*MAPW* 40). However, most critics with ecclesiastical affiliations, both Protestant and Catholic, tended to condemn Arnold on the grounds that he was not competent to deal with theological issues and in any case was no friend of Christianity. The title of John Tulloch's review in *Blackwood's* – 'Amateur Theology' – was representative. Like many of the other religious critics, Tulloch concentrated on Arnold's denial of a personal God: 'If Christian theology teaches that "God is a person," it is not merely that any bishops have thought or reasoned so, but because all the revelations of the Divine, "the not ourselves," in history and in human life, have pointed towards this conclusion.'[6]

An exchange between Arnold and the *Spectator* on this issue is revealing, both in terms of Arnold's Biblical project as a whole and his method of interacting with his critics. A *Spectator* review of the first instalment of *Literature and Dogma* in the *Cornhill* focused on Arnold's comparison of his own 'scientific' '*stream of tendency*' definition of God with the Biblical mode of personification, which, Arnold admitted, was more proper in the Biblical text. The reviewer suggested that if Biblical personification was more proper, then it must be more scientifically exact. In a footnote inserted into the text of the complete book, Arnold disagreed, and compared the case to Wordsworth's calling the earth 'the mighty mother of mankind', while geographers call it 'an oblate spheroid'. 'Wordsworth's expression is more proper and adequate to convey what men feel about the earth, but it is not therefore the more scientifically exact' (*CPW* 6:190n). In the first of two articles on the book, the *Spectator* responded: 'Wordsworth did not either produce, or intend to produce, the effect of making us *trust* in the Earth as if she were a person who could answer our appeals.'[7] Besides anticipating the charge that Arnold sought to substitute poetry for religion, this exchange reminds us of Arnold's own unfulfilled yearning to define a meaningful, felt connection between humankind and nature in his early poetry and his revision of Wordsworth's Romanticism that in a way anticipates his revision of Christianity. In the final phase of his career Arnold would return to Wordsworth as a major critical concern.

To Arnold one of the most interesting reviews of *Literature and Dogma* was written by the Italian scholar Angelo de Gubernatis. Gubernatis was scornful of Arnold's attempt to salvage the supposed moral and religious importance of the Hebrew scriptures: in Italy such a book would have been impossible.[8] This judgment actually reinforced Arnold's central justification for his book. In his view the English public simply did not understand the extent to which the modern spirit in Europe had dissolved the authority of the Bible as a practical source of wisdom. Unless Arnold's essentially conservative critical effort were successful, the Bible in Britain would be doomed to the same fate, and it was his English critics that Arnold felt compelled to answer.

As usual, Arnold read his critics carefully, and by April 1874 he wrote to his French friend Ernest Fontanès that he was prepared to answer the 'principal objections' to *Literature and Dogma* in a series of articles for the *Contemporary Review* (*LMA* 2:134). In the meantime, however, he had suffered another personal loss. The death of his mother in September 1873 marks an important transitional time in Arnold's intellectual as well as emotional life. As we have seen, Arnold was particularly dependent on his mother's approval of his foray into religious criticism. Shortly after her death, he wrote of her to Lady de Rothschild: 'She had a clearness and fairness of mind, an interest in things, and a power of appreciating what might not be in her own line, which were very remarkable, and which remained with her to the very end of her life.' Then he refers to a letter she had written to him upon the publication of *Literature and Dogma*. 'It was a wonderful letter. I can think of no woman in the prime of life, brought up and surrounded as my mother was, and with my mother's sincere personal convictions, who could have written it; and in a woman past eighty it was something astonishing' (*SL* 240–1). Finally, it was not the dead father who restrained the son through filial duty to the living mother; rather it was the son who carried forward the mother, and through her, the legacy of the father, towards new formulations of thought and belief. At the deepest level, Arnold's mother profoundly influenced every aspect of his literary career, not primarily because she exercised a psychological power over him in their personal relationship, but rather because Arnold internalized a certain version of his mother which was central to his intellectual as well as emotional life. The traditions of Fox How functioned in Arnold's private mythology much as Christianity did in his vision of culture. One did not forsake one's institutions but rather accommodated them to historical development.

Although he had intended to do so earlier, it was a full year after his mother's death before Arnold was prepared to answer the critics of *Literature and Dogma* in print. As he saw it, there had been two 'main objections' to the book (his refusal to affirm a personal God and his use of the Fourth Gospel), but he was prepared to discuss these objections in considerable detail, publishing a series of articles which ran in the *Contemporary Review* during the period October 1874–September 1875. Once again Arnold played the part of the reluctant controversialist: 'I really *hate* polemics', Arnold wrote to his new editor James T. Knowles when he returned the proofs of the second article; nevertheless, his projected four articles turned into seven. As in previous projects, Arnold was frustrated by his time-consuming duties as school inspector, and he missed some of his deadlines for the *Contemporary* articles: he complained to Knowles in May 1875 that 'my schools keep me so busy day after day that I cannot get the collectedness necessary for giving literary form to what I have to say; all I can do is keep on reading and thinking about my subject'.[9] From the beginning, Arnold made it clear to Knowles that he planned to publish the collected articles as a book with Smith & Elder. Arnold added a Preface, and *God and the Bible* was published in November 1875.

Arnold devotes the first three chapters – 'The God of Miracles', 'The God of Metaphysics' and 'The God of Experience' – to the question of a personal God. In answer to his many critics, Arnold amplifies his position that there is no evidence for supporting the belief in an anthropomorphic God: 'men do not know enough about the Eternal not ourselves that makes for righteousness, to warrant their pronouncing this either a person or a thing' (*CPW* 7:160). Against critics like Henry Dunn, who had challenged Arnold's emphasis on conduct as the essence of religious experience and the source of true happiness (*MAHC* 250), Arnold dismisses all metaphysical language as fraught with insoluble semantic problems. For Arnold, the discerning reader knows when to read the Bible literally, when it speaks of righteousness as salvation, and figuratively, when it refers to God as a talking, thinking being.

Arnold devotes the second half of the book – 'The Bible Canon', 'The Fourth Gospel from Without' and 'The Fourth Gospel from Within' (which combines his sixth and seventh articles) – to the question of the authenticity of John. As Coulling points out, Arnold virtually ignored much of the commentary on his book and chose to emphasize only a few key points in order to reassert his central concerns; nevertheless, it is curious that he chose to write so much about an issue that did not seem central to most of the criticism. Arnold's interest in this Gospel may be partially explained by the special emphasis that his father had placed on it (*MAHC* 257). Undoubtedly he was attracted to the issue as another opportunity to demonstrate clearly how a 'disinterested' literary critic could resolve certain Biblical questions more effectively than could traditionalist theologians or German specialists 'carried away by theorizing'. Arnold decides that the final version of the Gospel is not by John himself but rather a redaction based on *logia* or sayings of Jesus composed by a later Greek Christian editor. Nevertheless, according to Arnold, when the sayings are suited to the character of Jesus, in his typically gnomic, Semitic style, we know they are genuine. When they are long and repetitious, they are probably the product of the Greek 'theological lecturer merely expanding a theme given by Jesus' (*CPW* 7:325).

In his conclusion, Arnold returns to his central argument that treating the miracles and supernatural elements of the Bible as 'poetry and legend' actually serves to restore the original meanings of Jesus's teachings:

> The immortality propounded by Jesus must be looked for elsewhere than in the materialistic aspirations of our popular religion. *He lived in the eternal order, and the eternal order never dies;* – this, if we may try to formulate in one sentence the result of the sayings of Jesus about life and death, is the sense in which, according to him, we can rightly conceive of the righteous man as immortal, and aspire to be immortal ourselves. (*CPW* 7:372)

In defending his religious position, Arnold was aware that not only his heterodox ideas were at issue: even some of the critics in general sympathy with his line of argument found his tone occasionally offensive in *Literature and Dogma*. For fifteen years he had been developing a controversial prose style that was often playful, sometimes verging on flippancy, in his continual battle with the Philistines. As we have seen, even his mother and favourite sister were bothered by his 'vivacities', but Arnold went on filling his essays with bits of outrageous satire. Although he shows some restraint in his religious prose, there are a few passages in which he must have known that his *manner* would give offence to many of his readers. In *Literature and Dogma*, several personal references to the Bishops of Winchester and Gloucester disturbed some of the reviewers, but the most egregious example was Arnold's parody of popular Christianity's 'fairy tale' of justification by substituting 'the three Lord Shaftesburys' for the three persons of God. Arnold asks his reader to imagine 'a sort of infinitely magnified and improved Lord Shaftesbury' who sends a younger Lord Shaftesbury, his son, to deal with a race of 'vile offenders', while a third Lord Shaftesbury works 'in a very occult manner' in the background (*CPW* 7:360, 575–6). The *London Quarterly Review* voiced an opinion shared by many when it called this parody 'the foulest opprobrium' in modern theological literature, and even A. P. Stanley called it 'dangerous and regrettable' (*MAHC* 240–1).

Arnold retreated slowly and grudgingly in the face of this storm of negative opinion. He excised several of his references to the bishops in the fifth edition of *Literature and Dogma*, probably because his chief target, Samuel Wilberforce, Bishop of Winchester (remembered today principally for his debate with T. H. Huxley on Darwinism), had died in the meantime. However, in the Introduction to *God and the Bible* he defends his attacks on the 'oracular assurance', the 'mixture of unction and metaphysics', the 'clap-trap' found in many of the bishop's public statements (*CPW* 7:153). In the same place, he claims that his use of the 'parable of the three Lord Shaftesburys' actually 'shows our indulgence to popular Christianity' because Shaftesbury is 'a man widely beloved and respected, and whom no one respects more than we do' (*CPW* 7:152). When Arnold finally excised the offending passage in the 1883 popular edition of *Literature and Dogma*, he claimed that he did so only because he admired Shaftesbury, to whom it had given pain.

Arnold was willing to absorb attacks on his bad taste and unseemly humour in order to make a strong impression on his readers. Soon after the publication of *Literature and Dogma*, he wrote to Smith of the three Lord Shaftesburys: 'though it makes people cry out, yet it has the advantage of fixing sharply in their minds what I mean'.[10] (*CPW* 6:452). Later he wrote in the same vein to his sister, who apparently had scolded him for 'treating with lightness what is matter of life and death to so many people'. He justified his method by arguing that:

> There is a levity which is altogether evil; but to treat miracles and the common anthropomorphic ideas of God as what one may lose and yet keep one's hope, courage, and joy, as what are not really matters of life and death in the keeping or losing of them, this is desirable and necessary, if one holds, as I do, that the common anthropomorphic ideas of God and the reliance on miracles must and will inevitably pass away. (*LMA* 2:138–9)

Because it is so easy to label Arnold a *cognoscente*, it is important to stress his commitment to a *popular* transformation of religious thought in England. During the Renaissance, many 'cultivated wits' had lost the Bible, but the 'great solid mass of the common people kept it'. Now '*the masses*', '*the people*' are losing it and thus 'can no longer be relied on to counteract what the cultivated wits are doing' (*CPW* 6:362). The cultivated wits of his own day included the German Bible critics, who in their precious analyses of scriptural texts missed the 'natural truth' of Christianity and the fundamental need for doing good in the world. There is a genuinely democratic impulse in Arnold's religious thought that contends with his tendency to patronize the unenlightened. It is more than a fear of the 'anarchy' that will result when common people no longer hold allegiance to a discredited creed; it is the teacher's desire to instruct, to tell the truth (in this case, the 'natural truth' – as he saw it – of Christianity): the same spirit that underlay his real concern about the fundamental quality of British education and projects such as his edition of Isaiah for schoolchildren.

At the same time, however, Arnold was becoming more concerned with the practical business end of publishing at this stage in his career. In particular he wanted to be more secure about the income he received from his books, and he decided that he would prefer to receive a fixed sum for an edition of a specified number of copies. In the spring of 1875, he complained to Macmillan about the relatively poor profits from *Essays in Criticism*, and Macmillan responded by arranging for a more expensively priced third edition of 2000 copies (500 of which would go to America at a lower rate), for which he paid Arnold the generous price of £175. The cooperative Macmillan also settled with Arnold on the new edition of the Isaiah *Bible-Reading* and the recent *Higher Schools and Universities In Germany* editions although he observed that the collected *Poems* of 1869 was not quite ready for a new edition (*MAB* 25–7). Arnold then accepted £250 from Smith for *God and the Bible* but complained that Smith was underestimating profits from the book. Smith did not appreciate Arnold's aggressiveness on this occasion and resented the author's attempts to compare him unfavourably with his other publisher. The two men quarrelled briefly, but then resumed their friendship.

After the success of *Literature and Dogma*, Arnold had high expectations for its sequel. Of the 2000 copies printed, 500 were sold to Macmillan for publication in New York. At first sales were brisk, but they faded as the months passed, and there was no second printing. An inexpensive 'popular edition', like that of *Literature and Dogma*, was issued in 1884. As a 'review of objections' to the earlier book, *God and the Bible* was naturally seen as somewhat derivative of and less significant than its predecessor. Nevertheless, the second book extends Arnold's range as a literary critic, especially in its investigation of John, and Arnold believed that it contained some of his best prose (*CPW* 7:439). The articles which made up *God and the Bible* received a fair amount of critical attention, but typical objections to both the arguments made by Arnold and his style had become familiar. The book itself, unlike its predecessor, did not stir a great deal of interest. In the *Academy*, Réville wrote, 'Apart from the very real pleasure of having read a work of high merit in point of form and originality, we are no farther forward than before.'[11] Some later theologians were more favourably impressed by Arnold's increased mastery of Biblical criticism (*CPW* 7:440–1).

At any rate, *God and the Bible* was Arnold's last unified book-length project of any kind, although his production of critical essays continued unabated. He was determined to return to the subject of 'literature proper' but could not easily pull himself away from religious studies. In late 1875, about a month after the book's publication, he was at work on a two-part lecture he would present in early January 1876 at the Edinburgh Philosophical Institution: 'Bishop Butler and the Zeit-Geist'. Arnold's poem 'Written in Butler's Sermons', written back in 1844, was a reminder that Joseph Butler, the eighteenth-century bishop who resisted Deist philosophy, had been required reading for Oxford undergraduates. While writing the essays of *Culture and Anarchy*, Arnold had begun to refer to Butler as a sound and intelligent thinker. Now more than ever, Arnold identifies with this man and 'his argumentative triumph over the loose thinkers and talkers of his day' (*CPW* 8:29). In terms of Arnold's familiar psychological dualism, this English theologian – whom his father had studied before him – balances the more exotic Spinoza as a major influence on his religious thinking. The lectures were published in the *Contemporary*.

Another lecture in early 1876, 'The Church of England', also reminds us of connections between Arnold's formative years and his mature religious thought. As Super points out, Arnold's argument for the Church establishment is very much like the Coleridgean one made by his father: the Church is *'a great national society for the promotion of goodness'* (*CPW* 8:67,394). Speaking to a group of clergymen at Sion College, Arnold knew that to many of them his views on Christian dogma were suspect or even dangerous, but he spoke to them as a 'preacher's son' and felt afterwards that he had established a good rapport. He published this lecture and a related but less important article, 'A Last Word on the Burials Bill' (dealing with a controversy concerning Nonconformists' dissatisfaction with burial services conducted by the English Church), in *Macmillan's*. In these publications Arnold was anxious to distance his position from those of the agnostic and anti-clerical groups with whom he was often associated by his critics. As further evidence of Arnold's tolerance and openness to conflicting ideologies, however, he was at the same time developing a closer friendship with the leading agnostic, T. H. Huxley, whom he admired for his intellect and sincere but good-humoured iconoclasm.

In another *Macmillan's* article late in 1876, 'A Psychological Parallel,' Arnold compared an account of a seventeenth-century trial of English witches with a sympathetic description of St Paul's enunciation of Christ's resurrection: both were rooted in excusable contemporary ideas. (He knew but did not reveal the fact that some of his own distant forebears were involved in the witchcraft trial.)[12] In what he conceived to be his final essay on a religious or ecclesiastical subject, Arnold reinforced his point that the 'objections to popular Christianity are not moral objections, but intellectual revolt against its demonstrations by miracle and metaphysics' (*CPW* 8:146). Arnold placed this essay first in a volume which combined it with the three earlier essays. *Last Essays on Church and Religion* was published by Smith and Elder in March 1877. Arnold took great pains over the Preface, announcing the end of his attempts to address questions of religion and the Church and summarizing his views in the most concise statement of his religious position that he ever wrote.

Sales for the book were even lower than for *God and the Bible*, however, and there was little critical comment. Writing in the *Academy*, Edward Dowden welcomed Arnold's decision to leave off his religious studies and expressed the hope that his future literary criticism would fulfil the promise of his early essays. Beginning with his initial excursions into social and political criticism, critics had been urging him to return to the aesthetic studies of literature and writers for which he was better suited. Arnold was now ready to take their advice – up to a point. Even before *Last Essays* was published, he had placed (anonymously) a substantial article on the Geneva critic Edmond Scherer in the *Quarterly Review*: 'A French Critic on Milton' appeared in January 1877. Arnold had been favourably impressed by Scherer, whom he compared to Sainte-Beuve when he met him during his European visit of 1859. A companion piece, 'A French Critic on Goethe', would follow in the same journal one year later. By this time it was not unusual for Arnold to receive £30 or more for journal articles such as this. Other 1877 essays included 'A Guide to English Literature', a review essay on Stopford Brooke's survey of literature, and an essay on 'George Sand' in which he reminisced about his visit to Nohant as a young man and discussed the qualities of the writer which had made her one of his early favourites.

Obviously Arnold was revisiting the scenes of his earlier literary experiences while he resumed some of the lines of inquiry he had marked out in *Essays in Criticism*. The perceptive essays on Scherer in particular were products of his old comparative literary method. But this did not mean that Arnold intended to stop writing articles on social, political and educational issues.

In the March 1877 *Nineteenth Century* he published 'Falkland', on the seventeenth-century statesman and the tragic principle in history. Appearing during 1878 in the *Fortnightly Review* were 'Equality', on the necessity of social equality in a democracy; 'Irish Catholicism and British Liberalism', on the failure of English Liberals to understand the Irish and their need for a Catholic University; and 'Porro Unum Est Necessarium', on the need for a State system of secondary schools. Neither was Arnold able to steer entirely clear of ecclesiastical and theological issues in these essays, in which familiar points about the narrowness of English Puritanism and the need to reform popular Christianity recur as refrains. Even more importantly, Arnold's concentrated study of the Bible as literature had had a fundamental effect on his views about the *status* of poetry. In announcing his 'career shift' in the Preface to *Last Essays*, he wrote:

> [I]n returning to devote to literature, more strictly so-called, what remains to me of life and strength and leisure, I am returning, after all, to a field where work of the most important kind has now to be done, though indirectly, for religion. I am persuaded that the transformation of religion, which is essential for its perpetuance, can be accomplished only by carrying the qualities of flexibility, perceptiveness, and judgment, which are the best fruits of letters, to whole classes of the community which now know next to nothing of them. (*CPW* 8:148).

Even while he was disengaging himself from the fray of religious controversy in early 1877, Arnold was preparing himself for a time in the near future when he would make some of the largest and most problematic claims for poetry ever made by an English literary figure.

Arnold declined re-nomination for the Oxford poetry professorship in February 1877, fearing that the 'religious question' would be raised in a way that would be unpleasant both for him and for the University. In other ways he showed that he was determined to keep himself free of obligations that might restrict either his time or his freedom of expression as a writer. He declined to be nominated for the Lord Rectorship of St Andrews University and refused to stand for a 'virtually certain' seat in Parliament (*MAAL* 380). His post as school inspector was a demanding one but at least it left him free to write what he liked. Although he continued a certain level of social activity, Arnold at this time became more detached from public life than he had been.

His personal life was hardly carefree, however. Although Richard, his only surviving son, had managed to pass the entrance exam into Balliol College, he was a very poor student and after a series of disasters failed to obtain even a fourth-class (the lowest) degree from Oxford. His son's utter failure at Balliol, where his old friend Benjamin Jowett was master, was a serious disappointment for Arnold, always a loving and devoted father, but even worse was his concern about Dick's prospects for a career. Without a degree Dick was not qualified for the clerkship in the Education Office that Arnold had had in mind. Given the death of three sons, it is no wonder that Arnold and his wife had pampered Dick, and now they were apprehensive about his future. In November 1877 Dick parted from his anxious parents and sailed to Melbourne, Australia, where he took a position as a bank clerk, leaving his father to contend with the enormous (mainly gambling) debts he had run up at Oxford. The Arnolds were now over £1000 in debt (*MAAL* 377). Years later, Arnold was still attempting to pay it off, and earning money for this purpose would be the principal motive for his American lecture tour of 1883–4.

Although Arnold's last two books on religion had not sold well, his reputation, shaped by the unusual path of his literary career, remained substantial. One measure of public recognition is the increasing number of parodies of Arnold published during the 1870s, from jokes in *Punch* to the character 'Mr. Luke' in W. H. Mallock's satirical novel of 1877 entitled *New Republic* (*MAPW* 47). According to Mr Luke, culture 'sets aside the larger part of the New Testament as grotesque, barbarous, and immoral; but what remains, purged of its apparent meaning, it discerns as a treasure beyond all price'.[13] But it was not only as a prose controversialist that Arnold was being talked about. His first collected edition of *Poems* (1869) had helped to solidify his reputation as an enduring poet, and, as he ended his 'religious' phase, he was ready to publish a new edition of *Poems* (1877) and his first edition of *Selected Poems* (1878). It was ironic that Arnold, actively engaged as a critic, watched the sales of his books of collected essays decline after the success of *Literature and Dogma* in 1873, while the collected poems he had written in the first phase of his literary life were selling better than ever. Of the

Selected volume, published in his new 'Golden Treasury' series, Macmillan wrote to Arnold at the end of 1878: 'Your little book has been doing wonderfully well of late & we are now in our third thousand, a fact that is edifying and encouraging' (*MAB* 51). The book, originally priced at 4s 6d (22.5p), remained in print into the third decade of the twentieth century.

Hutton's important 1872 review essay on Arnold's 1869 poems in *The British Quarterly Review*, focusing on Arnold as a Nature poet and comparing him with his predecessors Wordsworth and Goethe, has an appropriate retrospective cast to it. Arnold dreamed of writing new poetry (perhaps as a professor at an American university) but busied himself with the practical task of rearranging the old. He took great care and presumably some pleasure in changing the order of poems and regrouping categories of poems, but in doing so he faced the growing reality that, like Wordsworth himself, he was essentially a poet of the past. The only 'new' poem in the 1877 edition was a revised version of 'Haworth Churchyard', which had previously appeared only in journal publication. The comparison with Wordsworth must have been on his mind when, a year after producing his own first selected edition of poems, he published his selected *Poems of Wordsworth* (1879). Arnold was amused in February 1881, when Disraeli at a social gathering engaged him in conversation and paid him the curious compliment of being 'the only living Englishman who had become a classic in his own lifetime'. Disraeli's statement might have been most appropriately applied to Arnold the poet; however, the context of the conversation as reported by Arnold suggests that Disraeli was thinking primarily of Arnold's critical prose: 'what I have done in establishing a number of current phrases – such as Philistinism, sweetness & light, and all that' (*SL* 259). Arnold could accept the compliment in this sense with considerable pleasure, first, because it conformed with his personal goal of creating an 'effect' on the British public through the use of key phrases, and second because, living classic or not, he was confident of producing more critical essays.

7

Mixed Essays (1879), Irish Essays (1882), Discourses in America (1885), Essays in Criticism, Second Series (1888)

By the summer of 1878, Arnold was planning a book that would collect together the eight essays he had published since the beginning of 1877: 'Equality', 'Irish Catholicism and British Liberalism', 'Porro Unum Est Necessarium', 'A Guide to English Literature', 'Falkland', 'A French Critic on Milton', 'A French Critic on Goethe' and 'George Sand'. He decided to place the retitled 'Democracy', previously published as the Preface to *The Popular Education of France* in 1861, at the front of the collection. However, *Last Essays* had not sold well, and when he offered a formal proposal to Smith in August, the publisher was not enthusiastic. Smith finally agreed to pay Arnold £50 for an edition of 1000 copies, which appeared in March 1879. In spite of the eclectic nature of the book's contents, Arnold was hopeful about its success because 'it has a good deal of literature mixed up with it' and would thus please readers who had been asking for more literary studies like those from the 'Essays in Criticism' period. As it turned out, *Mixed Essays* was at least moderately successful, and a second edition was called for in June 1880.

Critics were ready to point out a lack of unity in the book, though Arnold argued in his Preface that there was a 'unity of tendency'. The reviewer for the *Athenaeum* defended this claim, pointing to Arnold's consistent emphasis on 'the supreme value of noble conduct and high demeanour'.[1] Arnold was so pleased that he wrote a letter of thanks to the editor. Similarly, Mark

Pattison, writing in the *Academy*, found unity in Arnold's distinctive approach to a variety of subjects. Pattison praises him for his characteristic 'urbane quality, a play of mind for the play's sake, a quality the possession of which raised the Athenians to the preeminence they hold in the annals of ancient civilization' (*MAPW* 329). Increasingly the critics were focusing on Arnold himself rather than the subjects of his essays, another sign that he was indeed already a 'classic'. This approach can of course lead to negative as well as positive judgments: Margaret Oliphant thought Arnold was guilty of either lack of discrimination or 'exaggerated self-importance' for collecting his disparate essays in this way.[2]

Although *Mixed Essays* does not incorporate Arnold's exchanges with his critics to the extent seen in the earlier collections that originated in literary journalism, there is an interesting one with his old friend and adversary Goldwin Smith that illustrates Arnold's methodology as a thinker and writer. Arnold had originally published 'Falkland' in conjunction with a plan to erect a monument at Newbury, near the scene of his death during the Civil War, to the Royalist hero Lucius Cary, Viscount Falkland. In early 1877 Arnold was absorbed in seventeenth-century religious history. He had been reading John Tulloch's *Rational Theology and Christian Philosophy in England in the Seventeenth Century* and had plans – never realized – for editing a collection of writings entitled *Broad Church in the Seventeenth Century*. In his mind Latitudinarians such as John Hales and Ralph Cudworth were connected to the tradition represented by Dr Arnold in the nineteenth century. Arnold also came to identify himself and his own religious views with John Smith and the Cambridge Platonists, who, he believed, had attempted to ground Christianity on verifiable spiritual experience and unify the dissenting sects with the established Church. In his discussion of the witchcraft trial in 'A Psychological Parallel', he argued that Smith understood the essential 'psychological truth' of Christianity. Given Arnold's ideological frame and institutional loyalties, it is not surprising that, when he came to his study of Falkland, he contrasted that 'sweet-mannered' hero, 'martyr of lucidity of mind and largeness of temper', with his false and dangerous Puritan adversaries and their hero Milton (whose shortcomings Arnold had recently discussed in his essay on Scherer's criticism). Expanding earlier arguments about the defects of English Puritans, Arnold described their victory in the war as a disaster which led to 'moral anarchy', the 'profligacy of the Restoration' (in reaction), and a lasting narrowness and 'intellectual poverty' in the English middle classes.

Goldwin Smith lost little time in responding to Arnold's essay. In a *Contemporary Review* article he not only quarrelled with the portrait of Falkland but attacked Arnold's overall negative view of the Puritans as unfair. In fact, he argued, Puritan morality had prevented the English Renaissance from being more corrupt and it remained 'the most moral and respectable element in the country'.[3] In his subsequent essay 'Equality', Arnold in turn referred to Smith as 'too prone to acerbity' and 'a partisan of the Puritans' (*CPW* 8:295).

While he was sparring with Smith, Arnold was getting together new editions of his own poetry (1877 collected and 1878 selected), and he was working on other editing projects, too. In the autumn of 1876 he had discussed with Macmillan the possibility of editing selections from Johnson's *Lives of the Poets*. The two men agreed that an inexpensive modern edition intended primarily for students was a good idea, although they did not entirely agree about the format of the book, Macmillan favouring more extensive annotations (*MAB* 126). Arnold did not get around to planning the actual contents of the book until the spring of 1878, and it was not issued until September of that year. Arnold's prefatory essay was published in the June issue of *Macmillan's Magazine*. The book turned out to be successful in the long run, with three new editions being called for during Arnold's lifetime, and it remained in print as a textbook for schoolchildren until 1948. But well before the Johnson project was complete, a new editing scheme emerged, one with considerably more critical significance. In January 1877, Macmillan approached Arnold with the idea of editing a selection of Wordsworth's poems for the Golden Treasury series, and Arnold, who had been reading and thinking about Wordsworth's poetry since childhood, naturally found the proposal congenial. Arnold was an eager if not gifted editor. He was finicky about establishing the texts of individual poems but made mistakes in proofreading (*CPW* 9:338). Because this edition was meant for the general public, Arnold and Macmillan agreed that the preface or critical introduction should be relatively short; nevertheless, this was naturally the most exciting part of the project for Arnold, and the resulting essay was one of his most important contributions to literary criticism. 'Wordsworth', published in the

Macmillan's of July 1879, actually appeared prior to the book, which followed in September.

Arnold's goal was to make Wordsworth's poems as widely read as Milton's, and in a sense his essay was intended to promote Wordsworth's reputation rather than offer a thorough criticism of his works. In a letter to his sister Frances he expressed his opinion that Wordsworth 'can show a body of work superior to what any other English poet, except Shakespeare and Milton, can show . . . [and] superior to the body of work of any Continental poet of the last hundred years except Goethe . . . This . . . seems to me to be the simple truth.' He believed that his method of arranging the poems by 'kind' rather than Wordsworth's own 'intricate way, according to the spiritual faculty from which they are supposed to have proceeded', would make Wordsworth 'come out better' than ever before (*SL* 253–4).

Several Arnold scholars have expressed the opinion that the essay on Wordsworth is Arnold's finest example of 'practical' literary criticism or study of an individual author. Whether or not one agrees with this assessment, the essay is certainly a central document in Arnold's literary career. In his retrospective account of Wordsworth's contributions to English poetry, Arnold tells us a great deal about himself. His method of organizing the selected poems according to genre reminds us of his preference for 'natural' classical form over Romantic eccentricities: 'We may rely upon it that we shall not improve upon the classification adopted by the Greeks for kinds of poetry; that their categories of epic, dramatic, lyric, and so forth, have a natural propriety, and should be adhered to' (*CPW* 9:43). When Arnold had collected his own poems for the 1869 edition, his categories had been 'Narrative', 'Elegiac', 'Lyric' and 'Dramatic'. Then, for the 1877 edition, he added 'Early Poems' and 'Sonnets'. He thought that the new order made his poems seem 'much more *natural* and not so mournful' (*MAB* 42).

Regardless of his insistence on classical genres, Arnold's nineteenth-century cosmopolitanism is evident in his attempt to place Wordsworth in the context not of English poetry merely but European poetry as well. Like Goethe, we should 'conceive of the whole group of civilised nations as being, for intellectual and spiritual purposes, one great confederation' writes Arnold in a passage reminiscent of his critical essays of the 1860s (*CPW* 9:38). (Arnold's attempt to transcend the merely national ideal extends to the consideration of French, German and Italian poetry as well as English, but hardly seems to take into account all 'civilized nations.') He of course declines to compare Wordsworth with the ancients, who '[i]n many respects . . . are far above us', but he tempers his old classicism with a qualification: 'and yet there is something that we demand which they can never give' (*CPW* 9:54).

Arnold used the project to adjust his stance once again in relation to the best of the Romantic heritage. It seemed to revive his old delight in the natural world: 'The effect of reading so much Wordsworth lately has been to make me feel more keenly than usual the beauty of the common incidents of the natural year, and I am sure that is a good thing' (See *CPW* 9:339). As we have seen, much of Arnold's early poetry originates in 'an attempt to revisit the Wordsworthian scene', as one critic put it,[4] with 'Resignation' as the central text. 'Resignation' ends not with an image of Wordsworthian joy but rather with 'The something that infects the world.' Arnold could not be another Wordsworth, but he recognized the central, enduring power of Wordsworth's influence. When Wordsworth died in 1850, Arnold memorialized him in verse as the poet with 'healing power', the one who could 'make us feel'. Now, in critical prose Arnold reconsiders Wordsworth's best poetry and shares the joy: 'Wordsworth's poetry is great because of the extraordinary power with which Wordsworth feels the joy offered to us in nature, the joy offered to us in the simple primary affections and duties . . . and renders it so as to make us share it' (*CPW* 9:51). But in order to help his predecessor achieve his rightful status as one of the greatest poets of the 'last two or three centuries' Arnold must save Wordsworth from the Wordsworthians, who admire him indiscriminately. Arnold boldly separates the most successful poems of Wordsworth's best period, 1798–1808, from the 'mass of inferior work' produced during his long career, acknowledges the superiority of the best short lyrics over the 'poems of greatest bulk', and insists that Wordsworth should not be praised as a systematic philosopher. When Wordsworth, who excels at communicating *felt*, poetic truth, tries to write in a philosophic vein, he descends into abstract verbiage.

Arnold must have been thinking of the message-hunting critics who had complained about not finding answers to life's questions or a systematic philosophy in his own poetry. And yet Arnold was far from taking a purely aesthetic approach to Wordsworth. While dismissing didacticism in poetry, Arnold adapts his old definition of poetry as a criticism of life (but now 'under the conditions fixed for us by the laws of poetic beauty and poetic truth'), and argues that *moral* ideas are a 'main part of human life'. Like other great poets, Wordsworth focuses on the question 'how to live', and the term 'moral' can be applied to '[w]hatever bears upon the question, *how to live*' (*CPW* 9:45). Arnold, too, had struggled with this central question in his own poetry, though he had refused to settle for final answers, and in his prose career he had increasingly concerned himself with the problem of *conduct*. When scholars make the inevitable comparison between Arnold's 1879 essay on Wordsworth and the one Pater published in 1874, they often emphasize Arnold's move to distance himself from Pater's 'art for art's sake' aestheticism. As already pointed out, Arnold's early criticism had been a central influence on Pater: Pater's 'code of treating life in the spirit of art' is 'a simplification and extension of Arnold's ideal of disinterestedness'.[5] Although some critics have argued that, in spite of his rhetoric about moral issues, Arnold in his 'Wordsworth' essay is still fundamentally a subjective, creative critic who is not so very far from Pater,[6] it is clear that the Arnold of 'Wordsworth' was much less attractive to aesthetes like Pater and Swinburne than the earlier Arnold had been. In an 1884 essay, Swinburne suggested that Arnold's theological excursions had led to false conclusions about the centrality of the question 'how to live' in literature.

He challenged Arnold's reference to this 'moral' issue common to Milton's *Paradise Lost*, Keats's 'Ode on a Grecian Urn' and Shakespeare's *The Tempest*. For Swinburne, a '"criticism of life" becomes such another term or form of speech as "prevenient grace," or "the real presence," or "the double procession of the Holy Ghost"', and he asserted that Keats was 'the most exclusively aesthetic and the most absolutely non-moral of all serious writers on record'.[7] J. A. Symonds was another critic who thought Arnold was confusing ethical with formal matters: 'The application of the soundest moral ideas, the finest criticism of life, will not save [poetry] from oblivion, if it fails in the essential qualities that constitute a work of art' (*MAPW* 344).

At least one other aspect of Arnold's defense of Wordsworth is worth mentioning. Arnold never published detailed critical discussions of living poets, but in attempting to re-establish the supremacy of Wordsworth in nineteenth-century English poetry, he sought to reverse the trend which saw Arnold's rival Tennyson draw 'to himself, and away from Wordsworth, the poetry-reading public, and new generations' (*CPW* 9:37). Although Arnold's comments probably had very little effect on Tennyson's reputation, the Wordsworth edition was an outstanding success. Nearly 4000 copies, at 4s 6d (22.5p), were sold within five months of the original publication date, and a second edition followed quickly. According to Super, this second edition was reprinted 37 times in the following 68 years (*CPW* 9:339), and in spite of Arnold's disagreements with aesthetes and Wordsworthians, there can be little doubt that he really did advance Wordsworth's critical reputation significantly.

In the late 1870s Arnold re-examined and expanded his views on poetry and literature. His review of Wordsworth's contributions to English and European poetry was only one of the occasions which stimulated him to think and write about the most basic assumptions underlying his literary criticism. In October 1878, T. Humphrey Ward, the husband of Arnold's niece Mary, proposed that Arnold work with him on his anthology entitled *The English Poets*. Arnold was reluctant, citing his usual excuse that 'I am a school-inspector with a very limited time at my disposal for letters.' For the same reason he had recently passed up the opportunity to write a monograph on Shakespeare for John Morley's 'English Men of Letters' series (see *CPW* 9:378), but eventually he agreed to write a general introduction, and then also introductory essays on the poets Gray and Keats for Ward. Following his usual pattern, he put off writing until the last moment, and when he began, he incorporated into the first part of his essay a short introduction he had already written for the poets' section of Dr Wallace Wood's edition of *The Hundred Greatest Men: Portraits of the One Hundred Greatest Men of History* (1879–80). *The English Poets* appeared in 1881.

Arnold's general introduction was the chief point of interest in Ward's anthology. Later entitled 'The Study of Poetry', it contains some of his best-known pronouncements about poetry and poets. It is pre-eminently an essay of judgment and evaluation. Quoting himself from the previous short essay on poetry, Arnold begins by making a very large claim for poetry:

The future of poetry is immense, because in poetry, where it is worthy of its high destinies, our race, as time goes on, will find an ever surer and surer stay. There is not a creed which is not shaken, not an accredited dogma which is not shown to be questionable, not a received tradition which does not threaten to dissolve. Our religion has materialised itself in the fact ... and now the fact is failing it. But for poetry the idea is everything; the rest is a world of illusion ... the idea *is* the fact. The strongest part of our religion today is its unconscious poetry. (*CPW* 9:161)

This remarkable passage, so obviously a product of Arnold's Bible criticism, immediately imports into his literary studies some of the controversy generated by the religious essays. It would draw responses, both positive and negative, from future generations of scholars and literary critics. And yet Arnold did not intend to write for scholars or professional literary men: he wrote for a general, middle-class audience with an interest in poetry but not necessarily a sophisticated understanding of it (*CPW* 9:379). In attempting to reach this audience, Arnold employed some of the critical formulations that had become familiar in his work and re-introduced and expanded some of the ideas he had introduced in the 1860s, beginning with the early Homer essays. Poetry is a criticism of life. The reader must see the poetic object as it really is, thus avoiding the fallacies of the merely personal and the merely historical estimate. Even Arnold's notorious 'touchstone method' is anticipated by his use of quotations in the Homer lectures: the best way to know 'truly excellent' poetry when we see it is 'to have always in one's mind lines and expressions of the great masters, and to apply them as a touchstone to other poetry' (*CPW* 9:168). In citing specific touchstone passages – Milton is the most recent poet quoted – Arnold eschews abstract system and invites (or challenges) his readers to accept his critical taste and judgment. His assumption is that reasonable people, without absolute standards, can agree on the quality not only of a poet's artistry but of his 'criticism of life'. To his credit, Arnold's surviving notebooks, filled with short quotations from the classics,[8] suggest that he really practised the method he advocated.

To an even greater extent than in 'Wordsworth', Arnold is concerned with ranking the English poets, or rather with deciding which ones should be singled out as truly 'classic', and some of his judgments were controversial even when he wrote them; today, in an age of highly problematical and shifting canons, they may appear very arbitrary indeed. He praises Chaucer yet decides that the fourteenth-century poet lacks 'high seriousness' and thus is not one of the 'great classics'. Burns falls short for a similar reason. Arnold's most striking evaluations concern the eighteenth century, which, he decides, was an age of prose, not of poetry. Although they may be masters of the art of versification, 'Dryden and Pope are not classics of our poetry, they are classics of our prose' (*CPW* 9:181). Gray, on the other hand (to whom Arnold also contributes a separate essay in the anthology):

> is our poetical classic of that literature and age; the position of Gray is singular . . . He has not the volume or power of poets who, coming in times more favorable, have attained to an independent criticism of life. But he lived with the great poets, he lived, above all, with the Greeks, through perpetually studying and enjoying them; and he caught . . . their poetic manner . . . He is the scantiest and frailest of classics in our poetry, but he is a classic. (*CPW* 9:181)

This passage is worth quoting because Arnold so obviously identified with Gray, a poet living in an 'unpoetical' age, who turned to the Greek classics for his models and achieved a limited and yet 'classic' body of work. Such ultimate decisions could not yet be made about recent, and certainly not about living, poets. In this essay Arnold considers no poet later than Burns because 'we enter on burning ground as we approach the poetry of times . . . near to us – poetry like that of Byron, Shelley, and Wordsworth – of which the estimates are so often not only personal, but personal with passion' (*CPW* 9:187).

Yet Arnold had been eager to write his essay on Wordsworth, and, as he corrected the proofs for his *English Poets* introduction in February 1880, he was planning not only essays on the Romantic Keats as well as the eighteenth-century Gray for the same anthology but also a selected *Poetry of Byron* with its own critical introduction. Clearly he was willing to risk the danger of injecting his own personal estimates into his re-evaluation of the English Romantics. The essay on Keats, completed by early May, is less substantial than some of the others from this period, but Arnold's shifting, ambivalent attitudes towards that poet over the years reveal something of his own deepest conflicts about the nature of poetry. In the late 1840s he complained to Clough about the harm Keats had done to English poetry, but four or five years later, Arnold wrote his most Keatsian poem, 'The Scholar-Gipsy'. Arnold had mixed feelings about that poem, of course, and beyond his own internal conflicts and uncertainties about his vocation, there was the troubling presence of the great but seriously flawed Tennyson as the continuator of Keatsian lyricism. Arnold's 1880 essay does not add a great deal to the critical insights about Keats and 'natural magic' in the 1862 essay on Maurice de Guérin, but now that Arnold is reconciled to the end of his own poetic career, there is less tension, less need to complicate his genuine appreciation of Keats. It turns out that Keats's 'yearning passion for the Beautiful' is not ultimately a passion of the sensuous or sentimental poet:

> For the second great half of poetic interpretation, for that faculty of moral interpretation which is in Shakespeare . . . Keats is not ripe . . . But in shorter things, where the matured power of moral interpretation, and the high architectonics which go with complete poetic development, are not required, he is perfect. (*CPW* 9:215)

However, Arnold was more interested in securing the reputation of Byron, an important early influence on his own poetry and whom in his 1850 elegy on Wordsworth he had honoured (along with Wordsworth and Goethe) as one of the three poets who had most set the tone for their age. As Arnold explained, 'When at last I held in my hand the volume of poems which I had chosen from Wordsworth . . . there arose in me almost immediately the desire to see beside it, as a companion volume, a like collection of the best poetry of Byron' (*CPW* 9:217). Arnold had an agreement with Macmillan to publish the book by May 1880, but it did not appear until the spring of 1881. Following the precedent set in the Wordsworth project, Arnold first published his critical introduction in *Macmillan's* as a freestanding essay. Arnold's task of selection was more difficult than it had been with Wordsworth because he found fewer appropriate short poems and had to choose the right '*bits*' of longer ones.

Although Byron had defects such as vulgarity and affectation and did not share Wordsworth's 'insight into permanent sources of joy and consolation for mankind' (*CPW* 9:236), he would come to be regarded with Wordsworth as a pre-eminent English poet because his personality is characterized by *'the excellence of sincerity and strength'*. Ironically, Arnold is quoting Swinburne here, and he gives him credit for defining Byron poetic's value, but Swinburne was angered by Arnold's praise of Byron at the expense of Shelley, who according to Arnold was an 'unsubstantial' poet, lacking 'a sound subject-matter'. Swinburne, already upset with Arnold's perceived moralism, would characterize Arnold's remarks about Shelley as 'criticism inspired by a spirit of sour unreasonableness, a spirit of bitterness and darkness' (*MAPW* 370). When Arnold's letters were published in 1895 and Swinburne learned that Arnold had referred to him in an 1863 letter to his mother as 'a sort of pseudo-Shelley' (*LMA* 1:227–8), Swinburne remarked that Arnold had been 'a sort of a pseudo-Wordsworth'.[9]

Arnold's exchanges with Swinburne had less lasting significance than another 'debate' he was having with a very formidable yet more amicable adversary. T. H. Huxley, the pre-eminent spokesman for science in Victorian England, had been Arnold's friend since the 'Culture and Anarchy' period, when Huxley dined at Arnold's lodgings and Arnold accompanied Huxley to Geological Society dinners (*MAAL* 351). Huxley was a talented man of letters as well as a scientist, and Arnold acknowledged his role as an important cultural voice. When he sent Huxley a copy of *Last Essays on Church and Religion*, Arnold enclosed a note saying that there were 'few people whom I send my things with so much pleasure, though I know you cannot always agree with me'.[10] The chief area of disagreement between the two men was the position of science in culture and education. Arnold often referred to the increasing importance of science in his time and even insisted on a 'scientific' basis of verifiable belief in his Biblical studies. In his 1868 report on European education Arnold called for a kind of balance: 'The rejection of the humanities by the realists, the rejection of the study of nature by the humanists, are alike ignorant' (*CPW* 4:300). But a passage in the same report makes it clear where the emphasis should lie when hard choices had to be made. The study of letters in itself is concerned with the human forces of 'human freedom and activity', the study of science with the non-human forces of 'human limitation and passivity' (*CPW* 4:292). Arnold's comments in his

General Report to the Education Department in 1876 explain his view that the study of letters *'moralises'* the individual so that he can make proper use of scientific data (*CPW* 10:463). In the Introduction to *Literature and Dogma*, he expressed his concern at the revolt of the friends of science against the 'tyranny' of letters.

If Arnold intended to promote the study of 'letters' or 'literature' in order to meet the challenge of the new science in British education, it was necessary to sort out his usage of key terms. In a speech he gave at Eton in May 1879, Arnold adapted his old definition of 'criticism', declaring that 'what a man seeks through his education is to get to know himself and the world', and in order to do this he must 'acquaint himself with the best which has been thought and said in the world'. Further, 'of this *best* the classics of Greece and Rome form a very chief portion, and the portion most entirely satisfactory' (*CPW* 9:21–2). Since the Preface of 1853, Arnold's ideas about the study of poetry had been closely related to his ideas about the production of poetry. In the late 1870s and early 1880s this linkage became more important than ever and, in the context of his exchange with Huxley, led Arnold to his most comprehensive and in a sense his culminating statement about the claims of literature and the humanities in human life. Arnold's renewed study of Wordsworth and other poets after his venture into Biblical poetry had inspired his most expansive claims for *poetry*. But his efforts to defend his concept of poetry as a 'criticism of life' led him to return to the broader term *letters* or *literature*. In his essay on Byron, Arnold reminded his readers that he had originally used the phrase 'criticism of life' (in the 1863 essay 'Joubert') in reference to literature in general. Arnold now explains that both poetry and prose can be described fundamentally as a criticism of life: 'In poetry however, the criticism of life has to be made conformably to the laws of poetic truth and poetic beauty' (*CPW* 9:228).

Having made these distinctions and qualifications, Arnold was prepared to meet the challenge presented by Huxley's lecture, later published as 'Science and Culture', which he delivered at the opening of Sir Josiah Mason's Science College at Birmingham in October 1880. Setting himself against 'the classical scholars, in their capacity of Levites in charge of the ark of culture and monopolists of liberal education', Huxley attacked the classical literary curriculum entrenched in English universities. His reference to 'our chief apostle of culture' is disarmingly sympathetic, and he accepts Arnold's idea that 'a criticism of life is the essence of culture' but insists on the centrality of modern scientific knowledge to that criticism. When Huxley sent Arnold a copy of his text, Arnold replied by claiming that he had always intended 'the best that had been known and said in the world' to include 'science and art as well as letters'.[11] It would be two years, however, before Arnold gave his full response.

Working on his various but related writing projects, Arnold had a productive year in 1880 and, in spite of his numerous critics, he could take satisfaction in his growing status as an important man of letters who was expected to leave a permanent mark on English literature. In May he had the pleasure of meeting J. H. Newman for the first time, if only for a few minutes at the Duchess of Norfolk's reception. At home Arnold was still dogged by financial worries, however, and he complained about shortness of breath, an ominous sign that his health was deteriorating (*MAAL* 391). In September he took a short vacation, travelling alone to join the party of Francis Sandford and A. J. Mundella in the Swiss Alps. As in the past, the cold air and mountain scenery reinvigorated Arnold. Sandford, an old Balliol friend, was now Secretary of the Education Office; Mundella, also a friend and an admiring reader of Arnold's poetry, was Vice-President of the Council and the superior of both Arnold and Mundella. Arnold had never before had such a pleasant working relationship with his superiors, and in Switzerland Mundella chatted informally with Arnold about education matters (*SL* 258). Nevertheless, the routine of school inspecting back in England continued to be a burden to a tired and ageing author who still had literary ambitions.

While he was completing his retrospective study of the English Romantics, Arnold continued to write and lecture on miscellaneous topics. In early October 1881 he wrote to George Smith:

> I find I have accumulated, – on Ireland, theatres, education, the future of Liberalism, and other matters, – enough for another volume of Essays, which might come out, with the title of 'Irish Essays & Others' (?) in February. Would you like to add this to the too numerous series of my prose volumes? (*MAB* 160)

Irish Essays, brought out by Smith & Elder in February 1882, included seven new pieces: 'The Incompatibles' (in two parts), 'An Unregarded Irish Grievance', '*Ecce, Convertimur ad Gentes*' ('Lo, We Turn to the Gentiles', a lecture on education given at the Working Men's College at Ipswich), 'The Future of Liberalism', 'A Speech at Eton', 'The French Play in London', and 'Copyright'. All of the essays had been previously published in *The Nineteenth Century*, *The Fortnightly Review* or *The Cornhill* during the period 1879–81. At the end of the volume, Arnold added the Prefaces to his *Poems* of 1853 and 1854, thus coupling essays from the latter stage of his career with his first venture into critical prose nearly three decades earlier.

The title of the volume comes from the lead essays on Ireland. Arnold had been made aware of political and economic problems in Ireland as a young man when he was working for Lord Lansdowne (*MAAL* 117–18). Although he was by no means a specialist in Irish issues, his interest in Irish and, more generally, Celtic literature had led to his series of Celtic lectures in the 1860s. They in turn had given impetus to a movement to create a chair of Celtic Studies at Oxford, which was in place by 1875. In addition to associations of Irish Catholicism with his brother Tom and with J. H. Newman, Arnold's awareness of Ireland was sharpened in 1880 by the appointment of his brother-in-law William Forster to the chief secretaryship there. Arnold was sensitive to the 'hateful history of conquest, confiscation, ill-usage, misgovernment, and tyranny' in English–Irish relations, and he believed, as he wrote in his Preface, 'that in order to attach Ireland to us solidly, English people have not only to *do* something different from what they have done hitherto, they have also to *be* something different' (*CPW* 9:312). Arnold advocated policies that would promote '*healing*' in Ireland, and in 'The Incompatibles' he argued that the recent Irish Land Bill failed to meet the 'moral grievance' of the Irish and met the 'material grievance in a roundabout, complicated manner'. Arnold quotes extensively from Burke's Irish speeches to condemn the narrowness of English politicians who lose sight of ' "the end and object of all elections, namely, *the disposing our people to a better sense of their condition*" ' (*CPW* 9:267). For Arnold the final goal of Irish policies must be 'to bring Ireland to acquiesce cordially in the English connection', and in order to do this 'it is not enough even to do justice and to make well-being general; we and our civilisation must also be attractive to them' (*CPW* 9:262). The 'unregarded grievance' of Arnold's second Irish essay concerns the sorry state of secondary education in Ireland. Irish policy is also one of the issues Arnold discusses in his essay on the future of Liberalism, where he predicts that Liberal governments will not be secure until Liberal statesmen understand that 'the need in man for expansion' includes 'equality as well as political liberty and free trade' (*CPW* 9:159).

Arnold's review of a performance in London by the *Comédie française* in the summer of 1879 was his first attempt as a theatre critic. It gave him the opportunity to compare Sarah Bernhardt with his old favourite actress Rachel, and though with its appeal for a British state theatre the piece reads more like a critical essay than a review of a performance, it led to more conventional reviews. The playwright Henry Arthur Jones thought Arnold's 'French Play' article was interesting and he addressed a letter to the famous critic, enclosing two of his own plays. Subsequently Arnold reviewed Jones's play *The Silver King* and then four other plays during the period November 1882–October 1884, publishing them all in *The Pall Mall Gazette* – now under the editorship of John Morley – as letters from 'An Old Playgoer'.

In his contribution to the widely-discussed copyright issue, Arnold hoped (in vain) that he might help to convince the Americans to protect the rights of English authors. In his testimony before the Copyright Commission in January 1877, Arnold complained that he had not been remunerated for the large sales of his works in America, with the exception of £50 from Ticknor & Fields of Boston (the publisher principally responsible for introducing Arnold's works to America) in 1866 in return for Macmillan's sending early sheets of *Essays in Criticism* and 'Thyrsis'. Among Arnold's works published in America without payment to him were his 1853 and 1855 poems (published as a single volume by Ticknor & Fields in 1856) and the religious books *Literature and Dogma* and *God and the Bible* (both published by James R. Osgood, also of Boston). In some cases, the American publishers were competing with Macmillan, whose American branch in New York imported copies of Arnold's books printed in England.

One of the most significant aspects of Arnold's Irish essays is his use of Burke. Problems in Ireland gave Arnold the occasion for reviewing the works of one of his favourite English prose writers: 'Our neglected [prose] classic is by birth an Irishman; he knows Ireland and its history thoroughly' (*CPW* 9:287). Although Arnold was sometimes put off by Burke's Conservative politics, he found much to admire in both the form and content of Burke's essays. The influence of Burke throughout Arnold's critical career is illustrated in his key reference to Burke's 'return upon himself' in 'The Function of Criticism' and his frequent citation of Burke's definition of the State as 'the nation in its collective and corporate character' (though apparently Burke never wrote precisely those words) in his essays on culture and education. He used sentences and phrases from Burke as 'touchstones' to test the truth or moral value of ideas about the English character and the English nation. Arnold's positive experience of editing Wordsworth and Byron probably contributed to his idea of publishing a collection of Burke's principal writings on Ireland, and *Edmund Burke on Irish Affairs* was brought out by Macmillan in June 1881, nearly a year before *Irish Essays*. Like the more substantial *Poetry of Byron* – published about the same time – it was not a commercial success, but it was part of Arnold's long, backward look at his literary and cultural roots during this late stage of his career.

The death of A. P. Stanley in July 1881 was another occasion for looking backwards. Stanley, Dean of Westminster, had been Dr Arnold's prize pupil and biographer, and Arnold portrayed him in his elegy 'Westminster Abbey' as a Broad Church activist who 'Hath run his bright career,/And served men nobly'. Arnold was also sympathetic to Stanley as a representative Oxford man, and although they occasionally exchanged sharp criticism, as when Stanley blasted Arnold for his infamous 'three Shaftesburys' passage, the two men had agreed on a wide range of religious and political issues. The elegy, printed in the *Nineteenth Century* of January 1882, earned him £100 and may be considered the last substantial new poem he published. He did, however, publish two additional elegies, to his pet canary Matthias (December 1882) and to his dachshund Kaiser (July 1887)!

Arnold was finally ready to answer Huxley's challenge on the relative merits of science and the humanities in education when he delivered the Rede lecture at Cambridge in June 1882. The lecture, published in the August *Nineteenth Century* as 'Literature and Science', in some ways the culminating statement of Arnold's claims for literature, is also, along with J. H. Newman's

Idea of a University, one of the classic defences of the humanities or liberal arts in education. Arnold's strategy is to lay his defence of the traditional classical curriculum and the category of *belles lettres* to one side while he defines 'literature' so broadly that it becomes synonymous with the formula he had employed in 'The Function of Criticism' and revised in *Culture and Anarchy*: 'the best which has been thought and said in the world'. Keeping in mind that Huxley had admitted the need for the study of modern languages and literatures along with science, Arnold argues that 'those who are for giving to natural knowledge . . . the chief place in the education of the majority of mankind, leave one important thing out of their account: the constitution of human nature'. 'Human nature' is 'built up' by 'the power of conduct, the power of intellect and knowledge, the power of beauty, and the power of social life and manners' (*CPW* 10:61–2). The 'social life and manners' category quickly drops out of Arnold's discussion, but he insists that only in the study of literature is knowledge related to 'the sense in us for conduct, and to the sense in us for beauty' (*CPW* 10:64–5): that is, in literature, the Hellenic 'sweetness and light' emphasized in *Culture and Anarchy* is related to the Hebraic conduct emphasized in the religious books. Scientific knowledge, by itself, is finally 'unsatisfying, wearying' to the majority of humankind.

Having made his case for 'literature', Arnold turns to his beloved classical curriculum. He must have sensed that he was much more vulnerable here, and hence his care in separating the issue of Latin and Greek studies from his more general argument. Still, he prophesies that because 'the instinct for beauty is served by Greek literature and art as it is served by no other literature and art', classical studies will prevail (*CPW* 10:71). Arnold, student of Homer and Sophocles and author of *Merope*, could not accept the inevitable eclipse of classical studies by the modern national literatures he himself loved.

Given Arnold's considerable posthumous influence on the English studies movement that flourished in the next century, it is interesting to note his lack of enthusiasm for the emerging academic discipline of English literature. In a letter of December 1886 to John Churton Collins, who supported the establishment of a chair of English Literature at Oxford, Arnold explained that he would be glad to see university students study 'the great works of English literature' and modern languages in conjunction with

Greek and Latin (*MAAL* 415). His cautious and qualified support is ironic in the light of Lionel Trilling's claim that Arnold 'may even be said to have established the teaching of English as an academic profession'.[12]

Arnold was pleased with his reception in the Senate House at Cambridge, and with comments he received after the lecture was published. Complimentary remarks from James Russell Lowell, the American minister to London, may have influenced his choice of this lecture as one of three he would feature in his American tour the next year. 'Literature and Science' would prove to be popular with his American audience, and Arnold delivered it so often there that he became bored with it.

His idea of lecturing in America, unlike the European journeys he had undertaken as an education official, did not arise primarily from intellectual curiosity or the pleasure of travel. Arnold made the calculated decision to take on an exhausting schedule for the American tour, delivering 65 lectures to a total audience of about 40 000 people in about four months, in order to pay off his debts. Arnold's self-deflating description of himself in an 1880 address at the University College in Liverpool suggests that he did not overestimate his appeal to public audiences:

a nearly worn-out man of letters . . . with a frippery of phrases about sweetness and light, seeing things as they really are, knowing the best that has been thought and said in the world, which never had very much solid meaning, and have now quite lost the gloss and charm of novelty. (CPW 10:74)

At home in England, Arnold's usual practice was to decline payment for his lectures, and when he believed he was supporting a particularly worthy group he sometimes even declined to be reimbursed for travel expenses (*CPW* 11:485–6), but now for the first time he was determined to make a substantial profit from his celebrity. (After all, it was only fair that the Americans should repay him for pirating so many of his books.) Most pressing was the debt of approximately £1000 owed to his publisher George Smith, who had lent him the money in 1878 in order to pay Dick's gambling obligations at Oxford and help finance the young man's voyage to Australia. By 1882 Dick had returned from Australia where he had found a wife but not the fortune which would have allowed him to pay back his father. Richard D'Oyly Carte, the leading impresario of English operetta, who had booked Oscar Wilde for an American lecture tour in 1881, organized Arnold's tour, which was then directed by Carte's American agents. 'I hate going to America' Arnold confided to his sister Jane (*LMA* 2:253), but once he made the decision to go, he threw himself into the project with his usual intensity. Accompanied by his wife and his eldest daughter Lucy, Arnold arrived in New York on 22 October 1883, and, one week later, delivered his first American lecture there.

Arnold had never shown a great interest in America and often expressed the opinion that any American influence on England was negative. In an 1848 letter to his mother he complained that he saw 'a wave of more than American *vulgarity* break over us' (*SL* 36). Arnold even welcomed the American Civil War as an opportunity to purify the 'American character', and in *A French Eton* (1864) he asks:

> And what were the old United States but a colossal expression of the English middle-class spirit, somewhat more accessible to ideas there than here, because of the democratic air it breathed, much more arrogant and overweening there than here, because of the absence of all check and counterpoise to it – but there, as here, full of rawness, hardness, and imperfection. (*CPW* 2:319)

Arnold had of course been interested in Emerson since his Oxford days, but he did not devote an essay to an American topic until 1882. He had begun to think about his first American essay as early as the summer of 1879 when he took notice of a review of *Mixed Essays* by Thomas Wentworth Higginson in the *North American Review*, calling attention to Arnold's neglect of American topics in his social criticism. His correspondence with Lowell after meeting him in 1880 and his developing plans for the America tour – originally in the winter of 1882 but then delayed until 1883 – provided further incentives. By early April 1882, Arnold was writing 'A Word about America', and it was published in the May issue of the *Nineteenth Century*. Making references to his recent reading of Henry James's novel *Roderick Hudson*, Arnold describes the American population as made up of Philistines, just like British Philistines (with the Barbarians left out entirely and the Populace nearly). Although he focuses

on the need for greater 'cultivation' in America, Arnold maintains an amiable tone – no doubt preparing for his American
audience – and sounds a familiar refrain when he recommends
reform of secondary education as 'the really fruitful reform to
be looked for in America' (*CPW* 10:22–3).

His reference in the 'Word' essay to the 'friends of civilisation',
who can accomplish a good deal though they are few in number, helps prepare the way for 'Numbers; or The Majority and
the Remnant', the first lecture Arnold would deliver in America.
In his poem 'Balder Dead' (1855) Arnold has the spirit of his
dead hero decide to build a new society in the Norse version
of the underworld with 'a small remnant' of workers. Honan
connects this idea with Dr Arnold's views on Isaiah and with
Coleridge's 'clerisy' of key religious and social leaders (*MAAL*
286–7). Arnold's 'aliens' in *Culture and Anarchy* also come to mind.
Drawing on both Isaiah ('Many are called, few chosen') and Plato
('The majority are bad'), Arnold deliberately challenges what he
must feel to be the not uncommon fallacy among Americans that
the majority is always right. Citing examples of flawed national
majorities past and present – including a restatement of his views
concerning the English–Irish problems – Arnold makes his notorious comments about the French and their worship of the 'great
goddess Lubricity' or Aselgeia, as the Greeks called her: 'That
goddess has always been a sufficient power among mankind . . .
But here is now a whole popular literature, nay, and art too, in
France at her service!' (*CPW* 10:155). Since the time of the Franco-
Prussian War, Arnold had suspected that 'wantonness' or sensu-
ality had corrupted the French 'national character' that he had
admired since his youth. Arnold's distrust of, and lack of indulgence for, primal instincts and drives is related to his lack of
appreciation for the 'daemonic' element in his literary criticism
and to his fear of political and cultural 'anarchy'. The object lesson
of the French is especially appropriate in the context of his
apprehensions about the power of the majority in a great modern
democracy like the United States. At the same time, he could
assume that his American audience – with the same Protestant
Puritan biases as his English Philistines – would not be put off
by allusions to French lubricity. Arnold remembered his father's
views on ethnology as he concluded his lecture with references
to the 'excellent German stock' from which Americans, like the
English, have primarily sprung. Though 'your majority must in

the present stage of the world probably be unsound, what . . . an incomparable, all-transforming remnant, – you fairly hope with your numbers, if things go happily, to have!' (*CPW* 10:164).

Although Arnold was a veteran lecturer, he was not used to the large lecture halls he encountered in America. When he first presented 'Numbers', to a crowd of 1300 at New York's Pickering Hall, his voice projection was inadequate, and he was distressed to learn that large numbers of people in the audience (including Ulysses S. Grant) were unable to hear him. He arranged for elocution lessons and trained for his next performance a week later in Boston, where (in a slightly smaller hall) it went much better. Arnold did not possess great skills as a performer, but as he repeated his lectures multiple times, he memorized the words, and this aided his delivery. Overall, Arnold was pleased with the reception of 'Numbers', and he delivered it eighteen times in America, often enough to make the text all too familiar to him but not nearly so often as the 29 times he repeated 'Literature and Science'.

Arnold limited himself to only three lectures on his American tour: the third and most controversial one was 'Emerson'. When Emerson died in April 1882, Arnold thought of editing a collection of his works for Macmillan, but he found that John Morley had already agreed to write a preface for such an edition. Arnold was invited to write an essay on Emerson for *Macmillan's Magazine*, but he was busy with other projects and deferred writing the essay again and again. Although he planned, for obvious reasons, to use 'Emerson' as one of his American lectures, he wrote to his sister Jane on the eve of his departure that he had not yet written a line, though he reminded her that 'I always found him of more use than Carlyle, and I now think so more than ever' (*LMA* 2:254). He spent much of his time on the ocean voyage reading Emerson's *Essays* and his correspondence with Carlyle, and in spite of his busy schedule he managed to finish the lecture during the first month of his tour. The draft he had completed by mid-November was so rough that a Boston printer refused to print a lecture copy from it. (Charles Eliot Norton, the Harvard professor of fine arts who became one of Arnold's closest American friends, had the job done for Arnold at the University Press.) Arnold presented 'Emerson' for the first time on 1 December at Boston's Chickering Hall. Although he was anxious about its reception in Massachusetts, he thought that

Emerson himself would have been satisfied with it and predicted that it would help the American's reputation in England.

Expressing his admiration for Emerson since his Balliol days, Arnold begins his lecture by linking the American with J. H. Newman and Goethe, and he closes by making large claims for Emerson: Emerson is finally superior to Carlyle, and his essays are the most important work done in prose, just as Wordsworth's poetry is the best work done in verse. Yet Arnold does not refrain from pointing out Emerson's limitations: he is not a 'great poet' and, furthermore, 'his style has not the requisite wholeness of good tissue' to qualify him as a great writer or man of letters (*CPW* 10:172). Although Emerson's family had no complaints about the lecture and the *Nation* described it as a 'great success', many of Emerson's admirers were displeased. The *Literary World* complained about Arnold's 'iconoclastic habit' of 'forever pulling down'.[13] Sensitive to this sort of criticism, Arnold decided to deliver the lecture 'Numbers' when he visited Emerson's home town of Concord, but he presented 'Emerson' a total of eighteen times in America, and again at the Royal Institution a few days after returning to England.

Arnold spent most of November and December lecturing in New England cities and college towns. During the Christmas season he visited Philadelphia, Washington, Richmond and Baltimore. In January he travelled west, stopping at Madison, Chicago and St Louis. Then, as he made his way back east, he took a more northerly route, through Toronto, Ottawa, Montreal and Quebec, before returning to New York. He set sail for England in early March 1884. Arnold's adventures in America had many odd and ironic aspects. He began his stay in New York as the guest of industrial magnate Andrew Carnegie, whose mother gave Arnold advice about his speaking style. (Carnegie had helped to encourage the American tour in the first place by hosting a dinner at London's Grand Hotel at which he introduced Arnold to some prominent Americans.) Although Arnold could never agree with Carnegie's ideas about measuring the quality of life by material accomplishments or quantifiable statistics, Carnegie admired Arnold and freely adapted Arnold's concept of culture in his philanthropic projects. But many Americans did not share Carnegie's views. Confronted with diverse audiences, Arnold sometimes made miscalculations in addressing them. The haughtiness and pomposity often associated with Arnold's image in

England (qualities emphasized in contemporary satires) made him even more vulnerable before an audience of nineteenth-century Americans who tended to express a general insecurity and defensiveness toward all things British. Especially in the Midwest, where his audiences were smallest and least enthusiastic, he was attacked for his perceived elitist manner. According to one account of his lecture in Galesburg, Illinois, Arnold 'stood for an hour uttering an unintelligible message to an uncomprehending audience'.[14] In an impromptu speech at a luncheon given in his honour in Montreal, he discussed the juxtaposition of the two nationalities in that city and made remarks about the narrow-mindedness of the Catholic, French-speaking population that created a local scandal.

Everywhere he went, Arnold was hounded by the American press, which he considered vulgar and intrusive. Even after his return to England, Arnold's negative opinion of American newspapers was intensified when he became the victim of a journalistic hoax. The editor of the Chicago *Daily News*, angry at the rival Chicago *Tribune* for pirating his foreign news reports, wrote a bogus story about a very ill-natured account by Arnold of his visit to Chicago – which had supposedly appeared in the *'Pall Mall' Journal* – and through a devious scheme arranged to have it picked up by the *Tribune*. When the *Tribune* printed the story, *Daily News* reporters fanned the flames by interviewing individuals who had been insulted in the *Tribune* article. The *Tribune* then published an editorial lambasting Arnold and describing his visit to Chicago as a miserable failure. Even after the hoax was exposed, this incident seemed to contribute to the overall unpleasant impression of Arnold's visit as it was discussed in American journals (*MAHC* 290). For example, the *Nation*, which had earlier commented favourably on Arnold's lectures, published an article in 1888 referring to his American tour as a mistake: 'He had no preparation for that sort of work, and was . . . very ill fitted to encounter the sort of treatment that American newspapers deal out to literary and scientific men who do not please their taste.'[15] But despite the hostile press during Arnold's 1883–4 tour, in the long run Arnold made a greater impact on America than any other British or European critic.

Most importantly to Arnold, the American trip was at least moderately profitable and allowed him to pay the old debt to George Smith. He was not satisfied with the management provided by Carte's associates, however, and thought that he might make three or four times as much money with less effort if he arranged things differently on a future tour of the United States. But his financial situation was improving in other ways as well. Just before his departure for America, he was granted an annual pension of £250 from the Gladstone government 'as a public recognition of service to the poetry and literature of England'. This was a welcome addition to his annual school inspector's salary of about £1000, though he accepted it reluctantly, knowing that the fund available for literary pensions was small and 'literary men . . . numerous and needy' (*SL* 261). In April 1885, however, he was not at all reluctant to accept Macmillan's offer of £500 for a new three-volume library edition of his *Poems*, 2000 copies of which were printed to sell at 7s 6d (37.5p: *MAB* 58). Before the end of the year, *Selected Poems* was ready for a new edition as well. Even though Arnold's reputation as a distinguished man of letters continued to grow, his literary income never matched that from other sources for any single year; however, the increasing commercial success of his poetry books (now much greater than that of his prose volumes) was gratifying to Arnold in his final years.

One unexpected side-effect of the Arnold family's visit to America was the engagement and subsequent marriage of Lucy Arnold to Frederick Whitridge, a young New York lawyer. In his first letter to his daughter as the American Mrs Whitridge in January 1885, Arnold told her that he was working on 'a long promised thing for Knowles – "A Word More about America." I often think of you, as I write it, and that it would be unpleasant for you if it gave offense over there; but I do not think it will' (*SL* 281). Although he had told American reporters when he set sail for Liverpool that he did not intend to write a book and probably not even an article about his impressions of America, he soon changed his mind. 'A Word More about America' was published in the *Nineteenth Century* for February 1885 and the following June it was collected and published with the original 'Word about America', 'Literature and Science', 'Numbers' and 'Emerson' as *Discourses in America*. Macmillan paid Arnold £75 for the English and American editions of 1250 each (*MAB* 59).

'A Word More' anticipates the more developed treatment of his views on America in 'Civilisation in the United States', the last essay he published during his lifetime; but it is about England

and Ireland nearly as much as about America. Arnold had decided that the 'political sense' was sounder in America than it was in England. Unlike the English, Americans had solved the 'political and social problem'. Arnold goes so far as to advocate a reformed House of Lords, on the model of the United States Senate, to which '[e]ach of the provincial legislatures of Great Britain and Ireland would elect members' (*CPW* 10:212). And yet in Arnold's opinion the Americans had not yet solved the 'human problem'. The quality of life in the United States was such that an Englishman of taste would rather live in France, Spain, Holland, Belgium, Germany, Italy or Switzerland. According to Honan, Arnold's subsequent anxiety that he may have offended the New York Whitridges by publishing these unflattering remarks about the United States (causing Lucy to cancel her planned visit home in 1885) may have exacerbated his heart condition (*MAAL* 410).

In early May 1885, Arnold was suffering from sharp pains in his chest. His doctor prescribed a strict diet but attributed Arnold's discomfort to 'indigestion' rather than heart disease. Fearing that he did not have long to live, Arnold thought about resigning from school inspecting, but he delayed his decision for another year. Although physical exertion of any kind was becoming increasingly difficult for him, he was determined to remain an active man. He did not wish to return to the Poetry Professorship at Oxford, however, and in October 1885 once again declined re-nomination, in spite of a memorial from Oxford heads of colleges and tutors and another from 400 undergraduates. In 1884, after his return to England, he had received the honorary title of Chief Inspector of Schools, and in 1885 he eagerly took advantage of one last opportunity to study European schools. Arnold would spend most of the period November–December 1885 and February–March 1886 studying primary schools on the Continent for the Education Department but, before beginning his tour, he saw the publication of *Discourses on America* (June) and his three-volume collected edition of *Poems* (August). These were his first important new book publications – though not his only publications – since the *Irish Essays* of 1882. In 1883, the second part of his edition of *Isaiah* primarily meant for English school children was brought out by Macmillan, completing the project he had begun in the early 1870s. Also appearing in 1883 was the *Matthew Arnold Birthday Book*, published by Smith & Elder, a collection of 365 mottoes for each day of the year selected from

Arnold's poems by his daughter Eleanor. As with Smith & Elder's 1880 edition of 212 *Prose Passages* selected from Arnold's work and his contribution to *The Hundred Greatest Men* (which brought him £50 per page), the primary motive behind this contribution to a popular genre of the time was to earn a little extra income during troubled financial times (*MAAL* 388).

Macmillan's monumental Library Edition of 1885 reflects Arnold's final scheme of arranging his collected poems by genre, with some concessions to chronology. Volume I includes 'Early Poems', 'Narrative Poems' and 'Sonnets'; Volume II includes 'Lyric Poems' and 'Elegiac Poems'; and Volume III includes 'Dramatic Poems' and 'Later Poems'. Some curious combinations and juxtapositions among the poems had resulted from Arnold's shifting classifications and arrangements through the years. Among the narrative poems were 'Sohrab and Rustum', the representative poem of 1853, and the early and exotic 'Forsaken Merman', which has a mythic quality like the other poems in this section but also bears some similarities to the Romantic narratives of Coleridge and Keats. For the first time, the 'Switzerland' and 'Faded Leaves' series are included in the same (lyric) section, though with intervening individual poems. Presumably because it incorporates elements of the classical elegy and because of its close relationship with 'Thyrsis', 'The Scholar-Gipsy' appears in the elegiac section along with poems that are (more strictly speaking) elegies. Arnold's elegies on his pet dog Geist and his canary Matthias, with the elegy on Stanley, are grouped together as later poems. The two dramatic poems are *Merope* – appearing for the first time since 1858, when it was published as a separate volume – and, after it, *Empedocles on Etna*, the poem that had precipitated Arnold's revulsion against the 'dialogue of the mind with itself', which in turn had led to his attempt at Sophoclean drama in *Merope*.

This final collected edition to be supervised by Arnold reveals not the growth of a poet's mind but a grand attempt to integrate individual poems into a solid whole, the poet's *oeuvre* presented to posterity. Arnold believed – or wanted to believe – that his poetry, full of powerful and representative ideas, would achieve at least a limited 'classic' status in English literature, but with good humour and a touch of self-irony, he lets two serio-comic elegies of pets stand at the end of the collection. The only two poems Arnold published after completing the 1885 edition were 'Horatian Echo', a 'relic of youth' dating from 1847 but previously unpublished, and 'Kaiser Dead', yet another elegy to a deceased pet (a mongrel dachshund): both of them in journals during the summer of 1887.

Arnold's third Continental journey to gather information on schools was hastily arranged, but he was pleased with '[t]his last touch of "affairs" before I retire' (*CPW* 11:386). His principal charge was to study the free schools of Germany, Switzerland, and France. He spent most of the winter of 1885 travelling alone in Germany and then took his wife and daughter Eleanor with him to France in early 1886. After his return to England and just prior to his retirement, he testified on the subject of English primary education before the Royal Commission on Education chaired by Sir Richard Cross, giving 1227 oral replies in the course of his testimony (*MAAL* 410). Repeating some of his old arguments against the Revised Code and the principle of 'payment by results', Arnold pointedly questioned the wisdom of instructing children in order to prepare them for a particular examination.

He finally retired from his inspectorship of schools at the end of April 1886, after 35 years of service. Looking back over his career, he was disappointed about the lack of official recognition for his work and his failure to receive timely promotions through the years, and he regretted that he had not had more opportunities to improve the English educational system (*MAAL* 413). His deeply felt reservations about the state of the British school system are evident in his essay on 'Schools', which he contributed to Ward's compilation entitled *The Reign of Queen Victoria* (1887). In it he was frank about the limitations of his brother-in-law William Forster's landmark Elementary Education Act of 1870. At the same time, Arnold felt a profound sense of freedom and release in his retirement. After many years of financial troubles, all his debts were paid, and his retirement and civil service pensions, along with payments from publishers, made him and his wife financially secure.

A few days after completing his last foreign schools report in May of 1886, Arnold set out for the United States once again, this time to join his wife, who was already visiting their daughter Lucy, pregnant with her first child. He remained there until August. Following his extensive foreign travels in 1886, Arnold was restless in retirement. He accepted lecture commitments that he later described as 'horrid' and spent much time at his rented house in London in order to maintain an active social life. Although the experience of the long American lecture tour had substantially improved his ability to speak audibly and effectively in public, Arnold grew increasingly bored with lecturing. Most importantly, he returned to essay writing with renewed vigour. From January 1887 to April 1888, the month of his death, Arnold published ten journal articles, and a final one appeared posthumously in May.

In May 1886, his essay 'The Nadir of Liberalism' in Knowles's *Nineteenth Century* had argued against Gladstone's support of Home Rule for Ireland, a policy Arnold believed would destroy the Kingdom by setting up a parliament in Dublin. After the defeat of Gladstone's Home Rule Bill in 1886, Arnold published a companion essay, 'The Zenith of Conservatism', in which he calls for reduction of freedom of speech and of the press in order to prevent rioting and general anarchy in Ireland. Here Arnold goes farthest in expressing his willingness to comprise democratic values to maintain order and stability, perhaps not so much an indication of his ageing mind as the application of some of the principles of *Culture and Anarchy* to a contemporary issue about which he cared deeply. Arnold was a Liberal Unionist, sympathetic to the Irish people but dedicated to the ideal of the 'more attractive civilisation' that joined Ireland to England, an ideal that he knew was unappreciated by the political Dissenters who were Gladstone's most passionate supporters. Knowles published two additional essays by Arnold on the Irish question, an issue which dominated the British Parliament for the remainder of Arnold's life.

As he approached the end of that life, Arnold became involved in yet another Celtic political issue. In the late 1860s, he had opposed the way the Liberals had proceeded in disestablishing the Church of Ireland, failing to transfer church property to the Irish Catholics and doing nothing to meet the religious needs of the people. 'Disestablishment in Wales', published in the Conservative *National Review* of April 1888, warned against making similar mistakes in Wales, where Nonconformists – who had allied themselves with the Anglicans against granting concessions to the Irish Catholics – now found themselves in a very different position, because the great majority of the population there was made up of Presbyterians, Methodists and Baptists. (Disestablishment eventually came to Wales after the end of the First World

War.) Arnold's contribution to this less-than-overwhelming issue is worth mentioning because it illustrates the general approach to cultural politics that he had developed in the sixties and kept until the end of his life. In a letter to Georg von Bunsen, son of an old friend of Dr Arnold, he explained that he agreed to the request of editor Alfred Austin that he contribute to the Conservative journal because he wanted to reach 'reasonable' Conservatives who might be open to new ideas, unlike the Liberals who had 'no idea beyond that of disestablishing the Church', and the 'old-fashioned Tories' who had:

> no idea beyond that of keeping things as they are. I am anxious that the endowments should remain for religion, that the Episcopalians should keep the cathedrals, since in the cathedral towns the Episcopalians are in a majority, but that the Nonconformists, who are all of the Presbyterian form of worship, should have the Churches and endowments, for that Presbyterian form, where they are in majority, as in many of the country districts. (*LMA* 2:431–2)

This letter, written by Arnold on his birthday, Christmas Eve, 1887 – the last birthday and the last Christmas Eve he would live to celebrate – is not especially noteworthy in itself, and neither is the essay he is planning here one of his more important works, yet the letter and the essay itself are representative of the frame of values that characterize Arnold's prose from the beginning to the end of his career. Arnold revered tradition and supported the idea of a State church, but in spite of the occasionally absolutist and transcendentalist rhetoric of his cultural pronouncements, he was at bottom a relativist who recognized the claims of diverse nations and sub-groups within nations. He was an Anglican ritualist with a very liberal theology who respected the Catholicism of Ireland and – though he was widely considered to be an enemy of the Nonconformists – the Presbyterianism of Wales, with which he was quite familiar from his earliest days as an inspector of Welsh Nonconformist schools. (In the past he had made enemies in Wales by arguing in his Celtic lectures that it would be better for the Welsh language to disappear as soon as possible, but at the same time he had celebrated the Welsh component in British identity.) Characteristically, Arnold makes elaborate inquiries of Bunsen concerning the intricate accommodations made between Catholic and Protestant rights in Germany since the end of the Thirty Years War. For him, unifying and meaningful cultural institutions were more important than claims of ultimate truth or validity. Eleven years earlier, he had written to his Catholic brother Tom:

> Catholicism is most interesting, and were I born in a Roman Catholic country I should most certainly never leave the Catholic Church for a Protestant; but neither then or now could I imagine that the Catholic Church possessed 'the truth', or anything like it, or that it *could* possess it. (*SL* 248–9)

Arnold's last two journal publications both originated as lectures. Keeping the promise made at the end of his 'A Word More' essay to say something further about the subject, he composed a lecture on 'Life in America' during the week of 20–7 January 1888 and delivered it to three different audiences, beginning with the Literary and Philosophical Society at Hull, a few days after finishing it. The *Nineteenth Century* published it as 'Civilisation in the United States' in April. 'Milton' was a short address Arnold gave the next month on the unveiling of a memorial window dedicated to the poet at the parish church of St Margaret's, Westminster, arranged by Arnold's old friend, Archdeacon F. W. Farrar. It appeared – posthumously – in the *Century Magazine* for May.

Arnold's disgust with American journalism following his tour of 1883–4 had continued to grow in the final years of his life, and he came to regard newspapers as the 'worst feature' of life in the United States. In his new essay he said, 'The absence of truth and soberness in them, the poverty in serious interest, the personality and sensation-mongering, are beyond belief'. (Fortunately, Arnold could not know what British tabloid journalism would one day become.) The newspapers were representative of basic flaws: 'What really dissatisfies in American civilisation is the want of the *interesting* . . . due chiefly to the want of . . . elevation and beauty' (*CPW* 11:368). Again thinking of his American daughter, now pregnant, who was scheduled to arrive soon for a visit home, Arnold was worried about the response of the American press to his blunt remarks; and he was right to worry. Even Arnold's friend George W. Smalley, London correspondent of *The New York Tribune*, wrote 'I have never read anything which I thought more deplorable' (see *CPW* 11:486).

For three decades Arnold had tried to balance two opposing impulses in his critical prose: on one hand, to offer his opinions freely and openly, even when they were likely to make people uncomfortable; on the other, to restrain himself from giving offence. In an 1868 letter to his mother, Arnold had written, 'The Spectator does me a very bad service by talking of my contempt for un-intellectual people; it is not at all true, and it sets people against one. You will laugh, but fiery hatred and malice are what I detest and would always allay or avoid, if I could' (*SL* 210). Now in 1888 his health was fragile, his combative spirit had waned, and he was troubled by the reaction to his American essay and the connection with his daughter. Although Arnold kept up a vigorous social life and did not like to concern himself openly about the state of his health, he knew how vulnerable he was. In the hot summer of his second American visit he had had such chest pains that he thought 'my time was really coming to an end' (*LMA* 423). On 15 April 1888, Arnold and his wife were in Liverpool, preparing to meet their daughter Lucy on her landing, when he suffered a fatal coronary thrombosis. He was buried at Laleham in a vault near the three sons who had preceded him in death.

Arnold had lived a full and vigorous life, and he literally fell in mid-stride, as he rushed to catch a horse-drawn tramcar (*MAAL* 421). Appropriately enough, he left behind him one last publication project in nearly final form. About three months before Arnold's death, George Craik, business manager for Macmillan, had written to Arnold, suggesting that he collect some of his 'great many Magazine articles' into another volume. Arnold, however, had been thinking about assembling a 'purely literary' volume entitled *Essays in Criticism, Second Series*, implying a continuation of the 1865 book that had been so successful (*MAB* 75). After Arnold's death, Frederick Macmillan contacted Fanny Lucy Arnold through her son Richard, proposing to publish the book and offering £200 for the English edition of 2000 copies and £25 per 1000 for any American printings (*MAB* 76). The Arnolds agreed and asked that Arnold's old Oxford friend John Duke Coleridge, a distinguished lawyer currently serving as Lord Chief Justice, be asked to write an introduction. John Morley helped to arrange the order of the nine articles, eight of which had already been chosen by Arnold.

It is somewhat misleading to think of the second series of *Essays*, published in November 1888, as a continuation of the first. All the essays in the first volume were written within a period of two years, and they are unified by Arnold's emerging critical sensibility while lecturing as poetry professor to a university audience. The second volume contains nine essays written over the period of a decade, and six of them had originally served as introductions to popular editions of poetry anthologies: 'The Study of Poetry', 'Thomas Gray', 'John Keats', 'Wordsworth', 'Byron' and 'Shelley'. The other essays were Arnold's memorial address 'Milton' (added by Frederick Macmillan), 'Count Leo Tolstoi', and 'Amiel'. He wrote the essay on the Swiss writer Henri-Frederic Amiel for the benefit of his niece, the novelist Mary (Mrs Humphrey) Ward, who had translated Amiel's *Journals*. Arnold valued Amiel – who knew Arnold's friend Edmond Scherer – chiefly as a 'charming' literary critic.

Most important among Arnold's later essays is 'Tolstoi.' Arnold had met Tolstoy briefly in 1861, when the Russian was taking a tour of English elementary schools. Later Tolstoy, who like Arnold rejected the supernaturalism of the Gospels, read Arnold's critical and religious writings. After reading *Literature and Dogma*, he sent Arnold a copy of the French translation of *What is My Faith?*. Arnold developed an interest in Tolstoy's novels, especially *Anna Karenina*, which he read avidly in 1887. The Tolstoy essay is exceptional for two reasons. First, Arnold generally avoided writing about living authors, his peers. (How different his career might have been if he had written critical articles about Tennyson's poetry, for example.) Arnold's excuse for making an exception in this case was the special interest in religious issues which he shared with the Russian.

Second, the essay is unique as Arnold's only substantive contribution to novel criticism. Surely one of the major weaknesses of Arnold's critical programme is his reluctance to engage in the study of fiction. It seems odd that the most important Victorian critic wrote so little about the English novel. This weakness can be linked to his early desire to write timeless poetry and avoid being 'sucked up for an hour even into the Time Stream' with Clough and his Oxford friends who admired *The Bothie* (*SL* 49). Critics from his own time to the present have charged Arnold with looking backwards to a dead past, avoiding the realities of contemporary life. Like Clough's poetry, novels dealt with the here and now, and in his 1853 review of Arnold's poetry, Clough had pointed out that most people prefer *Vanity Fair* and *Bleak House* to poems after classical models. As we have seen, Arnold remained attached to the 'touchstones' of classical poetry in his literary taste, though no critic was more topical in his social criticism. In fact Arnold, like so many of his contemporaries, frequently read novels for entertainment, and his journals and letters contain many references to them. Following his youthful fascination with the exotic George Sand, Arnold read widely in popular English fiction, often recommending entertaining novels to friends and family members and making allusions to his favorite novels in his letters. In an 1885 letter to his daughter Lucy, for example, he joking compared himself to Mr Woodhouse in Jane Austen's *Emma* (*LMA* 2:335). However, he did not have a very high opinion of Dickens's work, thought Thackeray was 'a first rate journeyman', and had once referred to Charlotte Brontë's *Villette* as 'a hideous undelightful convulsed constricted novel' in a letter to Clough (*SL* 83). Yet Arnold is sympathetic to Tolstoy and praises *Anna Karenina*, not as a work of art but as a 'piece of life.' This judgment is striking since Arnold had hardly emphasized realism in his previous literary criticism.

In order to understand Arnold's susceptibility to Tolstoy, it is necessary to take into account the fact that the Russian's novels were available to English readers only in French translations. Arnold, who had developed an excellent reading knowledge of French during his youthful enthusiasm for Sand and Senancour, did not call for or expect English translations in the foreseeable future (although he thought that English readers might soon be learning to read Russian). He naturally compared *Anna Karenina* to Flaubert's *Madame Bovary* and other French novels. As already noted, Arnold had come to believe that French decadence in the latter half of the nineteenth century was expressed in the national literature of France. Arnold, ever the comparativist, contrasted the Russian realism of Tolstoy – which he associated with the profound soul-searching of Tolstoy and his character Levin – to the 'petrified feeling', the 'atmosphere of bitterness, irony, impotence' he found in the works of the French naturalists (who had gone beyond Flaubert in this direction: *CPW* 11:292–3). Arnold valued the religious ideas and sensibilities expressed in *Anna Karenina* more highly than the later autobiographical essays like *What is My Faith?* in which Tolstoy had attempted to 'pack' his

Christianity into a set of commandments: 'Christianity is a *source*; no one supply of water and refreshment that comes of it can be called the sum of Christianity' (*CPW* 11:302). Ironically, Arnold did not realize the extent to which the Russian novelist's own moral vision had been influenced by his reading of English novelists (including George Eliot and Dickens). Nevertheless, in emphasizing the realism of Tolstoy and promoting the current 'vogue' of the Russian novel, Arnold – near the end of his life – displayed an especially progressive aspect of his critical intelligence. An article published in the *Westminster Review* a few months after Arnold's death gave him credit for establishing Tolstoy's reputation in English-speaking countries.[16]

Written when he was only in his forties, Arnold's poem 'Growing Old' paints a rather bleak picture of those who have outlived their productive years, 'frozen up within, and quite/The phantom of ourselves'. This was not to be Arnold's fate: he died an active man, physically and intellectually, who was still growing as a writer.

Conclusion

Nearly everyone agrees that Arnold is a central figure in Victorian literature, yet his place in literary history is difficult to define. Tracing Arnold's literary development through his life helps us to understand the peculiar nature of his accomplishments.

For a long time it has been usual to acknowledge the fairly narrow emotional range of his poetry and yet concede his position as the third most important Victorian poet (after Tennyson and Browning), or the third or fourth (when Hopkins is added to the group). But the seemingly premature closure of his poetic career and his transition to critical prose are always complicating factors, especially since his persona as critical essayist appears to be so distant from that as post-Romantic lyricist. If the current consensus is that Arnold's literary influence has been primarily as a critic, that claim is also difficult to explain. In spite of his willingness to make sweeping literary judgments, it is not as a practical critic that Arnold made his greatest contributions. He helped to set up Wordsworth's modern reputation, but he offered little insight into whole periods and genres of English literature, including Renaissance drama and eighteenth-century poetry. He had practically nothing to say about English fiction, although he was intensely interested in *moral* issues, which are so prominent in the novel. He could not appreciate Shelley's brand of Romanticism and – although he did not publish his opinions in this case – seriously undervalued the poetry of his contemporary Tennyson. Although his contributions as a comparativist were formidable, some of his more interesting studies are of relatively minor French authors. And yet it would also be misleading, especially in the context of current post-structuralist criticism, to call Arnold a great theoretical critic. Arnold proudly called attention to his unsystematic approach.

T. S. Eliot's famous phrase that Arnold was primarily a 'propagandist for criticism' rather than a critic points to Arnold's limitations as a practical literary critic, but it also provides a clue as to the nature of his strengths and his real significance in English literature. It is often observed that Eliot inherited Arnold's position as England's pre-eminent man of letters, but Eliot did not fully appreciate and he did not significantly extend Arnold's pioneering work in expanding the *functions* of criticism (to quote from the original title of Arnold's landmark essay). Today, because some of Arnold's assumptions about a universal human nature, the intimate connection between the moral and the aesthetic, the possibility of 'disinterestedness', and the role of the state as the organ of a society's 'best self' are out of fashion, and because he is often seen as representative of an outdated, repressive and patriarchal social order, his place in literary history is often obscured or misrepresented. However, in extending literary criticism to cultural and political criticism Arnold anticipated the direction of literary studies in increasingly democratic societies. In making large claims for 'criticism', 'culture' and 'literature' in the widest sense, he opened up the way for such disparate groups as Edwardian aesthetes, Leavisites, New Humanists, and post-modern culture critics, as well as their traditionalist opponents. Although he himself was no academic critic and always insisted on classicist and comparativist approaches to literature, he helped to provide ideological justification for the proliferation of English departments in British and American academic institutions. (I am not claiming that this is necessarily a positive development.)

Arnold's intellectual habits and literary tastes were formed in a historically specific millieu, and the *Zeitgeist* moves on, though some argue that Arnold can still be usefully adapted to current issues. For example, Joseph Carroll glosses Arnold's 'culture' as '*Western civilization regarded as culminating in Victorian gentlemen with a predominantly classical education and refined literary tastes*' but believes that 'with little difficulty many of Arnold's specific cultural values can be . . . assimilated to a relativistic Darwinian model'.[1] The prospect of recovering through science a sense of 'human nature' available to literary representation is particularly provocative and ironic in light of the Arnold–Huxley relationship and the subsequent attack on the fundamental concept of 'humane letters' that has come from modern literary theorists.

However, this is not the place to discuss modern applications of Arnold's ideas. It is probable that Arnold's intellectual tolerance and strategies for moving beyond sectarianism and the claims of personal autonomy with the aim of finding unity in diversity will continue to look interesting in a time of contentious cultural and political debates.

Suggestions for Further Reading

A list of the editions of Arnold's works and the secondary sources referred to most frequently in this volume (along with notes on Nicholas Murray's recent biography and Cecil Y. Lang's first volume of a new edition of Arnold's letters) appears under the heading 'Abbreviations of Frequently-Cited Sources' before the Preface. Good general introductions to Arnold include Fraser Neiman, *Matthew Arnold* (New York: Twayne, 1968), and Stefan Collini, *Arnold* (Oxford: Oxford University Press, 1988). A few additional, important critical studies are listed below. For an annotated bibliography of the most significant contributions to twentieth-century Arnold criticism and scholarship (up to the year 1991), see Clinton Machann, *The Essential Matthew Arnold* (New York: G. K. Hall, 1993). A reliable survey of criticism through 1972 can be found in David DeLaura's bibliographical essay 'Matthew Arnold' in *Victorian Prose: A Guide to Research* (New York: Modern Language Association, 1973), pp. 249–320. An annual review of Arnold scholarship and criticism appears in the journal *Victorian Poetry*.

Ruth apRoberts, *Arnold and God* (Berkeley: University of California Press, 1983).

Paull F. Baum, *Ten Studies in the Poetry of Matthew Arnold* (Durham, NC: Duke University Press, 1958).

A. Dwight Culler, *Imaginative Reason: The Poetry of Matthew Arnold* (New Haven, Conn.: Yale University Press, 1966).

David J. DeLaura, *Hebrew and Hellene in Victorian England: Newman, Arnold, Pater* (Austin: University of Texas Press, 1969).

John Holloway, *The Victorian Sage: Studies in Argument* (London: Macmillan, 1953), pp. 202–43.

William Madden, *Matthew Arnold: A Study of the Aesthetic Temperament in Victorian England* (Bloomington: Indiana University Press, 1967).

David G. Riede, *Matthew Arnold and the Betrayal of Language* (University Press of Virginia, 1988).

G. Robert Stange, *Matthew Arnold: The Poet as Humanist* (Princeton, NJ: Princeton University Press, 1967).

Lionel Trilling, *Matthew Arnold*, rev. edn (New York: Columbia University Press, 1958).

Notes and References

1 Juvenilia

1. For an extreme version of this view see Nathan Cervo, '"Dover Beach", "Sohrab and Rustum", "Philomela", and "Stanzas from the Grande Chartreuse": The Iconography of Detritus', *Arnoldian*, 11 (Winter 1984), 24–31. Cervo contends that the poems listed in his title are 'grounded in an Oedipal complex'.
2. W. H. Auden, 'Matthew Arnold', *Another Time: Poems* (New York: Random House, 1940), p. 58.

2 Life and Work, 1841–53

1. The most influential general study of Arnold's poetic imagery is A. Dwight Culler's *Imaginative Reason: The Poetry of Matthew Arnold* (New Haven, Conn.: Yale University Press, 1966).
2. F. R. Leavis, 'Literary Studies', in *Education and the University* (London: Chatto & Windus, 1943), pp. 66–86.
3. See, for example, Leon Gottfried, *Matthew Arnold and the Romantics* (Lincoln: University of Nebraska Press, 1963).
4. See, for example, E. D. H. Johnson, *The Alien Vision of Victorian Poetry: Sources of the Poetic Imagination in Tennyson, Browning, and Arnold* (Princeton, NJ: Princeton University Press, 1952).
5. *Unpublished Letters of Matthew Arnold*, ed. Arnold Whitridge (New Haven, Conn.: Yale University Press, 1923), p. 15.
6. See, for example, Sir Edmund Chambers, 'Matthew Arnold', Warton Lecture on English Poetry, *Proceedings of the British Academy* (1932), 23–45.
7. C. B. Tinker and H. F. Lowry, *The Poetry of Matthew Arnold: A Commentary* (London: Oxford University Press, 1940), p. 291.
8. *North American Review*, 77 (July 1853), 1–30.
9. See Vinod Sena, 'W. B. Yeats, Matthew Arnold, and the Critical Imperative', *Victorian Newsletter*, 56 (1979), 10–14.
10. *The Correspondence of Arthur Hugh Clough*, ed. Frederick L. Mulhauser (London: Oxford University Press, 1957), II, 477.
11. Walter Bagehot, 'Wordsworth, Tennyson and Browning', in *Literary Studies* (London: J. M. Dent, 1911), II, 316.
12. *Christian Remembrancer*, 27 (April 1854), 310–33.

3 Life and Work, 1854–61

1. 'A Raid Among Poets', *New Quarterly Review* (January 1854), 40.
2. John Holloway, *The Victorian Sage: Studies in Argument* (London: Macmillan, 1953), p. 203.

3. Most notably, William Robbins in *The Arnoldian Principle of Flexibility* (Victoria, BC: University of Victoria, 1979).
4. Stefan Collini, *Arnold* (Oxford: Oxford University Press, 1988), p. 5.

4 Essays in Criticism (1865), New Poems (1867)

1. 'Essays in Criticism', *North British Review*, 3, new series (March 1865), 81.
2. Privately held letter dated 1 December 1864, from Arnold to his mother, quoted in *CPW* 4:345.
3. Two particularly suggestive and provocative commentaries on the poem are Norman H. Holland's psychoanalytical essay 'Psychological Depths and "Dover Beach"', *Victorian Studies*, 9 (1965 Supplement), 5–28, and Anthony Hecht's poem 'The Dover Bitch (A Criticism of Life)', *Transatlantic Review*, 2 (1960), 57–8, reprinted in *The Hard Hours* (London: Oxford University Press, 1967), p. 17.
4. See David J. DeLaura, 'Arnold, Clough, Dr. Arnold, and "Thyrsis"', *Victorian Poetry*, 7 (1969), 191–202.
5. Quoted by DeLaura, 'Arnold, Clough'.
6. Howard Foster Lowry (ed.), *The Letters of Matthew Arnold to Arthur Hugh Clough* (New York: Oxford University Press, 1932), p. 21; A. Dwight Culler, *Imaginative Reason: The Poetry of Matthew Arnold* (New Haven, Conn.: Yale University Press), p. 253.
7. 'Matthew Arnold's New Poems', *Anthenaeum* (31 August 1867), 265–6.

5 Life and Work, 1868–71

1. See Bernadette Waterman Ward, 'Ernest Renan's Averroism in the Religious Thought of Matthew Arnold', *Nineteenth-Century Prose*, 22, 1 (1995), 34–53.
2. The well-known titles of chapters in *Culture and Anarchy* cited here and below actually appeared for the first time in the second (1875) edition of the book. Chapters in the first edition were untitled.
3. For a concise account of the evolving meanings of 'culture' in nineteenth-century England and Arnold's role in this process, see David J. DeLaura, 'Matthew Arnold and Culture: The History and the Prehistory', in *Matthew Arnold in His Time and Ours: Centenary Essays*, ed. Clinton Machann and Forrest D. Burt (Charlottesville: University Press of Virginia, 1988), pp. 1–16. Also see DeLaura's 'Arnold and Goethe: The One on the Intellectual Throne', in *Victorian Literature and Society: Essays Presented to Richard D. Altick*, ed. James R. Kinkaid and Albert J. Kuhn (Columbus: Ohio State University Press, 1984), pp. 197–224.
4. See David DeLaura, 'Arnold and Carlyle', *PMLA*, 79 (1964), 104–29, and 'Carlyle and Arnold: The Religious Issue', in *Carlyle Past and Present: A Collection of New Essays*, ed. K. J. Fielding and Rodger L. Tarr (London: Vision Press, 1976), pp. 127–54.
5. Privately held letter of 16 December 1868 quoted by Super (*CPW* 5:412).

6. See especially the Samuel Lipman edition of *Culture and Anarchy*, which prints the original 1869 text in unaltered form, along with modern commentary.
7. Eugene Goodheart, 'Arnold, Critic of Ideology', *New Literary History*, 25 (1994), 415–28.
8. Sidney M. B. Coulling, 'Matthew Arnold and the *Daily Telegraph*', *Review of English Studies*, 12 (1961), 178.
9. George A. Sala, *Life and Adventures* (London: Cassell, 1895), I, 18–19.
10. *The Nonconformist* (7 February 1866), 119.
11. See J. Holloway, *The Victorian Sage: Studies in Argument* (London: Macmillan, 1953), pp. 215–19.
12. *Introductory Lectures on Modern History* (Oxford: J. H. Parker, 1842), p. 180.
13. David DeLaura, *Hebrew and Hellene in Victorian England: Newman, Arnold, and Pater* (Austin: University of Texas Press, 1969), p. 230.
14. See George W. Stocking, Jr, 'Matthew Arnold, E. B. Tylor, and the Uses of Invention', *American Anthropologist*, 65 (1963), 783–99.

6 Religious Writings, 1870–7

1. W. H. G. Armytage, 'Matthew Arnold and W. E. Gladstone: Some New Letters', *University of Toronto Quarterly*, 18 (1949), 222.
2. 'Arnold on Puritanism and National Churches', *Edinburgh Review*, 133 (April 1871), 399.
3. 'Mr. Matthew Arnold and the Nonconformists', *Contemporary Review*, 14 (July 1870), 540–71.
4. Leslie Stephen, 'Mr. Matthew Arnold and the Church of England', *Fraser's Magazine*, 2, new series (October 1870), 414.
5. J. H. Newman, *The Idea of a University* (London: Longman, 1947), p. 107.
6. 'Amateur Theology: Arnold's *Literature and Dogma*', *Blackwood's Edinburgh Magazine*, 113 (June 1873), 685, 689.
7. 'Mr. Arnold's Gospel', *Spectator*, 46 (22 February 1873), 243–4.
8. Angelo de Gubernatis, '*Rassegna delle Letterature Straniere*', *Nuova Antologia di Scienze, Lettre ed Arti*, 2nd series, 3 (December 1876), 880–1.
9. Super quotes from unpublished letters from Arnold to Knowles (*CPW* 7:436–7).
10. Unpublished letter quoted by Super (*CPW* 6:452).
11. '*God and the Bible*', *The Academy*, 8 (18 December 1875), 618–19.
12. See Gilbert Geis and Ivan Bunn, 'Matthew Arnold and the Lowestoft "Witches"', *Nineteenth Century Prose*, 20, 1 (1993), 1–17.
13. W. H. Mallock, *The New Republic: or, Culture, Faith, and Philosophy in an English Country House* (London: Chatto & Windus, 1878), p. 31.

7 Life and Work, 1878–88

1. 'Mixed Essays. By Matthew Arnold', *Athenaeum* (8 March 1879), 303.
2. 'New Books', *Blackwoods' Magazine* 126 (July 1879), 90–1.
3. 'Falkland and the Puritans. In Reply to Mr. Matthew Arnold', *Contemporary Review*, 29 (April 1877), 925–43.
4. Herbert R. Coursen, Jr, '"The Moon Lies Fair": The Poetry of Matthew Arnold', *Studies in English Literature, 1500–1900*, 4 (1964), 569–81.
5. See David J. DeLaura, 'The "Wordsworth" of Pater and Arnold: "The Supreme, Artistic View of Life"', *Studies in English Literature, 1500–1900*, 6 (1966), 651–67.
6. George Levine, 'Matthew Arnold: The Artist in the Wilderness', *Critical Inquiry*, 9 (1983), 469–82.
7. 'Mr. Matthew Arnold and Puritanism', *British Quarterly Review* 52 (July 1870), 187.
8. See *The Note-Books of Matthew Arnold*, ed. Howard Foster Lowry, Karl Young and Waldo Hilary Dunn (London: Oxford University Press, 1952).
9. *The Complete Works of Algernon Charles Swinburne*, ed. Edmund Gosse and T. J. Wise (New York: Wells, 1925–7), xiv, 85.
10. W. H. G. Armytage, 'Matthew Arnold and T. H. Huxley: Some New Letters, 1870–80', *Review of English Studies*, 4 (1953), 349–50.
11. Armytage, 'Matthew Arnold and T. H. Huxley', p. 352.
12. Lionel Trilling, 'Literature and Power', *Kenyon Review*, 2 (1940), 433–42.
13. 'Matthew Arnold's Visit', *Literary World*, 14 (15 December 1883), 446.
14. William T. Beauchamp, 'Plato on the Prairies', *Educational Forum*, 5 (1941), 285–95.
15. 'Matthew Arnold', *Nation*, 46 (19 April 1888), 316.
16. 'Count Tolstoy's Life and Works', *Westminster Review* 130 (September 1888), 282.

Conclusion

1. Joseph Carroll, *Evolution and Literary Theory* (Columbia: University of Missouri Press, 1995), 370.

Index of References to Arnold's Works

General Index

171